C000078790

Sexy

SEXY
IS ON THE INSIDE

JA HUSS

Edited by RJ Locksley

ISBN: 978-1-936413-92-8

Standalone Books

Three, Two, One (321): A Dark Suspense

Meet Me In The Dark: A Dark Suspense

Wasted Lust (321 Spinoff)

Sexy

Rook and Ronin Books

TRAGIC

MANIC

PANIC

TRAGIC, MANIC, PANIC BOX SET

Rook and Ronin Spinoffs

SLACK: A Day in the Life of Ford Aston

TAUT: The Ford Book

FORD: Slack/Taut Bundle

BOMB: A Day in the Life of Spencer Shrike

GUNS The Spencer Book

Dirty, Dark, and Deadly

Come

Come Back

Coming for You

James and Harper: Come/Come Back Bundle

Social Media

Follow

Like

Block

Status

Profile

Home

Young Adult

Losing Francesca

Science Fiction Series

Clutch

Fledge

Flight

Range

The Magpie Bridge

Return

1

"Life is a game and everyone's a player. Whether you believe it or not, the only thing that matters is the score. I can help you score, Katie."

The girl looks at me dubiously. She's tall and beautiful, with blonde hair, blue eyes, and a smile to die for. She works in her family's corporate law office in San Francisco. She makes low six figures, gets four weeks of vacation a year, and has a small but desirable apartment in one of the best neighborhoods.

Most women would say she's got it all. But you never know what's on the inside. And right now, Katie is a mess.

"It feels like cheating, Fletch."

Not everyone calls me Fletch, but all the girls I work with do. They see me as a friend. Someone on their side. A confidant. They share their innermost secrets and I listen. I'm there to wipe their tears. I hold hands, dish out praise, and cheer when they win.

And they always win. Because I'm a winner and everyone I take under my wing is a reflection of me.

"Katie, listen to me, sweetie. OK?" I place a fingertip under her chin and make those sad eyes meet my gaze. She's been destroyed by an asshole she trusted, and today is the day that asshole overtakes all the years of praise and happiness and beats her down. She thinks it's her fault he's an asshole. That she wasn't enough. But the truth I hammer home is that he's not good enough for her.

This is my job. I take these women at their lowest and build them back up. She met me a few months ago through a mutual friend. I'm here to take that sting of defeat away and turn it into whatever it is she thinks she wants.

"I'm not just a player, Katie, I'm a professional. And for the right price I'll guarantee you a win. You want Mr. Let Me Lick Your Abs to lick you back? I'm the chess piece. You wish Mr. Corporate Moneybags would buy you bling? I'll put him on the game board. You need Mr. String You Along to get strung up with jealousy? We'll checkmate together, baby, and he'll never know what hit him. Think about it. A guaranteed win."

"I'm just not sure he's worth it."

"Him? Jesus Christ, no, Katie. Not *him*. He's an asshole. Sweetie, we're talking someone brand new, OK? Anyone you want can be yours… if you sign the contract."

She takes a deep breath and lets it out, still undecided.

"I can do it," I tell her. "I can change your life, make your dreams come true, and he'll never even know he was played. But it all comes at a price. Because sexy doesn't sell, sweetie. It's for sale."

"OK," she finally says. "OK." This time it comes with a smile. "I'll do it. I'll sign. Where's the contract?"

Yes, I cheer silently. "Here you are, babe. Just read it over, initial each stipulation, and then sign at the bottom. And here"—I hand her a business card—"is the bank account number. As I explained before, I only accept wire transfers."

My dressing room door opens and lets in a chorus of cheers from the ladies waiting to see the show. Mitch walks over to my rack of outfits and browses through it.

Katie is still reading her contract, but she's not too worried about it. I've outlined it all in previous meetings and she comes from a long line of lawyers, so she knows legit when she sees it. She skims it, signs, then hands it back with a new hope shining through her sad depression. "This is gonna work, right?"

"I promise, sweetie. Or your money back."

"OK, when do we start?"

"I'll be in touch." I take her hand and pull her to her feet. I bring her to me, just enough to make it personal, and lean into her neck so I can whisper, "Forget about him and think about me. For the next few months I'm your whole life and I won't ever treat you like he did."

She turns her head and kisses my cheek. "Thank you, Fletch. So much."

I watch her ass as she walks out of my dressing room—because hey, I'm an ass man and I can't help myself—and then gather up her contract and stuff it into my briefcase.

"Got another sucker, huh, Novak?" Mitch asks as he peruses my rack.

"Fuck off, you dick. And get your own costumes."

He sighs. "The one I wear for my first gig was ripped off last week, remember? I haven't had time to find a replacement."

"Whatever. I'm gonna run this up to my room," I say, holding up my briefcase. "Be back in ten."

"Don't be late. Chandler is in a shit mood tonight."

I ignore that. I can handle Chandler. Besides, I'm the star of the show.

I open the door and again there's a roar from the crowd as Chandler warms them up after our first group act. Steve goes solo first, then Bill. I come on third, the main attraction for fifteen whole minutes, and then Mitch and Sean finish it up before we all come back on stage for the finale.

I head away from the noise and slip through the backstage door. Not all the guys in the show have a suite at the Landslide Hotel and Casino Resort, only Chandler and me, since we're the senior members of the cast. But it's a damn good perk and comes with a private elevator to the North Tower penthouses where they comp rooms for the high-rollers.

I press the button and step in when the doors open. The ride up to the fifteenth floor is quick, since this is a dedicated elevator for the upper floors, and then I step into the dimly lit hallway and walk the length of the corridor to the end where our suites share the same alcove and flash my keycard.

Inside the AC is chilly and welcoming. Lake Tahoe doesn't get hot, but hot is relative, right? And August is hot just about everywhere in America. I place my briefcase on the desk and then open it up and take out Katie's file. I've got three weeks of surveillance on her already, which is kind of ironic, considering what she does at her law firm. But let's face it. When I told her I was a professional, I meant it. I knew she'd end up being a client the first night we were introduced. She had the look of fear back then. Today she had the look of desperation.

I add her to my collection and then close the safe, ready to head back downstairs, when I notice the light flashing on the room phone.

Hmmm. No one calls me on the room phone but management. So I hit the speaker button and press pound seven to get my voicemail.

"Mr. Novak," Amy, the resort manager, says in her businesslike tone, "there was a meeting this afternoon. I had it on your calendar and you missed it. I'm sure, as always, you have a good reason for that? I expect to hear it tomorrow at nine AM sharp." She pauses for a moment to sigh. "And Fletcher, just so you know, it had better be monumental."

There's a click and the computer voice starts giving me options before I can disconnect the call.

Fucking management. I hate that corporate shit they do. And I hate these monthly meetings even more. But I have a show to do, so I push it away and head back downstairs. The ordinarily quick lift takes a few minutes and is filled with rich, drunk gamblers by the time it gets to my floor, so when I finally walk back through the stage door, Chandler is already calling my name.

"Fletcherrrrrrr…" he roars above the crowd of cheers.

"You're late again, bro," Bill says, walking by with his costume in his hand, sweat falling down his face after his dance routine. His hard body is rippled with muscles and his wet-look thong is stuffed with dollars.

But I'm a professional, remember?

I take the small set of stairs two at a time and push the curtain aside, just as Chandler says my name again. His expression is one of annoyance as he looks at the curtain, but then he realizes I'm here and it turns to relief. "Novakkkkkk..." he says, placing the mic in the stand and walking off stage on the opposite side.

I throw up my arms, allowing the tight white t-shirt to stretch across my chest and rise up from the waistband of my tattered jeans a little. The spotlight flashes directly overhead—just one brief tease of what's to come—and the audience goes wild at that little bit of skin. But before they can do anything else, the stage goes dark again and the music starts bumping.

I don't talk on stage. No one wants to hear what I've got to say. They only want to see what I can do with this body. Hardened from years of sports and diligent gym visits. Lean muscles accentuated with a grace that you only get with a decade or more of martial arts training. That's all they want. That's all they see. I'm just something to look at when I'm up here.

So I give them exactly what they expect. A show.

I start dancing, my hips moving to the beat of the song. Another flash of light from above. Another round of screams. And then silence as I freeze.

Whistles and catcalls start. But I hold my pose—fingertips on the back of my shirt, ready to oblige their insatiable need for the sight of bare flesh tonight. Then another flash. I drag the shirt up in that brief glimpse, and then darkness mimics my pause. The next flash they see my abs, the dream six-pack that's mostly genetics, but I do my share of crunches. Then another flash and I give them the pecs, flexing the muscles and making them dance a little. And in that final flash, I rip the shirt over my head.

The front row stands, waving their dollar bills in the air, begging to shower me with money.

I twirl the shirt several times, taking in the throngs of women with their hands up, ready to catch the prize, and then throw it to a little redhead just as all the lights come on to the beat of the bass. I train my eyes on the crowd, ready to start the real show, and then the lights switch from me to them, lighting up their faces—red with the heat of five hundred woman jostling for position in the room. All of them there for me in this moment. It pans to the left side, and I use those three seconds to search for my star. Then down the middle. My eyes train on a woman in a light-colored suit sitting dead center before I lose her in the darkness and switch to the right side.

But she's the one. She's my star tonight. And she has no idea how hard I'm about to rock her world.

I stride down the catwalk, the thumping music penetrating my boots and sending shockwaves up my legs. I train my eyes on the woman in the suit and take in her male companion, the only other person at her front-and-center table. Gay, I deduce, after half a second. He's too well-dressed in that fashionable way that only a gay man has. Best friend, probably. Safe.

She has a neutral expression as I stand on the stage just above her, but her upturned face is an aphrodisiac that I can't deny. It's soft, unlike her eyes, which say guarded. But I'm used to that. It's my specialty.

I extend my hand and she shakes her head no, her lips pressing together. Her gay friend pushes her a little, trying to persuade her to accept my offer, but she shakes out another no.

The crowd starts jumping when they realize she doesn't want to participate, so I move on and save her for later. I walk to the left where a girl in the tell-tale bachelorette veil is trying to squeeze in one more night of fun before she gives herself to the man of her dreams forever.

This time when I extend my hand, the new star reaches for it eagerly. I grip her wrist and bend down, wrapping my other hand around her waist, and easily lift her up on stage with me.

She glances back to her friends, blushing, but I wrap my hands around her waist and pull her back into my chest. My hips are doing their own dance against her ass, making her blush even more. A palm comes up to her mouth to continue the act.

I lean into her neck and yell over the music. "Wanna play the game with me tonight, sweetheart?"

She nods enthusiastically as her friends go crazy down on the floor.

Thought so.

I dance around her, touching her in places that would make her fiancé mad with jealousy—if he were here, and he isn't—and then I spin her around and place her hands over the taut muscles of my waist. She lets out a breath of surprise but the blushing is gone and all I see now is desire.

She wants me.

Maybe that man she's gonna marry is perfect. He could be a millionaire with a huge house. His job might be something so far above me, I'd look like an insignificant ant under his shoe. He might have a Harvard education and enough investments to put ten kids through college.

But right now, in this moment, all she wants is me.

I do the dirty dance with her, my body pressing against hers. The sweat is already pouring out of me, dripping down my stomach and pooling into the band of my tattered jeans. But her fingertips relish in it. They drag up and down the hard muscles of my abs. And I let her get her feel. I let her touch me anywhere she wants, waiting to see how far she goes. When she reaches around for my ass, that's the signal. I place my hand on her head and press. She gives in easily and falls to her knees in front of me, looking up, her mouth poised in front of the zipper of my jeans.

I bump against her face and the crowd roars.

She blushes again but doesn't pull away.

Fuck. They never pull away.

I grab the back of her head and push her face into the soft fabric. And even though my whole body is nothing but heat, I can feel her panting breaths as the humidity seeps through the denim covering my dick.

Just as she presses into me, just before I really get turned on, I push her away. She teeters backwards for a moment before catching her balance, and then I walk around her, dancing.

She pivots with me, but I move quickly and straddle her thighs, placing her head in my hand while pushing her backwards with the other one. She falls with my push, allowing me to lay her out on the floor. Those eyes, man, they're still trusting. Still eager.

I dance over her, bending my knees, getting lower and lower with each thump of the bass, and then I drop my knees on the floor and straddle her face. Undulating up and down just an inch or two from her mouth.

She'd suck me off right here if I let her.

But of course, I'm not gonna let her. This is a show. It's fake. And everyone in the room knows this. Especially me.

She starts stuffing her dollar bills into my pockets, but I have to give her one more thing to dream about tonight, so I grab her hand and place it over my crotch.

I'm not hard. I never get hard for this fake shit. It's a job. And I do it well.

She screams with delight as I rub her hand over me and then before she can enjoy it too much, I step back and pull her to her feet. I get behind her again, dancing against her ass again, and yell into her ear, "Thank you, baby. You're a good sport!"

She turns and screams, and before I know it, she's kissing me. Long and hard. Sloppy and demanding.

I grab her by the shoulders and laugh it off, but secretly I'm pissed I didn't see it coming. Most of the brides-to-be don't take it that far, which is why I push a little harder with them.

I back away and raise her hand in the air as Chandler comes out on stage to talk her back down from her stripper-induced euphoria. I take a bow and let them cheer for a few seconds before casually jogging offstage, passing Mitch in the hallway wearing the costume he just pinched from my closet.

He claps me on the back, laughing. "You're losing your touch. She got a sloppy kiss in."

"Fuck you," I say, heading to my dressing room. I close the door and relish the relative silence as I collapse into a chair.

But the kiss bothers me. I'm the one in control out there. The whole show is based on the fact that we're entertainers and in a room filled with hundreds of out-of-control women, we're the ones in control. And she got me.

I shake my head and take a swig of water, logging Mitch's music, picturing his act as I wait for my next appearance.

I've been doing this for about nine months and I've seen

and heard pretty much everything. But tonight was the first time anyone's ever got a kiss in.

A knock on my door pulls me out of the funk and then Bill enters. "Hey," he says, "Chandler wants to see you backstage."

"There in a sec," I say, and he leaves. I know what Chandler is gonna say. Every once in a while the girls take it too far. But it never happens to me. Sure, *I* take it too far. That's my job. But we are never supposed to let them take that control away. So I'm expecting a lecture from Chandler when I make my way back out after Mitch's act is over and Sean's act begins.

"You missed a meeting today," he says as I walk into the main office backstage. "And you're lucky that corporate never showed up or you'd be out on your ass, Fletcher. They're tired of you."

I get this lecture every month like clockwork. Lots of people would like me to go away, but the fact is, I make them money. And since the world is filled with greedy assholes whose only desire is to count that pile of money they hoard in a corner, they keep me around. "I just forgot, man. I mean, look. I work here when I work here. I get paid per show. I'm expected to show up for rehearsals and shit from nine to noon, Tuesday through Friday. Then I'm off until Saturday night's show. I use those hours, man. I'm a busy guy and you know that. So if they want to pay me to show up when I'm off, let's put that shit into the next contract."

"You're not gonna get another contract, Fletch."

His words are not angry, just matter-of-fact. We're friends. We both grew up on the North Shore of Lake Tahoe and we've been friends for a long time now. He got me this gig when I came to him nine months ago and told him what was up. He's had my back a few times and I've had his. But we've grown apart the last few months. He's got a steady girl now, maybe thinking about getting serious, and I'm… not. I'm too busy surviving, still finding my stride. I can't get excited about life plans when I'm struggling to keep up and hold it together.

"You won't, Fletcher. Not if you keep this shit up."

"Chandler, I'm the star of the show. Most of those women come here asking about me. We all know that. And I'm not trying to be a dick, but I'm a contributor. I'm part of its success. And for fuck's sake, if I've got the afternoon off, then I've got the afternoon off. Leave me alone and let me do my thing."

"I get it," he says, slumping down in his seat. "I do, man, but you have to try a little harder."

Try harder. Jesus Christ, I don't know how much harder I can try. I don't say that, of course. But it pisses me off that people think I'm lazy.

"Not that you don't work hard, man."

Yeah, buddy. Too little, too late. But again, I let it ride. Because fuck it. Fuck everyone. Fuck the fucking world. "Look, the meeting was rescheduled for tomorrow morning during working hours. So everyone will be happy. OK?"

We fist-bump and I leave with just enough time to make it backstage before Sean finishes his act. The rest of us line up and wait for Chandler to bring us all back out on stage together. This is the fun part. For me at least. Because this is when I look for a possibility. A girl I might like to fuck tonight. I've running a dry spell lately. No one's caught my eye in more than a month. So I'm horny. I need a slutty, forgettable girl to wipe this fucking day away.

2

Chandler cues us with his intro and then the curtain lifts up. The spotlights are going wild on us. Smoke, some flames for good measure, and the smell of chicks in heat get me pumped for the finale. We walk out on stage together. All the guys have ditched their costumes and they're all dressed like me. If you can call ratty jeans and boots a costume.

I've done studies on what the ladies like, and this getup is it.

We break into our dance when the thumping turns to music and the screaming starts. Some of them are practically begging for attention. Chandler whips his shirt off—this is his only act since the new girl put her foot down—and since he's been here the longest and has the most promo time, he gets an extra enthusiastic cheer he joins in off to the side.

Then the spotlights begin weaving around the crowd. This is my favorite moment. The moment when I get to choose. The moment filled with tonight's possibilities.

I zone in on that redhead who caught my t-shirt off to the left. She lifts her shirt up, showing her tits. But she's looking at Mitch like she wants to suck his cock right here, right now. So I move on. There's a blonde in the back, standing on a table, weaving her hips like she's way too familiar with this job I'm doing. Stripper. I'm not into strippers.

That makes me grin with the irony.

Another blonde off to the right is waving a fistful of twenties at Chandler. He's not looking to get laid by anyone here. He's got his girl and he's happy with her. But I don't like being second choice.

I look down the center of the stage and find the girl who said no earlier. She's sipping a drink that might be gin, or vodka, or hell, water for all I know. Her gay BFF is having way too much fun as she sits there stoically. Steve is gay, and it's pretty apparent when he does his act since it's to the YMCA tune. So I'm pretty sure her BFF's got his eye on him.

But that girl. She is blank. Like no expression.

I feel a little surge of adrenaline just thinking of her refusal. Not many people tell me no. And it's been a long while since I heard that word from a girl in the crowd after an invite to come on stage.

So she's my target when Chandler gives the cue for us to go find our last pick of the night. We go in order. First Steve, who can't pick a dude even if he wanted to because this is a ladies' night kinda gig. He hits up a cougar, like he always does.

Bill goes for grannies. He likes to make them blush and he gets a kick out of sticking their hands down his pants.

I head right to suit girl. She sees me coming and shakes her head no, but I'm in control. That last girl might've got a kiss in, but I *am* in control. I dance around her table, flirting with all the other girls as they stuff their dollars into my pockets, trying to cop a feel. One girl manages to get her hand inside the waistband of my jeans, but I grab it and rub it up against my lower stomach so she doesn't get far.

I weave back and forth in the middle of the audience, playing with ten or twelve women before the spotlight finally lands on me. And then I run straight towards suit girl who is too busy checking her watch to notice until I jump up, my boots clanking down on the bottom rung on either side of her bar stool, and grab her hair.

She looks up at me in shock, her mouth open, her eyes wide, and her head tilted up.

I am instantly hard.

"What are you doing?" she squeals.

"Yeah," the gay BFF screams. "Woohoo! Get him, Tiffy!"

I laugh at her name and then lean down into her ear as my hips gyrate back and forth, brushing against her thighs. "Tiffy," I growl in a gruff voice. "I'd have pegged you for a Jane or a Ruth. Something serious and boring."

"Get off me," she growls back.

"I'm not on you, sweetheart." And I'm not. I'm still standing on those chair rungs, hovering. But I let go of her head and point to my abs. "You wanna lick me?" I laugh.

"I do!" another girl says, jumping up and down with a fistful of dollars off to her right. "I do!"

"Come on, Tiffy. Lick me. Everyone wants to lick these abs.

Just open your mouth a little wider and I'll crash these rock-hard muscles into that sweet wet tongue."

Her BFF plants her hand on my hip, and she turns her head away from me to yell at him. I take her other hand and place it over the length of my cock. She gasps, tries to pull away, but I am focused on her now. Winning her over. Getting her attention. And hopefully meeting her after the show for some fun because she's damn cute.

Plus… I'm getting hard under her touch, reluctant as it is.

She freezes when she realizes what's happening, so I grip her hand tighter, forcing her to squeeze me. "Fuck, yeah, Tiffy. You feel good. Where you staying tonight? Here?"

She swallows hard, still holding onto my cock, even though I've eased up on her hand. Then she nods.

"What room, sweetheart? I'll drop by later."

"Penthouse Three!" the BFF screams. "Penthouse Three!"

I laugh at him as I lean down and breathe into Tiffy's ear. She shivers and her shoulder automatically comes up to push me away. But her hand is still on my cock. "Jesus, you better answer the door, because I like the way that feels."

Then I jump up, my boots finding the top rung of her stool, grab her head, and smash her face into my cock. Her hot breath beats against the soft denim of my pants, and just when I think my dick can't get any harder, it grows for her.

Her eyes dart up to mine and I see so many things. Vulnerability first. Then surprise. Then fear. She pushes me back and I jump off, letting all the other girls around me get their share as they fill my pockets with money.

I give a wink and she looks away—ashamed, or embarrassed,

or both.

But I know she'll answer the door.

They always answer the door.

XOXOXOXOX

Once the show is over, we spend the next hour flirting with anyone who approaches. Not all approach. It's not as bad as it sounds. I mean, we charge money for that shit, so not everyone cares to shell out thirty-five dollars for a photoshoot with male entertainers.

So by the time I get out of there, take a shower, pull on some jeans and a t-shirt and get an elevator up to penthouse three, it's pushing midnight.

I hesitate ready to knock. She didn't look like a party girl. She looked professional, I recall that much, in that cream-colored suit and a low-cut button-down blouse that was the color of tangerines. It was fluttering a little from the fans above her head that keep the room at a manageable temperature. She had on a gold locket too. Maybe not the kind that opens up and has a picture in it, but it was a heart shape. Her hair was long. I could tell even though it was pulled back in some sort of fancy updo because there were a few long tendrils spiraling down her neck and dragging across her shoulder when I leaned into her. She smelled fresh. Not like heavy perfume. Almost sweet. Like the resort gardens at night when the air is cool.

A nice girl, maybe.

What if she's asleep?

But then her determined look and firm no the first time

I approached her comes back to me. She gave in a little at the end but I bet it was only because there was no easy way out. I bulldozed over her.

So she's not a pushover. She's probably more of a conformist.

I knock. What do I have to lose?

The door opens after only a few seconds and then she's peering back at me. Her eyes are green. I didn't remember that. Maybe because I wasn't looking so much at her eyes downstairs. Tendrils of hair are still dragging along her neck and her blouse is still flirting with me from the air-conditioning vents above the door.

"Hey," I say in my sexy voice, one arm leaning against the doorjamb, nonchalant-like.

"Hey," she says in her sweet one.

"I wasn't sure if you'd still be up."

"And miss an opportunity to get to know the infamous Mr. Fletcher Novak?" She chuckles. "Not a chance in hell I'd miss that."

Hmmm. "OK." I chuckle back, but it comes off as nerves. Why does she make me nervous? "So…"

"So what did you have in mind tonight?" She bats her eyelashes like she's flirting with me.

Is this the same girl? I squint at her. Yeah. That's her. Same suit. Same hair. But her new attitude? It's throwing me. "Ummm, well, we could go have a bite to eat?"

Bite to eat, Fletcher? What the fuck are you talking about? This is a booty call, not a date.

"I already ate. I typically do that at dinner time." She smiles all flirty-like again.

"Oh. OK. Well, we have different ideas about dinnertime, I guess. I work late, so you know"—*Why am I defending myself?*—"I eat late too."

"What do you usually do when you knock on a patron's door after the show?"

I let out a nervous laugh. "Well, you know, I don't really do this often."

"No? So I'm special?"

"I picked you out of a crowd of hundreds of screaming women. So yeah, Tiffy." I use her name and it catches her off-guard. She looks surprised that I remembered. "You're special."

"It might've been because I was sitting in the front center table. Maybe I was just the first girl you saw?"

Oh, I get it. She is insecure. She wants me to make her think this might lead to more than just a one-night fuck. But I can tell by her body language she wants to fuck me just as much as I want to fuck her. She just wants me to work for it.

Well, I can work for it. I'm not a total douchebag. So I swipe a finger gently down her cheek and tuck one of those long flowing strands behind her ear. "You were the prettiest girl in that crowd, I guess." And it's not a lie. She is totally different from the kind of girl who usually shows up to see the Mountain Men dance. More put-together. More professional. Not there for anything other than curiosity. In fact, I bet the gay friend wanted to go to the show and dragged her along for the ride.

"God," she laughs. "You are a player, Mr. Novak."

"I can play," I say softly, leaning in to kiss her lips. It's a small kiss. Just a little tender peck. "If you want to play. But if you're interested in getting to know me better, then you've got my full attention."

"Really?" she asks, leaning in to kiss me back this time.

"Yeah," I breathe into her mouth. "Really."

"In that case, why don't you come in? Because I'm dying to ask you questions." She bats those long lashes again and I am mesmerized by her emerald eyes. She swings the door open to reveal a dimly lit hallway leading into the penthouse. I enter, my eyes on the far window, and then wait for her to close the door and lead the way.

"Would you like a drink, Fletcher? You might need one."

"Huh?" I follow her a few steps, put off my game once again by the change in her voice. "Yeah, sure."

Her heels click on the travertine tile floor as she walks briskly towards the living room. I follow, my eyes on her ass as I try to figure out what her angle is. But as soon as I look up again, I stop.

"Hey," I say, putting my hands up. "I'm not into group shit." There's a man in a suit. A very nice suit, even I can see that. And the gay best friend standing at the bar on the far side of the room. "What's the deal here?"

"The deal, Fletcher," Tiffy says as she pours two glasses of Scotch from a decanter sitting on the bar, "is that you missed a meeting with me this afternoon."

What the fuck?

"And since I'm really not used to getting stood up by *employees*"—she emphasizes the word—"I thought I'd pop in on your show and see you in action. I mean"—she walks back over to me with two drinks in her hand—"I've heard so much about you."

I look at the drink she's offering and decide I need it. It

goes down smooth in one gulp and lights a fire in my throat afterwards. "You set me up."

"I did not."

"Mr. Novak," the suit says, inserting himself between me and Tiffy. He looks familiar, but I'm off balance right now, so I don't have the time to give it more thought. "We're from corporate. I'm Cole Lancaster, general manager of the western division grouped under Preston Resorts. And you've met Tiffy here. Tiffy *Preston*," he says, enunciating her last name so it's clear just who she really is. The boss' daughter. "Her father, the CEO, has instructed me to train her to take over the hotel when I'm promoted to COO next quarter. The Landslide Hotel and Casino is our last stop after the recent mergers into the Preston family. We've heard a lot about you from Amy, and to be honest"—he says it with a laugh—"we thought she was just fucking with us."

"I'm not following," I say through gritted teeth. But I'm not having any trouble following. Amy hates me. She always has. But she was just an assistant manager when I was hired by her predecessor nine months ago. She had no say in that decision. And since I've packed that house two nights a week every week since I started, once she took over three months back after the merger with Preston, she had to admit I was good.

"This unprofessionalism that you exhibit, Mr. Novak," Tiffy says, taking over. "The tardiness, the missed meetings, the diva attitude. It's not a good refection on my father's company. But I get it, Fletcher. I really do. You're a performer. You have an ego that must be stroked and nurtured." She shakes her head, closes her eyes, and laughs before she can continue. She's making fun of me. "But propositioning patrons of this hotel for sex is something we will not tolerate."

"I never propositioned you for sex, honey. You're the one who propositioned me. I asked you to dinner." Holy fuck. God loves me tonight. Because I can't even remember asking a one-night fuck out for dinner before five minutes ago.

She looks over at Cole, who shrugs. He knows I'm in the clear for that. So I keep going. "In fact, you set me up. What I do on stage, what I did with you, that was an act, princess. I'm an actor out there. And you liked it so much you wanted more. Your assistant there—" I point to the BFF.

"Claudio," he purrs at me with a smile and a wink.

"—Claudio screamed out your room number. And since he works for you, he's part of this setup. So why don't you take your self-righteous attitude and give it a little adjustment. I could just as easily say you sexually harassed me."

"My God, please," she screams, her face burning a bright red.

"Tiffy," Cole says with a hand meant to shut her up. "Stop."

"Yeah, stop," I growl. "Save your breath for tomorrow's meeting. Because I'm out of here. Thanks for the drink. We can pick this up again on the clock." And I hand the empty glass off to a smirking Claudio as I exit the room.

3

The door slams behind him so loud, it makes me jump. I am instantly pissed that he had that effect on me. Especially after what he did tonight. How dare that man? How dare he—

"Tiffy," Cole says, walking to the door and looking out the peephole. "This is a problem."

"Which part?" I ask. "The part where he gyrated his hips in my face tonight? Or the part where he placed my hand over his..." Jesus. That really happened. And I didn't pull away.

"No, Tiff. The part where he says you propositioned him. What exactly did you say to him when you answered the door?"

"What? You're kidding me, right? That jerk has been using his... position to..." Damn. I can't even have this discussion with Cole.

"To pick a booty call out of the audience," Claudio offers up with a smirk. "Is that what you were trying to say, Tiff?"

"Yes," I say. "Yes, thank you, Claudio. That's what he's been doing, Cole! And my father is going to have another heart attack if he finds out how dirty this show is."

"Oh, relax, girlfriend," Claudio says, filling up his glass with Scotch and then pouring more into mine. "Your old man has been around more than one block. He knows exactly what's going on here. He could've shut this show down months ago and he didn't."

"Yeah, he thinks he knows. But he has no idea that the star of the show is using his hotel to drum up…" Shit. Why does Cole have to be here? I can't even with him.

"Sex," Claudio offers again.

Oh my God. I'm really having this conversation in front of Cole. I might die of embarrassment.

"Yeah, Tiff," Cole says as he gives my arm a comforting pat. "Your father isn't the one I'm worried about. Did you proposition Novak at the door?"

"What? No!"

"Did he ask to come in? Or did he really ask you to dinner?"

"He did, but—"

"Shit," Cole says, making a serious frown that causes his eyebrows to knit into a furrow on his forehead. "We're going to have to tread carefully here."

"I did not proposition him! I asked him if he wanted to come in! That's all!"

"I don't think that's all, Tiff," Claudio says before taking a long gulp of his drink. "You did kiss him."

"What?" Cole exclaims.

"No! Look, Cole. He was just being all…" Fuck. Why can't I talk about this stuff with him? I've known the guy for eight years, since I was a teenager and he just started working for my dad. And yeah, I have a little crush on him, but holy mother, I can't even think about sexy stuff with Fletcher Novak without blushing in front of Cole. "You know, playerish and stuff." *Playerish?* Something is seriously wrong with me.

"Flirty?"

"Shut up, Claudio! You're making things worse here."

"OK," Cole says, gathering up his laptop from the table near the bar. "We're just gonna go to bed…"

I lose track of his words as I stare at his mouth. He said *bed*. I'm like a fourteen-year-old boy.

"… and regroup in the morning. I have a call I have to take at eight-thirty, so if you see him before I get there, do not engage. Got it?"

"Got it," I say with a nod, finally managing to pull myself together.

"Goodnight then, Tiffy." He leans down and kisses me on the cheek like he's done a hundred times before. I have been holding my breath ever since the very first time he did it, hoping it would progress into something more. Like a real date. Not a business meeting, or a working lunch, or even one of the many corporate parties we've attended together. A relationship.

But Cole must be the most patient guy in the world. Because that innocent cheek kiss has never strayed. Much to my dismay.

"Good night, Cole," I whisper softly as he leaves my room.

"Oh my gawd," Cole says with a dramatic wave of his hand in front of my face. "I'm gonna throw up if I have to keep watching this desperate plight of yours. He's not interested in you, honey. That kiss will never change. He thinks of you like a sister."

"Just stop, OK? He does not think of me like a sister. He just hasn't had a chance to see the grown-up me, that's all."

"Pathetic," Claudio says, bouncing his ass down on the couch and kicking his Jimmy Choos up on the glass-top coffee table. "You're pathetic. Trotting around like a bitch in heat. That man is not interested. I mean, what good is a gay friend if you don't trust his manstincts?"

"Manstincts? Really?" He is always making these ridiculous frankenwords.

"What?" Claudio says, giving me one of those famous smirks that make men melt. "It's a good one. And it applies," he says, closing his eyes and lifting his face up like he's so superior. He feels superior the way most people feel hungry. Three to six times a day. "Because I know what I'm talking about. I see what you cannot. Cole is not interested in you."

"Oh," I say, plopping down on the couch next to him with my drink. He always makes me feel better. "And you're the expert in what straight men want, I suppose." I wrap my hand around his biceps and curl into his chest.

He wraps his arm around my shoulder and starts playing with my hair. "I am, Tiffy. Give up on Cole, please. It hurts my heart to think you might waste your life on that guy. He's all wrong for you. He's not even straight."

"Liar," I hiss softly into his suit coat. "You say that all the time, but even my gaydar knows he's into women. Besides, I've seen him date a few. He's not gay."

Claudio sighs. "Yeah, you're probably right. But a guy can

hope."

I pull away and look up at him.

"No, no, no, you sweet idiot! I'm not interested in him! He's portly."

I giggle. "He's not portly. He's muscular."

"OK, slightly chubby."

"Asshole. I like him like that."

"Pfft. No. He's not one of those giant men. You know, the big and tall guys. I call them linebackers. Those guys are hunky."

"Right? I totally agree."

"Cole isn't on the football team, Tiffy. He's that nerdy kid who wants to run the film projector."

"You're an idiot."

"Now, that Fletcher. Mmmm. Mmmm. Mmm. He's better than a linebacker. He's like a combination of linebacker and tight-end. Yeah," Claudio says, still playing with my hair. "Fletcher Novak is a tightbacker. I'd like to get a look at his back end, that's for sure."

"Perv. And that guy is not better than Cole. Not at all. He's a stripper, for Pete's sake."

"Mm-hmm. Exactly."

I giggle, thankful that Claudio and I have been a team since we graduated college four years ago. He wasn't interested in grad school, but my father said I needed an assistant, and Claudio was more than happy to step in and run my life. I love him for it too. He's more than my assistant though. He's been my best friend since high school. We've been inseparable since the ninth grade and as soon as I finished my MBA two years ago, my father hired me as a junior account executive and I kept Claudio. I run fourteen hotel accounts in Northern California and Nevada, and Claudio is my right-hand man.

But he's wrong about this Novak guy. I can see through Fletcher Novak a mile away. He's a player. And I hate players. He's also a slut. I hate them too. And a stripper? Please. Who wants to date a stripper? I mean, I get watching them for a few hours. But date one? No way.

"OK, toots, I gotta hit the sack. I'm gonna have so much fodder for my wet dreams."

"Gross, Claudio! No!"

He pushes me off him and gets up laughing. "Night, babycakes. Sleep tight." He turns back to me and winks. "And don't say I didn't warn you when you dream about the stripper instead of the spare tire."

I throw a pillow at him, but he dodges and jogs away to his end of the penthouse suite.

He's wrong about Cole. And Cole is not fat. Not even chubby. He's just thick, that's all. He's muscular, but instead of being lean, he's got some extra weight on him. I kinda like it. When he puts his arm around me it feels soft and comforting.

Fletcher Novak is nothing like Cole. And I don't mean that in a good way. He's crass and he sells himself on stage every night. What a stupid way to make a living.

And after reading through Amy's reports on him, I just know he's up to something. She didn't have any details, but she said she's heard rumors that he's some sort of pimp.

Imagine! A pimp working in my father's casino. He'd definitely have a heart attack if that got out.

No. Fletcher Novak needs to go. And I have plenty of reasons lined up to fire his ass tomorrow.

4

I toss and turn in bed as I imagine how tomorrow might go. Cole's reservations are playing on my mind. I fluff up my pillow and close my eyes for the millionth time.

But the only thing I see is that stupid Fletcher Novak. I know I'm right about him. And asking him to come inside my room wasn't a proposition. He was the one propositioning me.

I fling the white cotton sheet off me and pad out to the living room in my bare feet and nightclothes to find my laptop. He's up to something here, I just know it. So I'm going to do what I should've done straight away. Google him.

I settle down at the bar with my laptop and put in his name. And oh, yeah, baby, he's there. Pages of results for Fletcher Novak. And all of them seem to have something to do with the Mountain Men Male Revue Show.

I scroll down and make a face. This asshole has a Wikipedia

entry. How can he be that big? He's a stripper, for Pete's sake. I click on it anyway. Who wouldn't? And up comes his face.

Fletcher Novak, no middle name. Hmmm. He's two years older than me and grew up here in Lake Tahoe, on the North Shore—in Incline Village—and his parents worked at one of the resorts while he was growing up. Mother and father both died when he was eighteen. Brother, unnamed, three years later.

I almost feel sorry for him.

Almost.

Went to Berkley. Really? He does not look smart enough to go to Berkley. Majored in psychology. Dropped out senior year.

I do a quick date check, and yup, that's the year his brother died.

The next thing on his biography is the Mountain Men show here in Tahoe. But the years between are missing. Another red flag. He was probably in prison. I wonder if we did a background check on him before he was hired? You'd think the Wiki geek who wrote this up would've found a little more info.

But maybe no one is that interested in him?

I'm certainly not. I just need to know what I'm up against. Because there is no way Fletcher Novak will still be part of this show after I get done with him.

I grab a glass and some ice and then pour myself a little bit of Scotch. Maybe a drink will calm my nerves and let me sleep. Get this asshole off my mind.

I sit back down on the barstool and click out of Wikipedia, going back to my search results.

He even has videos and all of them seem to be of the strip show.

My finger hovers over the pad of my laptop. *Don't click those, Tiffy. You do not need to see him in action to get the info you need.*

Truth. But I can't help myself.

I click and the video opens up. The music is loud, so I scramble to turn it down and look over my shoulder, hoping I didn't wake up Claudio. He would never let me live this down if he caught me.

The MC of the show, Chandler something, calls out the names of each Mountain Man, and they appear on stage one by one, lining up along the back curtain as the women in the crowd start screaming. Then the music thumps, the dancers do some fist-bumps, and they start walking slowly forward on the stage, each one unfastening buttons down their dress shirt.

Wow. That's sorta sexy. Not Fletcher, per se, but the whole act. There's smoke and lights. The film quality is good too, like this might be a paid promotion. And the guys seem focused and serious.

When they get to the edge of the stage, the shirts come off and are thrown aside. Then they all reach down, grab their pants, and pull them off in unison.

The crowd of crazy lust-filled women goes wild.

My eyes go big.

Jesus. Every one of them is in metallic silver briefs. And their… yeah, it's all packaged up into one nice neat little—maybe not so little—ball.

Oh my God, I said *ball.* I giggle and take a long sip of my Scotch.

Then each of the guys is featured one by one. Fletcher is last. The star of the show, it seems. How does a guy do all this in only nine months? It's like he's got his own PR campaign going.

But that speedy intro is not enough for me. There's something about him. Something that says he's hiding something. And that gap in his Wiki profile was the first clue.

Yes, Fletcher Novak is not what he seems. That might not even be his real name.

So I go looking for more videos. And there are plenty. Some professional ones just like the last one. But lots of them are from women who went to the show. Fletcher has more than all the other guys put together. And in all of them he has the same charming smile, the same wandering hands, and the same raunchy hips in a strange girl's face as he had for me.

It was an act. *No,* I correct myself. That *is* his act.

I go back to all the other guys and watch their routines in various clips. They have their own style. And in most of the acts you can tell they are singling out women to make them feel good. Some who look reserved and nerdy. Some who are heavier than the rest of their companions. Some who are older. Some who are even very old. That makes me smile. It's sweet to give a grandma a thrill, I think.

But Fletcher picks the sluts. They are all sexy, just like him. They have confidence and big tits. They scream his name and paw his body when he approaches.

I know why he picks them. Because he wants to fuck them afterward.

So why did he pick you, Tiffy?

I fill my glass again and gulp it down.

Why did he choose me? I'm not any of those things he looks for. I was frowning, buttoned up in my work suit, and out to get him—but not in a sexual way.

Hmmmm.

It wasn't innocent, I know that much. He wanted to fuck me. And if I wasn't Tiffy Preston, and if I wasn't sent here to check the place out, and if I wasn't—such an uptight prude—so serious, I might be in bed with him right now.

Warmth floods between my legs and I blush, even though no one is here to see me, let alone read my thoughts.

He is sexy, that's for sure. But he's a liar too. I just know it.

I pour some more Scotch and go back to my search results, paging through videos until I get one that has different lighting and style from the ones with the show and there's a girl on the still image.

Now we're talking.

I click it and she whirls around, slapping Novak in the face with a crack. "Asshole," she screams at him.

"Haha," the girl behind the camera laughs. .

It cuts away to another scene, which plays out the same way. An angry girl, a slap across the face for Fletcher, a laugh from the cameraman, and a fuck you from Fletcher.

He seems to have a pattern.

And let me guess who these girls are. The one-night stands after they realize he's a bullshitter.

Oh, fuck, yes. I have this asshole now. All I have to do is walk in to that meeting today and show this to Cole. Then he'll be on my side and Novak will be history.

I gulp the rest of my drink and go back to the videos. There might be more evidence, after all. And I need to watch every single one.

5

"You whore!"

"What?" Oh my God. My head. It's spinning.

"You stinky whore! You stayed up all night getting drunk and watching videos of that dreamboat? I should slap you."

"Why are you yelling? My head."

"Tiffy," Claudio says, pulling me up off the bar. I stumble trying to step down off my stool and fall into his chest and knock us both down. "You're gonna pay for this, toots. I swear. You've got a meeting in one hour and you're still drunk! What the hell happened last night after I went to bed?"

"I don't know."

"Get up off me, you ungrateful—"

"Stop insulting me!"

Claudio manages to push me aside so he can scramble out from under me, then stands there, tapping his slippered toe in front of my face. "You're going to blow this, Tiffy. And you're the one who dragged me up here in these godforsaken mountains to help you fix this hotel. I could be on vacation right now. I could be sucking down margaritas with Raul in the Bahamas."

"I know. I'm sorry. Help me up." I reach for him, but no help comes. Claudio is a grudge-holder. And he's right. I did drag him away from that trip with Raul. But Raul is an asshole. He can do better. I feel justified. "Fine, don't help me up. I can get up myself."

I brace my hands on the floor and manage to make it to my knees. But then my head starts spinning and I have to take a break. I'm not sure how long I kneel there looking like I'm waiting for someone to take me doggie-style, but in the end, Claudio gives me a hand before I make it to my feet.

"Thank you," I squeak. My stomach is a mess and it starts to rumble loudly.

"Your meeting is in forty-five minutes, Tiffy. Now what?"

Shit. Shit, shit, shit. Fletcher Novak's final hour is upon him and I'm not even coherent. "Call Cole and tell him he should take care of it."

"No can do, girlfriend. He's been texting you all morning. In fact, he called just before you woke up and said he might be a few minutes late to the meeting. You need to handle this. And if I was a betting man, I'd predict that Novak has something up his sleeve. He's not going down without a fight."

"He uses audience members for sex after each show, Claudio. We both know that's happening."

"But it didn't happen last night, Tiffy. He asked you to dinner and you invited him in. So you're the one who looks like you're out to seduce him."

"Ridiculous."

"I agree." Claudio laughs. "He's ridiculously handsome. And these videos!" He takes my seat at the bar and starts clicking on the videos of the Mountain Men I was watching last night. "They are all delicious."

My phone rings and I stumble over to the coffee table to grab it before flopping back on the couch. "Tiffy Preston," I say, not even looking at the screen.

"Thank God, Tiff. I've been trying to call you all morning."

"Sorry, Cole, I was sleeping pretty hard."

"I guess," he says. "You feeling OK?"

"Yes, yes, yes," I say. "I'm perfect."

"Good, because I've got my hands full with a problem in Reno hotel. I have to drive down there and take care of a personnel issue this morning so I'm not just going to be late for the meeting, I'm gonna miss the whole thing. But I'll be back soon. Can we have a late lunch today?"

Lunch. Yes! Finally, after all these years of waiting, Cole is asking me out. It might only be a day date, but that's—

"Tiffy? You still there?"

"Yes! I mean, yes to both. Yes for lunch and yes, I'm still here." I chuckle. "Obviously."

"OK, good. I'll see you around two then. Sound OK?"

"Sounds great, Cole. Looking forward to it." I end the call and smile up at a waiting Claudio. He's got his hands on his hips and he's tapping that toe again. "We have a date!" I smile so big, my cheeks hurt. "A real date. Late lunch, you whore. So there. I told you he was interested in me."

"Hmmph," Claudio pouts. "And why wouldn't he be? You're hot, Tiffy. A little bit of a prude for my tastes. But you're damn fine in the beauty department. And you're the daughter of a bazillionaire. What's not to like? You are ten steps up for boring, pudgy Cole."

"He's not pudgy! He's just a big guy."

"Whatever. I think you had the right idea last night. Dreamboat Novak is where I'd put all my efforts."

"He's a stripper, Claudio. Gross. And we both know he's fucking strangers after each show. That's two one-night stands a week. Just gross."

"Well, that's easily dismissed. If one clean bill of health is all that's standing between you and the most delectable slab of abs I've ever seen, I'll make him a doctor's appointment today."

"You," I say, pointing my finger up at him, "will stay out of this. You understand me? I don't need your help in the relationship department. Remember the last guy you set me up with? Mr. Hot Buns?"

Claudio snickers. "He was a fireman. I hate firemen, said no one ever. You're a freak."

"He was an arsonist, Claudio. He started fires just to put them out."

"Same difference. I'm just saying, a man with a giant water hose in his hands is hot."

"He was hot, all right. And so was that car he drove."

"So I misjudged one guy. Give me a break. You've misjudged plenty on your own."

I shoot him a dirty look for bringing that up. "No. I'm going after Cole and now that I finally have his attention, I do not want you to mess it up. You hear me?"

"Fine, fine." Claudio throws his hands up and sighs. "But he's a mistake. I'd just like to go on record that Cole Cookie-dough Lancaster is a mistake."

"And stop calling him fat! He's just a—"

"Big guy. Got it." Claudio rolls his eyes at me. "You better get in the shower, you've got thirty minutes now."

Shit.

6

I'm taking deep breaths to hide the fact that I just ran the entire length of the casino in order to make it to the admin buildings when I arrive at Amy's front vestibule. "Hi, I'm Tiffy Preston. I have a meeting with Amy at nine," I tell the secretary behind the desk.

"Oh, yes," she says, pushing her glasses up her nose. "She's just finishing up with her eight o'clock, so go into the conference room and it will just be a moment."

"Thank you," I say sweetly. People expect me to be a bitch since I'm the CEO's daughter, so I try not to meet their expectations even if I'm in the mood to tear someone's hair out. Sure, I'm a spoiled rich girl. But I'm not a raging control freak. If there's one thing my father taught me, it was to delegate to people who knew more than you in areas you were weak in. And since Amy is the expert here at the Landslide Hotel and Casino,

I'm happy to delegate as much as possible to her and remain an observer. Especially since I have a helluva hangover.

Whew. I let out one last long breath as I open the conference room door and step inside, thankful I have a few more minutes to gather my thoughts about—

"Hey, there, Tiff," Fletcher says with a smug grin as he turns from the view at the huge picture window. He checks his phone. "You're late."

I check my watch. "Two minutes."

"Two minutes is two minutes, right? Didn't you say something to me last night about being late?"

"You are an actor on stage. Things are timed, Mr. Novak." I set my bag down on the table and begin pulling out my laptop. "You can't afford to be two minutes late."

"And I wasn't. I was two seconds late. So don't you find it unreasonable to be angry over two seconds?"

"Again, Mr. Novak, you are in showbusiness. Two seconds is too long."

"I agree."

"What?"

"I said, I agree. It won't happen again. I've been giving this a lot of thought, and you're right. Two seconds is too many. I'm going to be early from now on."

I give him a sidelong glare. What's he up to? "Well, good. Then once Amy gets here, we can drop that issue and start discussing your breach of contract regarding these girls you… date."

"What breach?" he asks with a smile, taking a seat across from me at the table. "Did I breach, Miss Preston?"

Grrr. I have not read his contract. I was, after all, watching him strip online while getting drunk.

"Because I know for a fact that my contract has no stipulation that I don't date show patrons. That would be ridiculous considering more than a thousand people come to watch me every week. It would severely limit my dating pool."

"Maybe so, Mr. Novak. But I'm positive that you are not allowed to act in a manner that embarrasses the hotel. And the way you take home—"

"Who do I take home, Miss Preston? Who?" He stares hard at me for several seconds and his jaw muscles tighten, telling me that this is something he takes serious issue with.

"Do you take them home?" I play it safe.

"I do not."

"Do you go to their rooms?"

"Yes."

"Do you…"

"Fuck them?" he asks, with another one of those sly grins. He averts his eyes for a moment, looking down as his smile grows. He flashes me a glance from underneath his dirty-blond hair that tumbles over his forehead. "If I want, Miss Preston. There's nothing in my contract that says I have to be celibate."

Then he winks. And laughs, not in a mocking way, but more like a chuckle, making his smile grow and a dimple appear in his chin. Jesus, he's really handsome.

The door bursts open and Amy rushes in with an armful of folders. "Sorry, Miss Preston. I was on a call with the accounting department. I wanted to make sure we had our numbers straight before we decided on any disciplinary action."

"I've been keeping track as well," Fletcher says, reaching

down under the table and pulling out a laptop. "I've got the total number of ticket sales since the first month I started." He flips his screen around so I can see it and then points to the graph. "As you can see, when I started the show we were barely half-full on both Wednesday and Saturdays. And once I took over as the central dancer and made changes to the lineup, fired the poor performers—"

"Wait. *You* fired? I thought that other dancer was in charge. What's his name? Chandler?"

"He is," Amy says. "Technically. But Fletcher is in charge of the dancers."

"I am, and have been since the first day I started performing in this nearly defunct show," Fletcher says with another one of those sly grins masquerading as shy. "When I come on board, I come to win. I did my research and found out what each dancer brought to the table and coached them on how to play it up. I know people, Miss Preston. I understand people. And I use it to my advantage."

Oh, please.

"I pulled the Mountain Men up from obscurity and placed this show on the map. In fact, I've been working on a plan to franchise the show. You know, hire more dancers to go on tour. Keep a troupe here in Tahoe, and then get an elite troupe for a hotel in Vegas. Your father owns casinos in Vegas, I presume?"

"Um…" Fuck a duck. He's smart. "Yes. We have four, actually."

"Right. And two have stage shows. We could technically…"

I drift off after that. Because he never stops talking. The full hour of our meeting is all about the genius expansion plan of the Mountain Men Male Revue Show. There is no more mention of Fletcher Novak's sexual escapades, disciplinary actions, or tardiness. Even Amy, who was clearly not on his side the last time we chatted before I came to the hotel to see for myself, is smitten with his plan.

"So what do you think?" he finally asks, turning his attention to me. "I've put together a business plan"—he rattles away on his keyboard for a moment—"and have just emailed it to Cole and your father for consideration."

That two-timing swine! He went over my head! But I will be damned if I will give him the satisfaction of knowing how much that pisses me off. "Great." I fake a look at my watch. "Well, I have another meeting at ten, so I'm going to move along. Thanks for your time, Amy." I shake her hand as I try for a quick escape. "And I'll be in touch, Mr. Novak."

I cannot get out of that room fast enough. I smile brightly at the secretary, and then pull the outer door open and practically run down the hall to get away from that vile man with the sexy grin.

I hate him. I mean, I hated what he represented when I walked into that meeting. But now I just hate him in every way possible. He did all that to make me look bad. Make himself look so smart. Make me feel—

"Hey, Tiffy!"

Oh, no, he doesn't. He does not get to embarrass me like that and then expect me to be civil in the fucking hallway. I make a beeline for the elevators and press the button. God loves me, because the doors open and there is no one inside. I rush in, hit the button for my floor, and then stand back against the mirrored walls.

But just as the doors are about to clang shut, a hand is there to ruin my escape.

"Hey," Fletcher says, getting in with me. "Didn't you hear me call your name?"

"I heard."

"So you ignored me."

"What do you want, Mr. Novak?"

"Well… I just… wanted to see if you liked that plan, that's all. I really have been working on it in my spare time."

"So you aspire to bigger things than taking your clothes off?" I wince, immediately regretting opening my mouth. *Expect the unexpected, Tiffy. Isn't that your motto? So why are you so pissed off that Fletcher Novak pulled the same stunt on you*?

I just am. That's all.

"Hmm," is Fletcher's only response to my outburst.

"I'm sorry," I say, taking a deep breath. "That was not… appropriate."

He's silent for a moment. "That's all right. At least you were honest."

I roll my eyes before I can stop them.

"I try to be honest too."

I huff out a laugh. "Right. You? Honest?"

"What's that supposed to mean?"

"You, Fletcher Novak, are a player. You're a bullshitter. You came into my meeting with your proposal when you knew damn well we were there to discuss you."

"We did discuss me."

"We were supposed to be discussing disciplinary actions! Not your dreams and aspirations."

"What do you know about my dreams and aspirations?"

"You just laid them all out for me."

"Now it's my turn to laugh. I gave you a gift. A way to move this dinky little show forward."

"And save your ass in the process," I sneer.

"An entire business plan for exponential growth."

"And I suppose you'd like to be one of the dancers who make it to Vegas? Right? You see your name in lights? You see money, and more slutty girls and one-night stands than you can count. That's your dream, and I'll tell you right now, my father might like your plan, but he will not like you."

"Why not? What've I ever done to him?"

"You're shady, and dishonest, and a cheat. He's into integrity, Mr. Novak." The doors open on my floor and I rush out, but Fletcher follows me. "What are you doing?" I say, whirling around to meet him face on.

"What's your problem? Was it the kiss last night? Did you like it? Was it the fact that you grabbed my cock and realized you wanted it? And then you saw that I could have anyone and you felt insecure?"

"Ha! You wish. I'm so much better than you. Believe me, that kiss meant nothing. And your… your…"

"Cock," he says with a smile and a wink.

"Was nothing…" And I run out of words because my mind is actually caught up in the *size* of his considerable… cock.

He laughs as the elevator doors close, leaving us in the hallway in front of my penthouse. He walks towards me, making me back up until my back is pressed against the door. "You liked it, Tiffy. You think I'm adorable."

“No,” I say, shaking my head. “I think you’re a player. I think you lie to women, tell them what they want to hear to get your way. And it’s not going to work with me.”

“Lie to them? No. I don’t lie. I tell them nice things, sure. I make them feel special, yes. And you know why I do these things, Tiffy?”

“To get laid!”

“To make them feel special. To wipe away all the bullshit some other man has already put into their heads. To make them smile. What’s wrong with making them smile?”

“You lie. You say things you don’t mean as a means to an end.”

“I do not. I say things that are true. I just refrain from saying the things that will hurt them. That’s all. I tell them they’re pretty because they are. I tell them they make me feel good, because they do. I tell them things that make them happy. Every bit of it’s true.”

“I don’t believe you. What woman wants to be used for a night and thrown to the curb the next day?”

“The women who come to a strip show and then go home with a stripper.”

“You’re an asshole.”

“You like it though, don’t you.” He takes a few steps closer to me, making me feel trapped by his glare and his words. “Did someone hurt you, Tiffy? Did some big, bad man hurt your feelings? Tell you you’re fat? Tell you you’re stupid? Tell you you aren’t good enough?”

“Stay away from me, Fletcher, I’m warning you.”

“I’m not even touching you, Tiffy. But you want me to, don’t you?" He takes one final step until we are barely an inch apart. "If I took you home I'd wipe all that shit out of your mind. I'll say you're pretty because you are. I'd say you're smart because you are. I'd say you're better than me because no man worth anything would want anything else. And that's all true, Tiffy. I'd leave out every negative thing about you. Is that telling you what you want to hear? Fine, maybe it is. But I like being nice. Sue me."

"You like getting what you want." He's so close to me, I can see little flecks of green in his blue eyes.

"True," he whispers. "I do. But I'm not out to hurt anyone in the process."

"Tell that to the discarded women you leave behind."

"They all know. Because I tell them. One night only. Take it or leave it." He smirks at me, and then places his hands on either side of my head, boxing me in. He leans forward so far that his hair dangles down and flashes against my cheek, making me shiver. "They always take it."

"They take it because they want *you*. No one wants a one-night stand."

"Fuck," he laughs, stepping back from me. The heat from his body disappears with him, and I have to take a deep breath to calm my heart. "I can't win with you, can I?" His eyes are bright and his grim is real. He's having fun right now.

I just stare at him.

And then his mouth is on mine. His hands are behind my head, pulling me towards him. His tongue does a little dance against my lips, begging me to open for him. I feel a rush of heat and a wave of dizziness as the moment captures me and holds me tight.

"Open your mouth," he whispers. "I want to feel your tongue."

"Stop," I say weakly.

He does stop. But I'm sorry I said it, because I want more, not less.

It's too late though. He bows his head and steps back. He gives me one more look before he turns and walks down the hall to the stairs.

"Fletcher?" I call softly, just as he disappears through the door.

I don't know what to do, so I do the only thing I can think of.

I go after him.

7

I wait inside the stairwell, backed up against the wall. The door flings open, almost smashes me in the face, and then I push it away and there she is.

Tiffy Preston was on my mind all goddamned night. Even before I knew her name. Her hot breath on the fabric of my jeans during the show last night. Her upturned eyes. I dreamed about those upturned eyes. Pushing my cock down her throat while she looked up at me. Maybe a little bit of mascara running down her face from tearing up with the effort of swallowing me whole.

“You!” she yells, as she pushes me solidly in the chest, making me take a step back.

My dick is already hard.

“What are you doing?” she yells. And if I didn’t already know this stairwell was soundproof, I’d be worried about how loud she is. But I know it’s soundproof. I’ve had other girls screaming up in here before.

And now it's her turn.

Because I need to get this girl off my mind and there is only one sure way to do that.

Fuck her.

Once I fuck her, she will cease to exist. That's how it's always been, and that's how it's gonna stay. One very simple solution to the problem that is Tiffy Preston.

"Say something, dammit."

"Why did you follow me?" I say it as calm as can be. Not one syllable betrays the way I want to push her over, drag that lily-white dress up her thighs, and fuck her from behind.

"What?" She blinks at me.

I almost laugh. But I'm so fucking horny. I'm so in need of release, and I need it to happen now. I don't want her to start feeling comfortable with me. I just want her to do as she's told. "Why, Tiffy?"

She bolts, reaching for the door handle and pulling back. But it's locked from the outside and she stumbles back a step when she realizes this. "We're locked in!" She whirls around to me. "What the—"

I cup my hand over her mouth. It's a creeper move, and she takes it in stride, so I have to give her credit for that. "Shhh. Just come with me."

I take her hand and start climbing the stairs that lead up to the roof. That door is locked too, but I press my back to it, making the keycard in my back pocket activate the mechanism, and then flash Tiffy a smile so she doesn't realize we're not locked in.

I can't have her bolting before I get my chance to erase her from my thoughts.

"What is this?" she asks, all innocent-like, when we step out into the fresh morning air.

"What's it look like?" I ask back, a little smile of satisfaction creeping up against my wishes.

"A garden?"

"Sorta," I say, leading her away from the door and the only way back down, so she can concentrate on what's gonna happen up here with me instead. "I guess they thought about a rooftop garden terrace at one point. But you know, we're like six thousand feet up in elevation and it's harder to grow things here than most people realize."

"You grew up in Tahoe."

"North Shore, born and raised."

"What do your parents do?"

"They're gone," I say, reaching for her face. I kiss her before she has a chance to say, *I'm sorry*, like everyone else. Mostly because I just want to imagine her lips around my dick, but also to shut her up about my family.

She kisses me back this time. The roof does it to them. Makes them think a) they are special and b) they are alone. When in fact there are several buildings nearby taller than the Landslide, so technically, lots of people can see us.

She pulls back from the kiss and I growl out my discontent as she stammers to find words. "How many girls have you brought up here?"

Shit, she was supposed to think she was the only one. "Not a lot," I say. She crinkles her nose at me, but it's not a lie. "I'm a spontaneous kinda guy, Tiffy. And getting up the roof stairs from the penthouse floor is not something you can do spontaneously."

"Oh."

She looks at me for a second. Not with suspicion for once, but maybe a little bit of relief. I kinda like it. "Come on, let me show you something." I pull her hand behind me, still laughing a little inside at how easy it is to take a girl from blind hate to blind lust. "See, they had all these raised gardens planned and everything." I wave my hand at the sections of concrete acting like flower beds. "For whatever reason, they abandoned the project and this is all that's left." It's not very impressive. Just some dead shrubs and whatever weeds grow up here in the summer. "But they do have this little potting shed."

"Oh, that's cute," Tiffy says. I look back and catch a smile.

I've never been up here during the day. Sneaking up to the penthouse floor isn't a daytime activity. But I didn't have to sneak. So here it is in full sunlight. I have to admit, it's a little shoddy-looking when it's not shrouded in darkness and only lit up by the stars. It's made out of stained gray cinderblock, the glass is dirty, and there's a layer of dust clinging to the panes. The metal door is a little bit rusty and it squeaks when I open it.

There's a storage box in the far corner, and I let go of Tiffy's hand to walk over to it.

"What's that?" she asks. "Your nookie stash?"

I look over my shoulder and smile. "Nookie?"

"You know what I mean."

It *is* my nookie stash, and she should be pissed off about that. But maybe the layer of dust over the footlocker box is all she needs to believe me when I say it's been a while. I flip the latch up and open the lid.

"Oh my God. It *is* your nookie box. How many times have you had sex on that blanket?"

I throw the blanket down on the ground. "Never, you sicko. I make them stand."

"Asshole."

"Hey, you asked. If you don't want to know about the secret life of Fletcher Novak, don't ask."

"Is that what you tell them? Don't ask?"

"I just told you, didn't I?" I regret my words the second they leave my mouth. She pulls away. "Sorry," I say, meaning it. I don't ever make the girls feel cheap when they've got my attention. It's one night, I make sure they know that. And I just told Tiffy that it's a one-time thing. But I don't have to rub it in. "I have not had sex on this blanket, OK? I use it for picnics."

"I've heard everything now." She snorts.

"Hey, I'm a romantic, what can I say?"

"You're playing me right now, aren't you?"

"Only if you want to be played."

"Why did you bring me up here?"

"Why do you think?"

We stare at each other for a few seconds. I can practically hear her thoughts. Her inner voice is telling her to run. Get as far away from me as possible. They all think that. But none of them can resist me. I'm not saying that to be obnoxious. It's just true. I have that 'it' factor. Something about me just screams sexy.

"Have you thought about me?" I ask. "Since last night at the show? Because I've thought about you."

"What did you think about me? That I'm your next victim?"

"No, actually." I smooth down the blanket on the ground of

the shed and then step towards her, taking her face in my hands and pulling her tight against my chest. "I've thought about your hot breath as you panted against my cock when I was standing on your chair. I thought about your upturned eyes, looking at me if I ever got the chance to get you on your knees."

She gulps air.

"Now tell me what you've been thinking about. Because you wouldn't be here if you didn't want to be."

"We're locked in," she whispers as my mouth moves in closer.

I kiss her softly. No tongue, just a small, tender kiss that makes girls melt. "You have a phone, Tiffy. One call to your BFF, Claudio, and you're free."

She stares at me.

"But even though I might be the biggest prick you ever met, you want me, don't you."

She swallows hard.

"And I want you. That's why we're here. I want you. So if you don't feel the same way, now's your chance to say so."

"I want…" She stops. There was a word on her lips, but I'm almost certain it was not my name. Jealousy heats me up in a millisecond. What kind of girl has another man's name on her tongue when she's gazing up into my eyes?

"What?" I say sharply. "What were you gonna say?"

"I want to be irresistible. Like you."

"What?" I have to admit, I'm surprised. And then I laugh. "Are you a virgin?"

"I'm twenty-six, asshole. I'm not a fucking virgin."

"Then what do you mean? I'm confused."

"You're just…" She sighs. "So good at this stuff. Seduction, right? I'm bad at it."

"Who do you want to seduce?" My jealous rage is back.

"No one. Not specifically. But you're so confident. And I'm so… not. I feel like I should take notes."

It's my turn to sigh. "What, you want me to teach you how to seduce someone?" The irony is not lost.

"Well, look. I hate you. I really do. You had me grabbing your cock last night and then I got accused of sexually harassing *you*. You made me feel like an idiot in that meeting with your plans and proposals. And now I'm up in your sex den, and I'm not sure what's happening." She looks at me with pleading eyes. "Tell me how you get all this control. How do you do it?"

I think about this for a few seconds, and then take a calculated risk. "How many blowjobs have you given in your life, Tiffy?"

"What?" She laughs, putting her hand over her heart like the word 'blowjob' is an assault on her virtue.

"Any?"

"I've given… one," she admits, and then averts her eyes.

I'm turned on again. "One? One is not enough. If you want to know how to control a man, you don't need to look any further than your own mouth. Men are drawn to lips. Every girl they ever think about sexually starts with an image of their cock in that girl's mouth. So if you want control, you gotta lead a guy to your mouth."

She takes a deep breath. "Go on."

God, why am I so annoyed that she's asking me for pointers? I can make her do anything I want right now. I should be celebrating.

"Please," she begs. "Tell me."

I place a hand on her shoulder and push. "Get on your knees."

She drops to her knees on the blanket without question and my dick grows inside my jeans. She looks into my eyes for a second, and then embarrassment takes over and she looks down.

"Look at me."

She does. Those amazing green eyes turn up and I almost moan.

"Now bite your lip a little. Get my attention." Fuck, she has my full attention as her white teeth take a little nibble of her lip. "That's nice," I whisper, dropping down on one knee in front of her. I take her face in both my hands and lean in for another kiss. "I can already picture my hard cock filling you up."

And then I stand back up and start unbuckling my belt. The metal clanks and the leather makes a zipping sound as I whip it off. "Bend over, put your forehead to the blanket and put your hands behind your back."

She does that hard swallow again, but then she does as she's told. I bind up her hands with the belt and cinch it tight enough to make her squeal. "Now," I say, placing a hand on her shoulder to give her a little push, "back to kneeling."

She struggles to right herself in front of me, but I help her when she needs it and then there she is.

Perfect.

Innocent.

And perfectly fuckable.

"In my opinion, girls use their hands too much. So lesson number one for giving a fabulous blowjob is to let the guy do his thing. Let him play with you first and keep your hands to yourself." I unbutton my pants with a small snap and then drag the zipper down. I reach inside, pull my hard cock out from my boxer briefs, and present her with it.

She stares at my length for a moment, and then her eyes shoot up to mine.

Holy mother. I want to come on her face and we haven't even started. "Don't open your mouth yet, Tiffy." I swear, she trembles when I say her name. "Just let me rub my cock along your lips."

She keeps her mouth closed as I bring my tip to her face. And when I touch her soft skin, her lips don't press together. They move, ever so slightly, as I play.

"You want to know how to make a man want his cock in your mouth, Tiffy?"

She nods. And then, even though I don't expect it, she says, "Yes, Fletcher. Tell me. Show me how to do it."

I have to stop for a moment. She is unbelievably sexy. "If your hands aren't tied behind your back, then you place a finger in your mouth. Tease him. Bring his attention to your lips. Make him imagine all the ways they can move. When you bite your lip, show him a little tongue. It drives me wild." Wait. "It drives *them* wild," I correct.

She smiles coyly at my slip-up. She knows she's beautiful, dammit. She's probably given a hundred blowjobs and here I am trying to tell her what to do. Shit, she's probably playing me.

I can't handle that thought. I can't handle the image of her blowing other men and taking me for a ride. So I stop playing with her mouth and aim my cock right for her opening.

Her lips wrap around me, slightly sucking. Fuck, yeah, this chick is hot. She looks up at me, her eyes half-mast and her cheeks flushed pink. I grab her head and bring her closer to me, little by little so she doesn't gag.

She inhales sharply through her nose, trying her best to be accommodating.

And that's it, man. I'm gonna blow.

I pull my dick out of her mouth and pull her to her feet.

"What?" she asks. "What did I do wrong?"

"Nothing," I growl. "Nothing." I spin her around and untie her hands, throwing the belt on the ground as I spin her back. I push her up against the door to the shed and hike her dress up her thighs. "I almost came down your fucking throat."

"Isn't that the objective?"

Objective? Fuck. I'm gone. She thinks she's part of some sort of training and I'm ready to explode. "Sexy Man's Rule Number One, princess. Never come before the girl."

She laughs as I pull a condom out of my back pocket, tear open the foil packet, and slip it over my shaft. "Sexy Man's Rules?"

"Yeah," I say, grabbing her hips and lifting her up so I can spread her thighs apart. "It's a column in some magazine Chandler gets delivered backstage. Now stop talking."

8

"Wait."

"Shit," he mumbles, taking a step back, letting my legs go until my feet touch the floor again. He takes a few deep breaths. "What's wrong?" It's not mad, which surprises me since he's so clearly ready to get on with things. And then he threads his fingers through his hair and gives me a look that says he's doing his best, but the only thing on his mind is fucking.

"I barely know you." It sounds very needy, even to me. And when his brow scrunches up, I know he's ready to walk out.

And I don't want him to walk out. Fletcher Novak might be a dickhead, but he's a seriously hot dickhead. And he's got more experience in his toe than any man I've ever been with. And the promise of pointers has me intrigued.

So I salvage this situation the only way I can. "Tell me what to do," I say, blushing as the words come out.

My reward is a smile. Not just any smile. Not just any Fletcher Novak smile, either. But something… very… genuine. His blue eyes light up, and smile wrinkles line his face. He looks almost boyish. If a rock-hard man like him could ever be boyish.

"Fuck," is his response. "You're like a fucking porn star right now."

I laugh. "I'm so not."

He grabs my face and kisses me so hard my knees go weak. My head spins, and then his teeth grab my lip and give it a nip. I pull back from the shock, but his hands tighten against my head, and he pushes his tongue further inside.

And we kiss. We pant and twist together. His hips find mine and start to grind. His hard cock presses against my belly, making me heat up from the core.

He draws back, still holding on to my face with those strong hands, and stares into my eyes. I feel like he can see inside me. All my insecurities and doubts. All my failures and faults. "You want to know how to make me want you, Tiffy?"

I breathe hard and nod. "I want to know how to make all men want me. I want to know how you do it. You're… hot. And charming. But you're bad in every way that girls hate. So why do they want you?"

"Why do you want me?"

I swallow. "I'm not sure. That's why I need to know. I want to be that girl. I want men to desire me the way I desire you right now." The lust in his eyes multiplies as my words sink in. "And I have no good reason to want you. I don't even like you."

He laughs at that and I'm drawn deeper into his spell. "That's what they all say."

"Why do they say it? Why do they let you use them when they know you're just playing? When they know there's not a serious bone in your body, that you're using them?"

"Why are you here?" He pets my cheek as he asks it. And that's why.

"You trick them. You're tricking me right now. Pretending to care with a tender gesture."

"Why is it pretending? If I'm here trying to make you happy in the moment? Why is that a lie?"

"Because you don't want me. You want to fuck me."

"Do you want me?" His laugh makes me wince. This is so easy for him. "You don't, do you? You're asking me to teach you how to make men desire you. Not how to make *me* desire you."

"You're already here."

"I'm here because you got my attention. So you're obviously doing something right." He watches me think about this for a moment. "But you want someone else, don't you? And that's the guy you're thinking of as I stand here with my dick pressing up against your stomach."

I can't even deny it.

"So you're using me."

I wait for him to walk off, but he doesn't. In fact, he does the opposite. He strokes my cheek again and I can feel that burning desire deep in my core. He leans in and kisses my mouth in a new way. A tender way.

I melt. I want him again. Even though I know the minute we leave this roof I will regret it, I want him to keep going.

"You touch him, Tiffy."

"What?"

"Whoever it is you want. You get him alone, and you touch his arm like this." He traces a finger down my bare skin and makes me shudder. "So softly, it almost tickles. And then you look him in the eyes and smile."

His smile, combined with that fingertip dragging down my arm, has me spinning.

"When you talk to him," he continues, leaning into my ear, "you get close. As close as you can. And you drop your voice to a whisper." His breath hits my neck and then finds its way into the shell of my ear.

I moan, my whole body pressing against him. "You make it seem easy."

"It's easy if you're right for each other."

"How do you find so many who are so right for you when I can't even find one?" I look up at him, begging him for this answer. "Why do some people draw love to them, and all I can find is… you?"

He laughs that off, but not as easily as before. "You don't get offers?"

I shake my head. "Not like this."

"Do you want me to stop, Tiffy?" He stares down at me, his fingers still working their magic on my arm. "Because I will." I look away, but he gently moves my chin back so I can't escape. "I don't want to, but I will."

But the truth is, I don't want him to stop. I want him to do everything to me. Everything. But for all the wrong reasons. Fletcher Novak is very hot, but he's not my type. And this makes me a user, just like him. I only want whatever will come from this experience and not the man himself. And I'll get in a lot of trouble with my father if he finds out I'm having this kind of relationship with an employee.

"Maybe we—"

But I stop. Because his hand slides under my dress and begins playing with my pussy. Rubbing my clit right through my panties.

"I know what girls like, Tiffy. And I know what guys like. We all like the same thing. To feel special. To feel good. And this feels good, right?"

I am practically panting, that's how good it feels.

He rips off the unused condom, throwing it aside, and then takes my hand and places it on his hard cock, gently moving it up and down until I make a fist around him. He's thick, and so hard.

"Guys like that, Tiffy." He takes my other hand, finds my pointer finger, then brings it to my lips. "Use your mouth, remember?"

I touch my lips, then lick my finger.

"Fuck," he groans. "Fuck, yes."

I pump him faster, squeeze him harder. He raises his head and arches his back a little before returning his gaze to me. "How close are you? I'm so fucking close."

"Close," I repeat, then hesitate.

"How do you like to come, Tiffy? With my fingers doing this?" He strums my clit in little circles and then drives a finger deeper, pushing inside me, right through my panties. "Or with my cock filling you up until you scream?"

"God, I don't know. I never really do that."

"Do what?" he asks, taking my finger that's still up to my lips and kissing it. He puts it inside his mouth and sucks, then slips it out and kisses my mouth. His mouth is hungry. It's rough again, the tenderness forgotten.

"Get off. I don't really get off."

Everything stops—his mouth, his fingers still trying to work their way inside through the barrier of my hundred-dollar lace panties—and he just stares at me. "You don't orgasm? Ever?"

I laugh, a little bit embarrassed. "I do, I mean, yeah. But only when I…"

He cocks his head at me. "When you…?"

I shrug.

"Masturbate?" he finishes.

I nod, blushing.

And before I know what's happening, he's swooped me up into his arms and is kneeling down on the blanket. He lays me down, then spreads my legs and positions himself between them. His cock is still stiff, and he pumps himself a few times absently.

"No more talking, OK?"

I nod, ready for that part of this to be over.

"Just close your eyes, relax, and forget all that bullshit we just talked about. Put all that out of your mind and just feel good for me."

And before I can even nod out a yes, he's got my knees up to my chest, my legs spread wide, and he dives between them. My panties are still on, and I stiffen, but he strokes my knee softly and whispers, "Be still."

I am still.

Until the heat of his breath passes over the thin layer of fabric that stands between him and what we both clearly want. I want him to rip my panties off so bad. I want to feel the texture of his tongue as it sweeps along my folds. I want him to push it inside me, fuck me with his mouth the way he made me fuck him with mine.

But he leaves them on, licking his way up and down the crease between my legs like an expert. His lapping makes them even more soaked than they were, and soon I can feel the pool of desire rushing out. "More," I beg. I need to feel more.

"Come then, Tiffy. I'll make you come twice. Three times, probably. But I want it to start like this. So just relax and let that feeling build until you can't contain it anymore."

Jesus Christ. No wonder he can get anyone he wants. His words are magic. Everything to do with that mouth is magic. He's making me crazy.

He pulls my panties aside. Just a fraction. Just enough to let the air sweep in across my clit. Just enough for the tip of his tongue to find its mark. Just enough to—

"Oh," I moan. Fuck, yes. "Ohhh," I groan out again. I grab his hair and push his face deeper into me.

My back buckles and my hips thrust up, like I'm the one fucking his face now. I rub myself along his scratchy chin, angling my body so that he hits me as I reach that climax and then sail away into the moaning of the most exquisite release I've ever experienced.

He licks me a few more times and then nips my inner thigh until I squeal. "Miss Preston," he whispers, "I do believe I owe you a taste." He scoots up my body, dragging that still very hard cock along my belly, right up my two-thousand-dollar pristine white dress.

Then his tongue is in my mouth. It's sweet with my own

desire. It's tangy, tasting of the most sexual moment I've ever had with a man.

"We're not done yet," Fletcher says, taking my hand and pushing it down onto his cock. I squeeze him, then flick my fingertip over the little bead of liquid, smearing it across his head as I close my eyes. "Have you ever had multiple orgasms?" he asks.

"No," I mumble sleepily.

"You're about to." He eases off me, flips me over on my stomach, and drags the zipper down my dress.

I don't care what he does at this point. I just want more. I have never had sex like this. Ever.

He slips my arms out of the dress and then slides it down my legs and tosses it aside. When I look over my shoulder, he's standing up, kicking off his boots. I watch him from that position and he grins as he takes his faded and ripped jeans off, one leg at a time.

I close my eyes as he eases himself over the top of my back. I open my legs to give him access, but he slaps my ass and says, "Close them back up, princess. I'll tell you when I want you to move."

Jesus. He's got my full attention once again. And I obey without questioning him because he is clearly the expert here.

He reaches down between my now closed legs. He fingers my asshole, just briefly, and then he thrusts his fingers inside my pussy, pumping in and out—quick and rough. He drags the pool of come and saliva up my ass crack, and then I hear the tell-tale sound of another condom being ripped open. He slaps it on and positions the tip of his hard cock between my cheeks.

I look over my shoulder nervously. "I've never—"

"Shhhh," he says. "I know. Just trust me."

I don't trust him, not for a second, but his cock eases past my asshole and slips right up into my pussy like it was meant for him. He reaches around my hip and lies down across my back, tilted to the side a little so he can continue playing with me as he eases his cock in and out. So slowly, I'm moaning for more without even realizing it.

It feels so amazing. My virgin ass is so sensitive to all the new touching. And even though this is just plain old pussy-fucking, it's new in every way possible.

The hand underneath me finds my clit and starts strumming in the same rhythm as his hips.

I lose it before I even know what's happening.

"You needed a good fuck, Tiffy. But holy shit, woman, you're driving me nuts with your little moans and squeals. I'd fuck you all day if I could. I'd eat your pussy out so much, you'd be sore. I'd fuck your ass and your mouth next."

I come. I come hard. Then he's flipping us over, positioning me on top of him. I lift up a little and he shoves his cock inside me.

"Ride me, princess." He reaches up and squeezes both my tits in unison, then tweaks my nipples until I gasp. "Harder," he commands, as I move slowly. "Faster."

I obey. I rock on top of him and then fall forward, drained beyond belief. He slaps my ass, and the crack of the smack wakes me up.

I push myself down into him. And he fills me up so much, I cry out from the pain.

"Shhh," he says, kissing my mouth. "Sorry," he whispers. "I just want to be inside you. All the way inside you." And then he pushes my exhausted upper body off him, so I'm sitting on top again, and twists my nipples until I groan. "Fuck, yeah," he says. "You like that, don't you, princess?"

I mumble out a, "Yes," but before I can say anything else, he tugs my upper body back down to his chest and starts hammering into me from below. His balls slap against my asshole so hard, I am breathless.

Utterly breathless.

He holds me down as I struggle to sit up so I can fuck him back. He grabs my hands behind my back and grips my wrists with fierce determination as he continues to pound. The little room fills with the noise of skin slapping skin and that's it. That added sensory input is all I need to wail out my third orgasm.

Fletcher comes at the same time, grunting into my neck. He releases my wrists and slaps my ass, then grips both cheeks as we reach the pinnacle of pleasure together.

9

When I wake up, he's gone.

I almost smile. Like for real. Jesus fucking Christ. That was amazing. My first one-night stand. Only it happened in the middle of the day. I have to laugh at that.

Fletcher Novak. He made me come three times.

I roll over and have a moment of fear that he might still be here watching me. That's enough to make me sit up and cover my bare breasts with my arms.

But he's really gone. And I breathe a sigh of relief until I spy a note on the footlocker.

Shit.

I reach for it and then squint my sleepy eyes at the sloppy writing.

Hey, princess,

It was fun and all, but you know me. I'm only into the one-time thing. So don't take it too hard, OK? Just accept it for what it is. And hey, I get points for leaving a note, right? I left the roof doors propped open with stones so you can get out of there all covert and shit.

Love ya,

Fletch

Holy hell. Thank God. I had a moment of fear that he might actually be interested in me. Sex on the roof is one thing, but dating an asshole like Fletcher is not in my future. At all. And I'm a little bit amazed that I feel this way. I mean, aren't girls supposed to feel used after this sort of thing? And I admit, there were a few moments during that whole thing where I might've felt a little vulnerable. But not now.

I feel… satisfied. And happy. And ready to try out my new moves on the guy I really want.

Cole.

Shit! I scramble for my bag, dropped carelessly on the floor as I entered the little shed, and check my phone for the time. One o'clock. I have to meet Cole in an hour.

I jump up and find my clothes and shoes, then shrug into them as I grab my bag and stumble my way to the door.

Wow. I had a one-night stand.

I grin a little at that idea. I mean, I have never done that before. But Fletcher Novak was the perfect guy to do it with, right? No-Strings Novak. It should be tattooed on his chest. Plus, he really did give me some tips on how to seduce Cole. I need to make a change. Cole just doesn't see me as girlfriend material and I think if I sexy myself up a little, I might be able to go from little sister to hot prospect.

I open the door and skip down the steps. I have not felt this good in so long I can't even remember. Sex. Who knew it was just what I needed?

I giggle a little at that as I get to the door that leads out to the penthouse hallway. I open it just a crack, peek out, and then slip into the corridor and power-walk to my room.

Jesus, I sure hope Claudio hasn't been looking for me. Fletcher was fun, but I'm never—like ever—gonna tell anyone I had sex with that slut.

I key the door, open it, listen, get silence, and then scoot inside, closing the door softly just in case.

"Claudio?" I call.

Nothing.

Sweet. I jog down the hall, throw my bag on the floor, and then take my clothes off and go into the massive bathroom. It's spectacular. It's got a huge tub. Which I'd like to take advantage of right now. I'd love to just soak up this good feeling, relax the muscles that were strained during my secret sex, and enjoy the afterglow.

But I can't. Date with Cole in T-minus fifty minutes.

We've had lunch lots of times and I'm sure he thinks this one will go the same way. Me pretending it's a date, him clueless as ever. But he's wrong.

I've got seduction tips from a semi-famous stripper. And I'm gonna use every one of them.

Well, maybe not all of them. Not the getting-naked ones. I mean, Cole isn't a one-night stand kinda guy. He's a serious guy. Career-minded. Stable, reliable, and maybe even slightly predictable. I like all that stuff.

But none of that says we will be fucking on the roof after we eat. No. Cole is a slow and steady kind of conquest. I need to take this one step at a time and the first step needs to be subtle. Just make him look at me differently. Make him see me as a possibility, even if it's only for one moment. If I could do that at lunch today I'd call it a success.

I start the shower, which is penthouse perfect. The temperature preset is hot enough to make you steamy, but not enough to burn. In other words, sublime. And it's a rain shower. So wow. Just what I needed after that romp on the roof.

I look in the mirror for a moment and run all of Fletcher's tips thorough my mind. Make him look at my mouth, Fletcher said. That was the big one. Make him look at my mouth and then bite my lip a little. Maybe if we have dessert I can stick my finger in some chocolate and then lick it off. Or maybe I can do that move men do in movies all the time and swipe some chocolate off *his* lip.

Oh my God, I'm dying to get started. We really need to have dessert. Chocolate is perfect.

I get in the shower and smile as I wash the musky scent of Fletcher off me and briefly wonder if I should feel guilty for fucking him as I plan my date with Cole.

Hmmm. It's kinda skanky. But necessary. It's research.

Besides, Cole and I are not a thing, so it's not cheating. And I know he dates. I don't date. So if we're not allowed to have fun before we date, then he's cheating on me.

I laugh out loud in the shower. He's the cheater if this fling with Fletch counts. And that's ridiculous, so it doesn't count.

Guilt trip over.

"Tiffy?" Claudio calls out from the door. "What are you laughing about?"

"Oh, hey," I call. "When did you get back?"

"I was looking for you in the casino. Where the hell did you disappear to?"

"I took a cab down to the shopping district," I improvise. I did that last night. Before the whole Fletcher thing at the show and while Claudio was getting his spa treatment in here at the hotel. But the shop wasn't going to deliver the dress until today since I didn't have time to wait for them to wrap it up.

"Oh, that package that came for you?"

"That's the one," I say, relieved my cover story has a bit of truth to it. "I'm wearing it to my lunch date with Cole. Go open it and tell me if you like."

"It's not a date, Tiff. You're gonna be depressed afterward, as usual, when you finally have to accept it."

"Just go look at it," I call before squirting shampoo in my hair and lathering it up.

"I like," Claudio calls from the living area a few minutes later. "Great color. Pink always looks good on you." He walks back into the bathroom and takes a seat at the vanity. The shower glass is as clear as the window with the mountain view in the bedroom, but this is Claudio. He's not even remotely interested in seeing me naked in the shower. In fact, he's checking his hair in the mirror. "So how did the Fletcher rendezvous go?"

"What?" I almost choke on the shower water.

"The meeting this AM. Did you fire him?"

I chuckle to myself.

"What's so funny?"

"No. he came in prepared with a proposal to take the show to the next level. And it was good, Claudio. I probably can't ignore it." I rinse the shampoo and work the conditioner in, and then rinse that and finish up. Claudio is putting makeup on when I step out of the shower wrapped in a towel.

"Do you like the eyeliner?"

I glance down at him as I walk past, my wet feet slapping on the Carrera marble floor. "You know I do. Especially when you've been drinking."

He gives me a smile. "When in Vegas…"

"We're not in Vegas, you dummy."

"Tahoe, Vegas, same thing. Slot machines and strippers everywhere I look. That one guy in the show is so gay, he walks on air. I have my eye on him."

"Oh, God," I say as I step into the bedroom and hold the dress up. It is the perfect summer dress, classic with a floral pattern. It's not quite sleeveless—there's a hint of a ruffle up there. And it's got two tiers, with the bottom one hitting me just above the knee. If I twirl, and I did twirl when I bought it last night, then it flares out and an interested man might even catch a glimpse of the perfect pink panties. Not too revealing, a lady doesn't show too much. And I think Cole likes conservative women. Soft, pretty women. Like me. I always have pink on. I imagine him loving pink.

I'm conservative in just the right ways. I like classic things. Especially fashion. And Cole wears classically cut clothes. Not those skinny pants trendy men wear with their suits. No, Cole likes a cut that flatters, but isn't too flashy. His style says business.

"Did you even hear me?" Claudio is asking with irritation.

"What? Sorry, I was lost in thought. Isn't this dress perfect? Cole is going to love it!"

He crinkles his nose at me in disgust. "I don't want to talk about Cole. He's boring."

"He's not boring. We like all the same things. Classic movies, quiet nights at home, and the symphony."

Claudio snorts at that statement and now I'm annoyed. "I've never seen the two of you at the symphony," he says.

"But he likes it, Claudio. I know him. I've seen his playlist at work. It's all classical music. I bet once we hit our stride we'd frequent the ballet and everything. Oh my God," I squeal, turning around to look at my BFF. "I bet we go see *The Nutcracker* together at Christmas."

"Girlfriend, you are delusional. I've seen him just as much as you and he does not look even remotely interested in a Sugarplum Fairy. But that stripper in the show, now that fairy can dance. Mmm, mmm, mmm."

"You're not helping, Claudio. I have confidence right now that this is gonna work out. I need your support."

He eyes me up and down and then tilts his head and gives me a sidelong glance. "You do have confidence. Where did that come from?"

"Gee, thanks. I've always had confidence. But now I feel like I have a plan. You said he sees me as a sister. Which I don't believe," I say, before he can put the kibosh on my momentum. "But maybe there is a smidge of truth to that. So all I have to do is change his mind and make him see me as a desirable woman. Right?" I beam a smile at him.

He scratches his head with one dainty fingernail. "OK. You know I'm on your side, and if you feel Cole is your forever man, then I'm there for you, sweetie. But—"

"No buts! Now let me get ready. I only have thirty-five minutes to turn into the woman of his dreams."

"Fine," he says, leaning in to kiss my cheek. "I'm gonna go stalk that hottie and see if he'll let me lick his abs."

I just shake my head. But my tryst with Novak really has given me a new perspective. Seduction is a skill. All I need to do is learn it. And I've got good tips to try out today.

Cole will be mine.

It's only a matter of time.

10

The ringing phone on the nightstand wakes me from the most restful sleep I've had in weeks. Fuck.

I smile. That was a good fuck. I left her up there all sweaty and flushed from the sex and then came back to my room and passed out. I was up all last night putting together that proposal. And it looks like it was worth it. Because Tiffy Preston was impressed enough to give me a brand-new once-over.

Not that I care about her. I don't. And now that I've had her, I can forget about her. She won't be firing me for dating show patrons. And she doesn't know about any of the other stuff I'm doing. So good. It was an excellent move taking her up on that roof. And I mean that in every way possible.

The ringing phone makes me turn over and pick up the receiver from the nightstand. Room phone means front desk. "Yeah?" I say, annoyed.

"Mr. Novak," Kristen from guest services says. "You have a visitor down here. Her name is—"

Shit. It doesn't matter who the girl is, it's someone I don't want to see again. Once is enough. "Tell her I'm unavailable at the moment."

"Sure thing, Fletch. Sorry to bother you. I know you don't like to get calls. But she's feisty. And she looks mad."

"Thanks for the heads-up, Kristen." I hang up the phone and check the time. I'm hungry. I skipped breakfast this morning and now it's well past lunch. So I force myself to get up and take a shower.

I think about work as I wash up. Not this stripper job. That's not work. Katie, she's work. I mean, the stripping pays decent. But the contracts, those are priceless. Katie is my only client at the moment, but I need her. So I better come up with a plan to get her the man of her dreams so I can keep things moving forward. We've got daily calls for the next week to plan shit out.

I get out, towel off, and then tug on a pair of jeans, a Mountain Men t-shirt, and my boots. Time to head out and see how my little world is turning downstairs.

I get to the bar a few minutes later and greet Sissy at the bar. "Hey, Sis. How about a Dos Equis and a large order of chicken nachos?"

Sis winks at me. "You got it, Fletch."

I wait for my beer and then turn around on my stool so I can see the whole bar and adjoining restaurant. This place isn't always so busy, but the Shakespeare Festival runs all summer in the Village up north, and people swarm to that shit, so the casinos are hopping right now. I grew up here, so I've seen every

Shakespeare play live, ten times over. If I'm having a dry spell with the stripper-lovers from the show, I can usually pick up a girl by quoting that old bastard.

Good stuff. Tahoe is filled with good stuff. And if I can just get this last little bit of shit together, I'd be able to enjoy it more.

But it's within reach. Finally, I feel like life is about to go my way. And I can't wait.

XOXOXOXOX

I study the room and the people as I wait for my food. Girls—plenty of lookers. Guys, mostly gamblers, and mostly local. Some rich professional types, here to play golf and pretend that they brought the family for the boating. And an energy in the air. An energy I have come to appreciate since I took this gig as a stripper.

It was a good move.

"Hey, Fletch," Britt, one of the day waitresses, says as she drops off my plate of nachos. "How's things?"

"Perfect, Britt. Thanks for the chips." I've never fucked a waitress. Or anyone who works here, for that matter. But I go out with them every now and then. Britt likes to rock-climb. Sis, the weekday bartender, likes rafting on the river. The Truckee River is not fast and challenging, so we usually get a big raft, some beers in a cooler, and spend the day floating down to the pool a few miles away.

I'd say they are friends. Decent friends, if pressed. I don't talk too much shop with them, but I don't talk shop with anyone, not even the other guys in the show. It's nice. And casual. Which is how I like my life. Casual. It says it all, right? Easy-going. Lighthearted. Fun.

Life and fun go together like shits and giggles. But it hasn't always been this way.

I shake that last thought out of my mind as I munch on my food and drink my beer. The past is the past. Complicated.

I don't like complications. I'm like the river. Smooth and peaceful. I don't get riled up, I don't get hung up, and I don't get serious.

At least with women. I've seen too much over the past ten years to fall into that trap.

I sit there and enjoy the view, the bustle of the casino out past all the tables, and the—

Wait a minute. Is that…?

Aw, fuck. Tiffy Preston is heading my direction and she's got a huge smile on her face. Jesus Christ, didn't she get my note? I mean, how much clearer could I have made it? One time only, Tiff. One time only!

Double fuck. She's waving. I give her a sheepish smile and sink into my chair. Do I wave back? I mean, she's the big boss' daughter. Do I have to be polite and shit? Why the hell did I bang the boss' daughter? She's an employee. Just like Sis and Britt. Why the fuck didn't I realize that before my cock got the best of me?

I know why. She kept me up all night working on that proposal. And she got me so fucking hard at the show last night. Add in the exchange at the door when I was ready to jump her and she ambushed me. Well, it was sorta well played on her part. She got me. And that business suit is so not my type.

I have no clue what I was thinking.

I slump down a little more in my chair and give her a wave,

hoping this convo won't get ugly. "Hey," I say weakly as she beams another smile, still making a beeline for my table.

"Tiffy," a voice booms from off to my right. The guy from her room last night. Cole. "I was starting to think you were standing me up."

Tiffy laughs and allows him to give her a polite hug as he puts his hand in the small of her back and leads her away from the bar towards a table on the other side of the restaurant.

Fuck. I sit there, a little embarrassed, then a little relieved that I didn't have to have that awkward conversation with her.

Dodged another bullet, Novak, I tell myself.

"I heard she tried to fire you this morning," Sis says, opening another beer and taking away my empty. "And you gave her a run for her money."

"Yeah." I chuckle, remembering the meeting. "It was fun. I got her all flustered."

"You usually do, Fletch." Another customer calls for Sis and she skips off down the bar to fill his order.

I got Tiffy flustered upstairs as well. She's quite pretty, if you're into those career women. Her dress this morning was sophisticated business attire. White, sleeveless, hit just below the knee, and absolutely no cleavage. Even her little white shoes were office-approved two-inch heels.

But now she looks… different. Her pink dress isn't exactly casual, but not professional either. It's flirty. It's short. And very low-cut. Her shoes have some little sparkly things on them and that is definitely a four-inch heel.

She's sexy.

Damn. Tiffy Preston doesn't look as buttoned up as I first

thought.

I picture her legs spread open before me. Her soft mewling as I licked her pussy. Her manicured fingertips digging into my hair.

Fuck. I'm hard again.

I watch her as that Cole guy pulls out her chair and then scoots it in as she sits. She's facing me, so I see her smile a little as he walks around to take his seat.

Hmmmm. What's going on here?

I study her face, waiting for her to notice me as they chat. But she only has eyes for him. Did she see me earlier? Is she trying to make me jealous by having lunch with another guy after fucking me? After I gave her three goddamned orgasms not three hours ago? Really?

"Pffft," I mutter under my breath. Gonna take more than that to make me look twice.

But then she licks her lips.

Wait. Did I just imagine that?

Nope. She's chewing on them too. And then her fingertip sweeps up and traces her plump lower lip as she casually pretends to wipe away a drop of the pink champagne Mr. Fancy-Pants greeted her with. Pink champagne? Who the fuck drinks pink alcohol?

Britt comes to their table with plates of lobster tail and a new bottle of champagne. She laughs with them and I get a little pissed off.

Is Tiffy practicing my seduction tips on that guy? That guy? Really? He's like ten years older than her. He's huge. Like six foot four at least. And he's got to weigh two-twenty. I bet he shops at Big & Tall. She cannot be serious. No way is she interested in him.

And that just pisses me off more. Because, oh, hell the fuck no. I do not dish out trade secrets to a one-night stand only to have her go use them on a worthless prospect. Anyone can see he's all wrong for her. He is not a possibility. Not at all.

I sit there at my table, sipping my beer as I process what's happening and how I feel about it. I'm not jealous. I'm not. I'm pissed off. Why the fuck did I give her tips? I charge good money for that shit. Hell, I made Katie sign a six-week contract and I haven't even given her one tip yet.

And yet Miss My Father Owns This Town is practically giving them away to every wandering eye in the whole place.

And that's a lot of wandering eyes. All the employees know who she is by now. Britt is chatting them up like they are old friends, probably taking notes.

There it is again. Holy fuck, Tiffy just licked her lips and practically winked at that guy. And Britt saw the whole thing as she set down a dainty cup of chocolate mousse in front of two-timing Preston.

Hell the fuck no. I never let my clients work my magic here at the casino. Otherwise I might lose business. Hell, I've helped more than one cocktail waitress hook a rich dude over the past nine months. They paid dearly for it. And signed a NDA. Trade secrets are trade secrets. And I have spent years coming up with my methods. I'm not gonna let her get away with practicing them on this asshole for everyone to see.

I push away from the barstool, straighten my t-shirt, and walk over to ask her just what the fuck she thinks she's doing.

11

"Do you want some?" I ask Cole, spooning out some chocolate mousse from the little dish they serve it in here. "It's so good." I pop the spoon in my mouth, savor the taste—which is not that good, but I'm working it—and then lick my lips and trace a fingertip daintily over a small spot of misplaced chocolate.

His eyes are trained on my mouth, just like Fletcher said they'd be. Damn, he was right about all of it. Cole has been responding to every trick. Not in an obvious way, of course. He's reserved. And you don't go from little sister to sexy girlfriend in one thirty-minute business lunch.

"Uh… ah… no, thanks, Tiffy." But he smiles warmly at me, then his gaze darts back down to my lips as I give them one last swipe with my tongue. "So the account in Reno is good. I took care of that little issue. But"—he smiles and shakes his head—

"we're a big corporation. And San Francisco is having issues with the new merger. Your father called me while I was in Reno and filled me in. He might need us to go back there and lend a hand."

Shit. I'm just getting started here with Fletcher's tips. If we go back to San Francisco, then we go back to our old life. Cole will never start seeing me in a new light if my father is there running interference. My father isn't exactly a jerk to my boyfriends—when I have one—but he's one of those overprotective types. He's always warned me about people who will like me for my money and not myself.

Cole is wealthy. He's from a very rich family with old money, like us. So Cole wouldn't be an issue in that department. But my father sees Cole as a family member. He's never hinted that we'd make a good couple. So it's much better to make this change away from home.

"Can't we do it remotely? I mean, a video call is pretty much the same thing as being there."

"Maybe," Cole says.

My optimism soars.

And then I see him.

Fletcher Novak is walking this way.

Shit. He's got a look on his face that I can't exactly read because I don't know him that well, but it doesn't look happy.

"Miss Preston," he says. Cole's back is to him as he approaches, so Cole has to turn in his seat. "Nice to see you again. You're positively glowing today. What happened to make you so happy?"

"Ah…" I laugh and dart my eyes to Cole. "Well, I'm just happy to be having lunch with my favorite co-worker." I beam a smile at Cole.

"Can we help you with something?" Cole asks with a hint of suspicion in his voice. "I mean, I'm not sure it's a good idea for us to socialize, Mr. Novak. I'm sure you can understand after your allegations last night."

Oh, shit. Fletcher's got a weird look on his face. Like he's about to say something I might not like.

"Tiffy and I worked—"

"Fletcher?" All our heads turn to a blonde girl as she grabs Fletcher by the arm and spins him around. She's seething mad. Her lips are pressed tightly together and she's clenching her jaw. "I called your room earlier, but they said you weren't there."

"Ummm..." Fletcher looks at me and for a second I think he might actually tell her where he was. "I didn't get the message."

"You lying piece of shit. I was watching the girl at the front desk when she called up to your room after I waited around for an hour to see if you'd show your pathetic face."

"Look, ah—" Fletcher stops short, like he's about to say her name but he doesn't remember it.

"Lisa," she spits out. "Lisa! How could you not remember me? You fucked me—"

"Whoa, whoa, whoa," Cole interjects, standing up from his chair. "Miss... Lisa?" He drops his voice and hopes she will do the same. "Is there a problem here?"

But Lisa doesn't answer him. She slaps Fletcher across the face so hard it makes a crack. And even though there are probably fifty people in this bar, it goes silent and everyone looks at us.

Fletcher doesn't even flinch. He just stares at me.

"Lisa Watkins. That's who I am. One of Novak's many, many, many one-night stands. And who might you be?" Her words snap out of her mouth, and Cole actually withdraws a fraction, thinking she might slap him next.

"I'm the general manager of this hotel, Miss Watkins. And if you've got a problem with one of our employees, then you can talk to me about it. But you may not assault him. We can talk privately if you like." Cole reaches for Lisa's arm, but she sidesteps him and puts her hands on her hips.

"I'm not going anywhere. And neither are they." She points to a group of girls standing off to the right with the same pissed-off expression on their faces.

"Oh, fuck," Fletcher mumbles under his breath.

"Do you know them?" Cole asks Fletcher.

"Know them!" Irate Lisa exclaims. "He's fucked them all too! He's nothing but a man whore, Mr. General Manager. And he's your employee. And I'm gonna make sure everyone knows that this show is—"

"OK," I say, standing up and interrupting her. "Miss Watkins, I'm Tiffy Preston, the owner"—which is not really a lie—"of this hotel. And I'm going to have to ask you to come make your complaints in private. We're not going to have a scene here in the restaurant. You're not going to assault my employee. And if you try either of those things again, I'll call the police and have security hold you until they come."

She takes a deep breath and then her anger gives way to frustration and what might be shame. "He used us, Miss Preston. He used us like—"

"I understand," I say, placing a hand on her shoulder and giving her a push towards the casino. "Let's talk about it in my office, OK? And then you can tell me everything in private."

Cole buttons his suit coat. "I'll come with you, if that's OK."

Lisa Watkins sniffles, and gives him a nod. "But we all have to come, Miss Preston. He did this to all of us."

I motion to the girls off to the side. "You're all welcome to come." I smile sweetly at Lisa and then she turns and begins to walk out of the restaurant. Cole follows her and I steal one quick glance at Fletcher.

He doesn't say anything. Not a shake of his head like they are lying. Not a word to defend himself. He just stands there and frowns. Looking very, very guilty.

I walk behind Cole and the group of girls as we make our way to the elevator that services the offices on the third floor of the East Tower. I think about Fletcher and what an asshole he must be to have slept with all those women. He probably left them the same note he left me this morning. And I can see how hurt a young woman might be if she had hoped for something more than just hot sex. Lord knows I'm thankful that I'm not even remotely interested in him. I mean, he has slut written all over him. I knew that going in.

But some of these girls look very young. Especially Miss Watkins. Twenty-one? Maybe twenty-two? And Fletcher is pushing thirty. He's got some experience and years behind him. Me as well. I'm no doe-eyed college girl.

It's sad really. That he feels the need to pump himself up with these young women. Use them to make himself feel better just because he can.

But on the other hand, he's a male stripper, for Pete's sake. How dumb can these girls be? He's only good for a one-night stand to begin with.

When we get upstairs to the reception area I wave them all into a conference room just as Cole's phone rings. He checks the screen, and then looks at me and winces. "It's your father. I have to take this."

"I can handle it. But Cole," I say, grabbing his arm real fast before he leaves. "Don't mention this to him. He doesn't need this on his plate too."

"Got it, Tiffy. I'll leave it to you."

"Thanks." I take a deep breath as he answers his phone and walks off. And then I plant a smile on my face, enter the room, and close the door.

XOXOXOXOX

Two hours later the last girl is just finishing up. It's been two hours of hell with the We hate Fletcher Novak Support Group of South Tahoe. Two hours of crying and threats to castrate my star stripper. Two hours of swearing and anger. Two hours of what-are-you-gonna-do-about-this.

I don't even have an answer. But I have to tell them something. "Ladies, first off, thank you for coming in and telling me your stories. As a woman, I know what it feels like to be objectified. And I know how bad it hurts when you feel misled by a man you thought was interested. But Fletcher Novak has no clause in his contract that prohibits him from sleeping with non-employees."

And I just fucked him, so I'm breaking more rules than he did, I don't add.

"But," I continue, "I assure you, I will take action regarding this matter. And his contract will be redrawn the minute I can talk to the lawyers."

"You're not going to fire him?" Lisa exclaims.

"Well—" I stutter.

"He deserves to be fired," a girl named Cathy says. "Now."

"Yeah," a few more echo.

"I can't promise that. You have to understand we are bound by labor laws. If he didn't break his contract, then I have to write him up and give him a warning."

"How about poor representation of your show and casino? Don't performers have that in their contracts?"

"We do not," I lie. I'm not sure why I lie. Maybe just because I need these girls to go away. I don't want them following up or pressing matters. I don't want my father to find anything out about this. I just want to clear the air, make the necessary changes, and then move on. "But I will be looking very closely at this issue. And I'm not saying he won't be fired, I'm just not saying he will. You understand this is an internal matter and he has rights too. So I need to respect them and push this through the proper channels. But I can tell you, the Landslide is not interested in a performer who presents a bad image of our establishment."

They mumble a few more complaints, but I wrap things up, give them one more assurance that things will be dealt with and usher them out of the hotel.

I watch them leave by the front entrance, and cringe when Lisa Watkins gives me an angry look over her shoulder. She's not satisfied.

And neither am I.

Fletcher really does need to go.

I turn back and walk into the casino, wondering what I

should do next. I wonder all the way back up to the office floor, and then I take my indecision back into the conference room and sit down.

"Leslie?" I call out for the receptionist.

"Yes, Miss Preston?" She gets up out of her chair and rushes in to see what I might need.

"Can you text me Fletcher's number?"

"Sure, ma'am. Let me go get it."

I stare out the window as I wait. It's late afternoon now and the sun is making its way towards the mountains on the west side of the lake.

Well, this day certainly started better than it will end.

I still can't believe I slept with Novak. What an idiot I am. And not because I feel used, like those girls. I don't. I'm not interested in a pretty boy like him, a man who thinks he can manipulate the world with his charm and good looks.

I just feel disappointed in myself because if my father finds out, he'll be disappointed in me for making a bad decision.

I'm not afraid of my father. I'm not afraid of being yelled at, or losing my job, or my trust fund. I just want to please him. And if he finds out I had such a monumental lapse in judgment, well, it will kill me to see his face.

M phone buzzes in my purse, and Leslie calls out, "That's the number," from her desk.

"Thank you," I call back. I get up, close the door, and press send as I walk back and take a seat in my chair.

"Yeah," he answers on the first ring.

"It's Tiffy."

"I know."

"Can you… come down to the conference room on three?"

"That's OK, Tiffy. I'll save you the trouble. I've already got a lawyer. He'll contact you tomorrow." And then I get the hang-up beeps.

Fuck.

I press send again and this time it rings through to voicemail.

Shit. Lawyers are bad news. If lawyers get involved, I'm screwed. My father will definitely hear about that.

But I can't let Fletcher get away with it. I really can't. What he's doing is wrong and he needs to know that.

I think the professional thing to do is to have an adult conversation. I mean, I haven't exactly been professional today. But as my father always told me, it's never too late to turn over a new leaf.

I get up and open the door. "Leslie? Does Novak have a room here?"

"Yes, ma'am. He stays on fifteen in the penthouse tower. He and Chandler both have a complimentary suite."

"What number?"

"Fifteen thirty-nine."

"Thanks." I go back in the conference room and grab my bag. I guess I will have to go to him if he's not going to take my call.

My heart races on my way up to fifteen. He's in the same tower as me, and all I can think of the whole way there is how much I want to go back to my room and take one of those long bubble baths I was craving this morning.

Gah, and then I feel guilty for what I did with Fletcher. How could I have fucked up so badly?

I stop in front of his suite room and then hesitate. Maybe I should just let legal handle this? I might make things worse if I confront him.

But no. I run all the reasons through my head why my father can't know about this, and then I rap on the hard wooden door.

I hear footsteps inside, and then a pause, which means he's probably looking through the peephole.

So I wave at him. "I just need to talk," I say in my most businesslike tone. "Five minutes, that's it."

The door opens a crack. "What?"

"Don't you want to give your side of the story?"

"I will, when my lawyer is present. I'm not gonna let you corporate people fuck up my life."

"Fletcher—"

"Save your breath, princess. Because I've got nothing to say. I don't want to lose this job just yet and if you think I'm gonna let some bimbo trash take it away from me, you're mistaken."

"I never said I was going to fire you, OK? I just want to hear…" What do I want to hear? "All the right things," I say with a heavy sigh.

He gives me a crooked smile. "You want me to lie and say I didn't fuck them? That it's their word against mine?"

"So you did sleep with them all?"

"Yeah," he admits like this is a foregone conclusion. "So fucking what? You're gonna come up here and lecture me on safe sex? I use condoms, as you well know."

"Hey—"

"Hey, nothing. I was upfront with you and I was upfront with them too. It might be a douchebag move to fuck around like that, but it's not illegal."

"Can I come in?"

He squints at me. "Why?"

"Because," I whisper, "I don't want to have this conversation standing in a hallway."

"Five minutes, you said. I've got you on the clock." He opens the door and I step in.

His suite is nice. There's a small foyer with a table and a door to a closet and a second bathroom. I'm familiar with the floor plan. "This is quite a perk we give you. Free room? It must be nice living in a luxury hotel."

"It is. Get to the point."

I walk towards the living area and take it all in. He's got a laptop open on the coffee table and tons of papers scattered around. He pushes past me and starts gathering them up and then tucks them away in an end-table drawer like he can't get rid of them fast enough.

"I have to admit, the story the girls tell is sad."

"Yeah, well, that's because they are sad people. They go to strip shows looking for a piece of ass and then act surprised when it's just sex? Come on. They're not pissed because I fucked them. They're pissed because I only did it *once*."

12

"Yeah," I say, about to get sarcastic. But I realize it's true. He's… hot. I mean, let's face it. Fletcher Novak has a six-pack, thighs that make you moan just thinking about them gripping your hips, fingers and hands that know just where to touch you, and a cock the size of a cucumber. So instead of being sarcastic, I just sigh and say, "You're probably right."

"What?" he asks, thrown by my surrender. "You believe me?" He stares me in the eyes and I get a little lost in the blue.

"What's not to believe? You're… desirable," I say, coming up with a better word than hot. "They got hurt. And I'm sure you were up front with them, since I got the Novak treatment this morning and you were perfectly clear with me. So yeah, I believe you. But that doesn't mean you're off the hook, Fletcher. I can't win here. You're gonna call a lawyer if I take action and they're gonna… well, who the hell knows what they might do. Tell the media? Write a letter to my father? Try to sue us for letting you assault them?"

"I didn't assault them, Tiffy. I slept with them. And it takes two to do that shit, right? So why is it always the man's fault? Why do I have to pay for doing the same thing they did? Why am I the bad guy when they came on to me? Hell, I didn't even have to go looking for them. *They* found *me*."

And he's right. Every bit of it is right. "It's a double standard. I get it. But that's not the point. The point is, you can't do that shit and work for this company. My father would blow a blood vessel if he knew you were acting this way."

"I'm a fucking male stripper. This is how I'm supposed to act."

"Well, none of the other guys in the show have a pack of angry women slapping them in the face in the casino restaurant. That's you. And I'm sorry, but I'm gonna have to—"

"I want to keep this job, Tiffy. I'm not kidding. I want to keep this job for a little bit longer and I won't let you force me out without a fight."

"What's that mean?" Seriously, can he be any more cryptic?

He stares at me for a second, like he's not sure what to say. But the indecision passes just as fast, and his answer pours out of his mouth like all the other lies. "I'm the one who decides to leave, Tiffy. And if I broke your rules, then you'd have cause to get rid of me. But I didn't. We both know that. So I'm staying and that's the end of it."

I walk away. I have no good way out of this. I need to just be a professional and do the job I was hired to do.

"Hey," he says roughly, coming up behind me. "I saw you

today."

"What?" I ask back, looking over my shoulder at him. "Saw what?"

"You at the table with Cole. He's the guy, right? You like him, don't you? You took notes this morning and then you used them on him at lunch. I saw the whole thing."

"We're not talking about me, Fletcher. I didn't do anything wrong."

"You fucked me this morning."

Shit.

"You liked it. And"—he chuckles—"you understood that it was just fun, right?"

"So what?" Dammit. Now he's gonna threaten me. He's gonna say, *Tiffy, I'll tell your father what a disappointment you are. I'll tell him you fucked a complete stranger on the roof of his hotel and you came three times.*

Jesus Christ. Why the hell did I ever do that?

Fletcher Novak will use this against me for eternity. Why didn't I think of all this before I let my vagina have a party with him?

"So let's make a deal."

"What deal?" I ask, spinning around. "I let you keep your job and you don't tell on me? No. I'm not gonna play that game. I'd rather tell my father that I fucked and get it out in the open."

"Wait. What the hell are you talking about? You think I'm gonna tell your father?" He laughs.

"Aren't you? Aren't you gonna threaten to ruin my life if I don't let you keep your job?"

He frowns and lets out a long breath of air. "You have a really low opinion of me, don't you?"

I stop a sarcastic remark once again. Because he's got a look on his face. A look that appears oddly similar to the same disappointment my father might have.

So I reconsider him.

He's smart, I know that much based on the proposal this morning. And he's got ambition. That's for sure. He's only worked here nine months and he's a star. He has a Wikipedia entry, I remind myself. I don't have that, and I'm the daughter of billionaire Randall Preston. And he's honest. I have to admit that too. He hasn't lied about anything. I mean, I don't care for his brand of truth, like, at all. But he still gives it to me.

"I don't, actually. I think there's a lot more to you than just taking your clothes off."

He smiles. It's the same smile from this morning when we were up on the roof. His eyes light up a little and his grin gets wide. "Then let me help you."

"Help me how? By not telling—"

"I'm not gonna tell a man I fucked his daughter, Tiffy. Just what the actual fuck?"

I stare at him. And blink a few times, trying to grasp what he's saying. "Then what?"

"You want Cole, right?"

I just shrug. "I like him a little. I think we'd make a good couple."

"Just admit it," Fletcher says, bringing his hand up to my cheek and stroking it softly. My insides do a little flip as I recall all the ways he touched me this morning. "You think he's hot. You were flirting with him using my trade secrets—"

"Trade secrets?" I laugh out loud. "What?"

"—and they were working. Probably be working right now if those psycho bitches hadn't come up and ruined it."

"Actually, Cole's in San Francisco—"

"I was being figurative, Tiffy. My point is, you know they were good tips. Look, you got dressed up, took that business suit off and did all the things I told you to. I'm good at this. So look, I'll patch things up with Lisa and the other girls, you agree that I should keep my job, and as a way to show my appreciation, I'll help you reel Cole in. What do you say?"

I give him the stink eye, sure that I'm being set up. "What's the catch?"

"What catch? I just told you. I keep working, I apologize for hurting those girls—even if it wasn't my fault—and help you get the guy."

"How will you make things right with those girls? They are pissed. They want you fired, Fletcher. I can't just ignore that."

"I'll find them guys too. New guys," he adds quickly. "Not me. Nice guys."

"What, you're some kind of matchmaker? Where the hell are you gonna get guys to date them?"

He walks across the room and opens a drawer filled with files. "I *am* a matchmaker. I have a secret side business. Because sexy doesn't sell, Tiffy. It's for sale."

I laugh out loud again. "Is that your tagline?"

"It's good, right?" He smiles at me, one hundred percent serious. "I'm a hookup genius, Tiffy. I will find a guy for each girl and I'll hook Cole for you too. I'm good at this, I swear."

"What is all that?" I ask, pointing to the files.

"Satisfied customers. Clients. It's a side job I started a few years ago and I've got seventeen real hookups. My first two are already engaged. And another five are heading in the same direction. The other ten are, well, works in progress. But all of them are still going. And before you blow up at me for having two sleazy jobs, ask yourself why women might need me. For real." He stares hard at me like he's waiting for an answer.

"Because… you know what men want, I guess. And you know what women want, obviously. You're pretty good in that department."

"Exactly. I don't force women to come look at me take my clothes off. I don't force women to hire me to find them a boyfriend. All I do is fill a niche. And you need filling, Tiffy. I can help you too."

I scowl at him. "You don't even know me. Or Cole."

He turns me around, takes my hands, pins them behind my back and pushes me up again the wall. "I know all I need to know, Miss Preston."

The switch from casual Tiffy to formal Miss Preston does a number on my heart. And when he pushes his hips into my ass, I have to draw in a tight breath.

"I know you want Cole to fuck you like I did this morning." His hand slips down to my waist and then slides along the little dent under my hip bone. "You want him to touch you, Tiffy?" He gathers up my flirty pink dress in a bunch and then he's underneath it, stroking my thigh. My pussy tightens and tingles with anticipation of what I know is coming. I should stop him. We cannot do this again. But everything about Fletcher Novak makes me want to say yes.

"You want him to make you come three times in a row? I can make him *want* to do that. I can change the way he sees you. I can deliver what you think you want."

And then Fletcher is pushing my panties aside and stroking my pussy.

"Wait, what are you doing?" I gasp. We cannot do this again.

"He's a big guy. He's got big hands, doesn't he?"

Oh my God, why does Fletcher have this effect on me? Why does he make me feel so good? "Mmmm," I mew out, totally embarrassed that I'm letting him get me started again, and yet utterly helpless to stop him.

"I bet two of my fingers equal one of his."

"Fletcher, we can't," I moan as he slips two fingers inside me.

"I bet you imagine he'll stretch you like this, right?"

I'm not even capable of talking right now.

"I'm sure his cock is small and puny and will be a huge disappointment—"

"Fletcher!"

"Because my cock is the king and always delivers satisfaction." Fletcher laughs, and I lean back into his chest a little. "But if you want him, I can deliver. I can. But I'm seriously not ready to leave this job. So princess, let me take care of things, OK? I'll make it all right. And we'll both end up happy."

I know it's wrong—not giving in to his plan, I'm all over that—it's wrong to want him to keep going. But I do. So I fake my reluctance. Just a little, so he will try a little harder to convince me. "I don't know..."

"Remember," he breathes into my neck, just the way he told me to do it—and holy fuck, that shit works again—"how it felt to be with a man who pays attention? I can make him pay attention, Tiffy." He continues to finger me, pushing in and out in a motion that is so slow, it's killing me with anticipation. And then he withdraws his fingers and I whimper.

He laughs into my neck. "Turn around," he says, making it more of a command than a request.

I turn slowly, my eyes on the floor. What am I doing? Didn't I just get done convincing myself it was a mistake to fuck him? And now I'm caught in that web again.

But he lifts my chin up with one fingertip, and waits for me to drag my eyes up to his.

When I finally do, he smiles. Relaxing me. "Put your hands above your head."

I blink at him again.

"Do it."

I gulp some air and do as I'm told. My breasts lift up, my nipples perky and hard. The hem of my dress hits me mid-thigh now, and then Fletcher presses his knee between my legs, making the throbbing that started to abate when he withdrew his fingers start back up.

"I'm good," he says.

I nod.

"Say it."

"You're good at this, Fletcher."

"Tell me to finish and I will."

God, I want him to finish.

"Don't feel guilt. It's fun."

"I do feel guilt. I feel dirty. But I still want you to finish."

That smile again. God, it's incredible. I love seeing him smile.

And it makes me realize that the normal smile he wears all day is nothing like the real one. It's fake.

"I'd like to as well," he says. "So just do as you're told and this one-day stand will end with perfection."

His hands slide under my dress, cupping my ass cheeks. He lifts me up and presses his body against mine, grinding his hips against me. Not enough to hit the sweet spot between my legs, just enough to make me crazy with want.

He kisses me. His mouth is soft and tender one moment, hard and pressing the next. His tongue glides against mine, tasting me from the inside out.

He pulls away and stares down at me with his eyes heavy with lust. Does he really want me? "It's still a one-time thing if we do it again in the same twenty-four hours."

Well, I guess that answers my question.

"Do you think Cole will fuck you the way I did?"

"Um… I hope so?" What the hell was that? Do I detect a hint of insecurity in Fletcher Novak? He's all over the place right now.

Kinda like me.

"I really should stop." He stills his hips, waiting to see if I'll encourage him to go on. We must be having the same struggle. We both want it, but know we shouldn't. "Tell me not to stop."

And because I was told to do as I'm told, and I'm rationalizing the hell out of this right now, I tell him. "Don't stop."

We're both rationalizing this, but neither of us cares. He lowers me until my feet find the floor and then he places my hands on his belt buckle. "Kneel down and take me out, Tiffy."

I glance up at him, meet his eyes for just the briefest of moments, and then glance down at my hands as they automatically pull the brown leather strap and start threading through the buckle.

He digs his hands into my hair, urging me to go faster. The buckle jingles as I get it loose, and then I pop the button open and drag the zipper down. I can see his hard bulge pressing up against his black boxer briefs and I can't touch him fast enough.

I place my palm on his hot cock.

He moans out, "Yeah. Fuck, yeah. Grab it, Tiffy. Squeeze it hard. And then place your mouth on it and lick me through the fabric."

I grip him hard like he wants me to, and then lean in and place my mouth on his length. His cock jumps from my touch, and that just makes me want to do more. I drag my tongue up and down his shaft, pressing on him with a little bit of force. He moans again and then his hands, still fisting my hair, begin rubbing my face into his cock. This time I'm more comfortable, so I let him control me. He rocks back a little, making me look up. I meet his gaze and he says, "Fuck, you turn me on. Keep going."

So I pull down the waistband of his briefs until he springs out, hard, and long, and hot. I look up at him again and he throws his head back and groans, like that gesture—me looking up at him with his cock in front of my face—turns him on more than my actual lips when they wrap around his tip.

"Swallow me," he whispers, pushing my head into his hips. I take as much as I can, but I'm not a porn star and before long I'm gagging.

"Breathe, Tiffy. Just breathe through your nose. Relax your throat," he says, dragging a fingertip up and down my neck. "I want you to swallow me so fucking bad."

I gag again, and saliva comes spilling out of my mouth, dripping down onto my dress.

"That's so fucking hot," he says.

And the fact that it turns him on to watch me drool spit makes me so turned on.

He thrusts once, hitting the back of my throat and making me struggle to get away. He lets go, understanding I've hit my limit, and then bends down like he did this morning and kisses me hard. "Tell me to fuck you, Tiff."

"Fuck me, Fletch."

He laughs when I call him Fletch. "God, what are you doing to me?"

"Everything you tell me to."

He stops smiling and stares hard, cupping my face with his hands. "I'm gonna fuck you now."

I nod and he stands back up, taking me by the hand and pulling me with him. He reaches under my dress and pulls my pink panties down, throwing them over his shoulder as he twirls me around and pushes me up against the wall again. "Open your legs."

I open them a few inches.

"Wider, Tiffy."

I spread out, and the air rushes in, teasing my clit and making me throb again.

He takes off his shirt and I stare at those perfect abs in the gray dusk of early evening light while he throws that aside too. Then he kicks off his boots, drops his pants, and flings them away.

He stands there naked before me. His perfect, god-like body

is all hills and valleys of taut muscle.

"Now you."

I swallow hard and reach to the back of my dress. "The zipper." It comes out as a hoarse whisper. But before I can explain that I need help, he reaches for my flirty skirt and drags it up my body, whipping it over my head.

"Fuck the zipper," he says, reaching for the front clasp on my lacy pink bra. "Who's got time for a zipper?"

13

She automatically crosses her arms, preventing me from taking off her bra. "Shy much?" I tease.

"A little."

"You weren't shy this morning."

"I didn't take my clothes off this morning."

"Hmmm," I say. "We'll have to work on that then. Men like a little blushing, but they like confidence too. So how about we start with lesson number one." I lean into her ear, thread my hands in her hair, and say, "You can practice with me."

Her shoulder comes up to stop the tickle of breath against her skin. "If we're going to have a professional relationship, then we shouldn't mix business with pleasure."

I can see her point. I can also see that it's a copout. But whatever. She wants to rationalize this, and I'm OK with that. Because I'm horny. I want her. And she's beautiful. "OK. But you've got to practice on someone. I can get one of the guys to come help you out. Mitch is a good decoy."

She pulls back a little. "What do you mean? Decoy?"

"To practice, Tiffy. There's so much more to this than licking your lips. You need real bedroom experience."

"I have bedroom experience, Fletcher. I'm not some stupid college virgin."

"That's not what I'm saying. But Cole isn't interested, right? I think we can both agree on that. So obviously you're not his type. We need to make you his type. What kind of girls does he date?"

She scowls at me, still with those arms covering her perfect breasts. "I don't know."

"You've known him a while, surely you've seen him with women. Right?"

"He likes blondes, I guess." She says it with an air of disappointment.

"I like brunettes myself. What else does he like?"

"They are tall. Taller than me." Another frown.

"Hey," I say, tipping her chin up. "Don't do that. Don't feel bad about who you are. My matchmaking works for two reasons. One, the women are confident. And two, the men understand that not everyone is blonde, Tiffy. Not everyone is tall. Not everyone who makes a match with me is even pretty. But all of them feel sexy on the inside. And that's all it takes. So forget about looks. Tell me what he likes about them."

She bites her lip and then sighs. "I think he likes their looks, Fletcher. And maybe status. I mean, one was a pro golfer. I know that. But another one sold him a yacht."

Yacht. What kind of douche has a yacht? "Maybe it's not golf and yachts that attract him, Tiffy, but the fact that they're…" I want to say snobby bitches. But I realize Tiffy might fall into this category as well. "Refined and cultured." *Good recovery, Fletch.* Besides, Tiffy's not snobbish. Sure, I can tell she comes from money. She has a polished sophistication about her. Nice clothes, precise speech, and dignity. Mostly it's the dignity. But she's polite, resourceful, and hardworking too. "And you're refined and cultured too. So this is an easy fit."

"Can I put my clothes back on?"

I laugh. "Why? We're just getting started."

"But we're not going to fuck again, right? I mean, that's pleasure and this is business."

"We don't need to fuck to work. But if being naked makes you uncomfortable, then that's something you might want to work on."

"Why? Cole is not a stripper, Fletcher. He's not going to morph into some sociopath BDSM guy and expect me to crawl on the floor and sit at his feet naked."

I picture that and actually get hard. "Have you ever done that?"

"No." She laughs. "No. I'm so not into experimenting. I like the normal stuff." She takes a few steps towards her dress on the floor, but I grab her arm and make her stop. "I want to get dressed."

"I want you naked."

"I'm sure you do," she quips with a tip of her chin. Superiority, that chin tip says.

"And that," I say, taking her face in my hands and kissing her softly on the lips, "is sexy. Confidence is sexy, Tiff. So if you've got it, flaunt it."

"Have I got it?" she asks, the insecurity spilling out again.

And fuck if that isn't sexy as well. "In spades, princess. More than you even know. Cole is stupid for not noticing what's right in front of his face. But maybe he's just one of those workaholic types."

"He is. He works like sixteen-hour days."

"So where did he take these women he dated?"

"Um…" She thinks for a few moments. "Well, I think they mostly came to see him at lunch and they dined in his office."

"So he likes lunchtime quickies." What a dick.

"Quickies? He didn't fuck them in his office, Fletcher."

"Tiffy, please. If a man invites a woman to his office for lunch, he wants to fuck her on his desk."

"That's not true! My mom had lunch with my dad—Oh my God." She waves a hand in front of her face. "Make it go away. I just pictured my mom and dad having sex on his desk."

I laugh at her naiveté. "Did Cole take them out on any real dates? Maybe they were whores?"

"Whores! Jesus Christ, Fletcher. Cole Lancaster does not date whores."

"Call girls, I mean. You know, high-class sluts? Cater to businessmen who are too busy to fuck?"

She screws up her face. "That is not a real thing."

I throw my head back and laugh. "OK, let's move on, pretending that Cole is not into whores or fucking on his desk. Where do you think he fucks the girls?"

"Do I have to think about him fucking other people?"

"No, I just need you to think up a place where he fucks any

people. So we can prepare for it."

"I think he fucks people at home in his bed, like everyone else."

I place my hands on her shoulders and pull her close so I can whisper in her ear. "Like we did this morning?"

"That's different."

"How?"

"It was a heat-of-the-moment thing. If we were really dating we'd have gone to one of our places and had sex—"

"Against the wall over there?"

"In bed, you dumbass. Not everyone is a sexual deviant like you. Cole is not fucking whores on his desk at lunch."

"OK," I say, giving in. "You know him better than me, so I'm gonna take your word for that. Let's move on. So when you get back to Cole's place, after he takes you to lunch at his desk, what do you do? How will you seduce him?"

"Won't he seduce me?"

"OK, Tiffy you're losing me, babe. Do you want this guy or not?"

"I do," she whines. "But why do I have to initiate things? I thought you could make him initiate things with me. Can't you? And can I please put my dress back on?"

"So you want to take the passive approach? And why put the dress back on? I'll just have to take it off again when I fuck you after this conversation."

"What?" And then she bursts out laughing. But my even stare makes her stop abruptly. "We're not fucking again."

"We are. We're naked. We're talking about sex. And we're horny. So we are most definitely fucking. I just wanted to get to know you better this time. So I know what to try next."

"What do you mean?"

"I'm trying to figure you out, Tiffy. So I know how to make you feel good about yourself. And now that I know you like to be guided, well…" I kiss her mouth again. I hold her chin in my fingers as my tongue sweeps inside her, and when I pull away, ever so slowly, she sighs. "I'll tell you how I like it so you know what to do back. I'll do things without asking you, so you don't have to make decisions. And I'll make sure you have the best sex of your life every time you're with me."

"Do you fuck them all?" she spits as she pushes my chest back and sends me stumbling. "Is that what this matchmaking business is all about?" She grabs her dress off the floor and before I can even say another word, she's got it pulled over her head and she's hunting for her shoes.

"Tiffy? What the hell?"

"This is a mistake. You're just trying to sleep with me. And I fell for it! Oh my God, you are such an asshole. I came in here to fire you—"

"And we made a deal, remember? I'm just trying to help you with your deal."

"By fucking me? No."

"OK," I say, pulling my jeans back on and zipping them up. "OK. We don't have to fuck. And the answer to that last question is no. I don't fuck these girls. Not one of them."

"So why me, Fletcher? Why me?"

"You picked me off the floor last night."

"No, you chose me. How delusional are you?"

"You had your eye on me the whole time."

"I'm your boss. I was there to discipline you. Of course I'm going to be watching you!"

"Well—" I'm speechless for a few seconds. And then the answer I need manifests. "Well, then I guess you've got moves, Miss Preston. Because your inner sexy was shining bright last night. I saw it from a mile away."

"Player!" she squeals. "God, you are so full of bullshit moves, I cannot even believe it."

"Tiffy," I say, my hands up, palms out, like a hostage negotiator trying to reason with a terrorist. "We made a deal. I promise you, this is business. And if you need me to keep my hands to myself, then I will. Done deal. No fight about that from me. But we both need this, right? You want Cole and I want this job. So don't walk away mad. Just meet me down in the lobby at noon tomorrow and we'll start your first lesson."

She huffs out a breath of air, shakes her head, turns away, turns back, and finally says, "OK. And you better make things right with Lisa and those girls you fucked over."

A few seconds later she's gone.

And I'm back to being the guy who fucks girls over just because they want me to fuck them.

14

I barely slept at all last night. I tossed and turned. Fretted and fussed. I am riddled with guilt. Why did I sleep with him? Why did I make this stupid deal? My poor father, if he finds out. And those girls. They will come back to haunt me, I'm sure of it. There is no way Fletcher Novak can make things right with them. No way.

I glance down at my watch. It's ten past noon. He can't even make things right with me, because he's already fucking up.

Calm down, Tiffy.

I take a deep breath and search the lobby one more time. But nope, I don't see him. So I grab my phone from my purse and dial Amy's receptionist, Leslie.

"Landslide management," she says in her professional voice.

"It's Tiffy. Do you know where I might find Mr. Novak at this hour? He was supposed to meet me and he's not picking up his phone."

"Oh, yes, ma'am. He's in rehearsals on Friday mornings. Until…" She hesitates. "Well, noon. Technically. But he's missed a few from what I've heard. Maybe they're staying late?"

"Where are rehearsals?"

"The North Tower basement. There's a key pad to the studio at the end of the west hallway. Your ID should get you in."

"Thanks," I say with a cheerfulness I don't feel.

I take a deep breath and head towards my tower and then take the elevator to the basement. There's a security guard at the entrance to the gym, but he tips his hat at me and says, "Afternoon, Miss Preston," as I pass by.

I find the west hallway, and it's not difficult. I can hear the stripper music a mile away. Goddamn him. How dare he leave me waiting up there? I really need to put an end to this ridiculous deal.

I swipe my card and pull the door open as my anger builds.

And then I stop. Dead in my tracks.

Fletcher Novak is doing some sort of striptease to a girl tied to a pole in the middle of the room.

"Yeahhhhhhh," Claudio yells. He's bound to the next pole over.

"Claudio!" I yell over the music.

"Whoooooooo," he screams again. His eyes are on that other guy. Presumably the gay one Claudio was referring to yesterday.

"Claudio!" I scream again, but the music cuts off halfway through my outburst, and it echoes in the silence.

Every head turns to me.

Six male strippers in various stages of undress. Claudio, who has an open mouth and wide eyes. He might even be blushing. And about fifteen girls, who I can only presume are groupies. Some of them have Landslide uniforms on.

"What the hell is going on here?"

"Tiffy," Claudio says excitedly. "We're stand-ins for the crowd for tomorrow night's new act." And then he does a not-so-subtle head tilt towards the stripper whose crotch is just inches from his face, and waggles his eyebrows.

"I'll talk to you later." I drag my gaze to Fletcher. "Why are you here when you're supposed to be—"

"Tiffy," he says, cutting me off. "Sorry, I got caught up in the heat of the moment and lost track of time." He smiles sheepishly at me. "What time is it?"

"Twelve twenty-one," I snap.

"OK." And then he leans down to his captive's neck and whispers something that makes her laugh.

I let out a long, aggravated sigh. "I'll meet you—"

"No, no, no," Fletcher says, jogging away from the girl tied to the pole in nothing but skimpy panties. "We're done. I was just playing around with her. Come on, I gotta change and then we can go."

He takes my hand and I don't even bother trying to pull away, because he's practically dragging me down a hallway.

"You can't mention that I'm mentoring you, Tiff. It's weird, ya know?"

Boy, do I ever. "About that—" And then I stop because he just ushered me into a men's locker room. There are hot guys everywhere I look.

"Pay no attention to them, Tiff. I have a private dressing

room back here."

I blush my way past one, two, three, four, five, six naked men and one, two, three four half-naked men, and then let him swoop me behind a closed door.

Jesus. This job cannot be real.

Fletcher whistles and looks me up and down. "You look hot, princess. Like smoking."

"Oh." I blush again. I'm wearing tan slacks that hug my curvy hips, a pale pink sleeveless silk blouse with a little flutter of fabric near the neck, and some crystal-encrusted pink Louboutins that I wore to my cousin's wedding in May. "Thanks." I think I look pretty hot too. I thought about what Fletcher said. About becoming the girl Cole wants. But this is me. The me not in a suit, at least. And I don't think Cole is that shallow. So I'm not going to change my ways to win him.

"I love it, babe. Fuck, yeah, you're hot in that fancy shit." He reaches into a closet and pulls out a garment bag. "But you said Cole was a yacht guy and dates golf pros. So we're gonna have to… adapt a little." He smiles as he thrusts the garment bag towards me.

"What's this?"

"Your outfit for today's practice lesson."

"I'm not—"

"Not me, relax. We're going to the golf course to hang out in the bar. Obviously, you will be alone and I'll be watching from afar, otherwise I'd cramp your style. This is your first chance to try out your tips on a stranger."

"But I only have the lips thing, Fletcher. And I had Cole interested in that yesterday." Jesus Christ, do I hear myself? I came here to tell him it's off.

"Relax," he says, placing his sweaty hand on my cheek. It should repulse me. He's sticky. And he smells.

But I like it. His whole body is glistening from his workout, if that's what that was. His hair is damp and has been finger-combed back across the top of his head. I glance down at his package and—"Fletcher!"

"Sorry." He laughs. "You just look fucking hot today, princess."

"Don't call me princess, that's so stupid."

He puts his hands up but he's still grinning.

"And stop looking at me like that. I don't want to change. I'm not going through with this. But you still have to make things right with those girls and I'll let you keep your job."

"Wait," he says, removing his hand from my cheek. "You're quitting on me? Why? You did good yesterday, Tiff. I just have one tip today, that's all. So you put them all in motion with one stranger at the golf course bar, and then once he's interested, you get up and leave. No funny business. He's not gonna touch you or kiss you or anything. Because you are a hot commodity. You are too good for this world. You are an angel among mere mortals. A goddess. No one is worthy of your company."

"I sound like a bitch. I know Cole won't want me to be a stuck-up snob."

"Not a snob. Just self-assured." And then he shakes the bag at me. "Go on, get dressed in that. It's not as sexy, but it's far more comfortable."

"What is it?" I ask, pulling the zipper on the bag to get a peek.

"Golf skort, polo shirt, and golf shoes." Fletcher beams another smile as he grabs a towel and wipes his face with it.

I prefer him sweaty, I realize, once that sheen is gone.

"If Cole likes the jocks, then a jock you shall be. Now, do you play golf?"

"No," I say, annoyed. "I can, but I hate golf. It's stupid."

"I agree. But today you will talk golf with a man in the course bar and you will like it. Cole likes it, so you like it."

I sneer my lip. Is that really how this works? I have to pretend to be someone else to snag a man?

But I don't say anything. Mostly because Fletcher just assumes I will do as I'm told, and he's already walking away, calling out, "Gonna get a shower. Be done in five." But also because I really do want to hook Cole.

I look around, find a corner where I can hide in case he comes back before I'm done, and start changing into Cole's future wife.

Five minutes later I'm transformed, sitting on a wooden bench, braiding my hair when Fletcher comes out of the shower, dripping wet, and wearing nothing but a towel.

He drops his towel like I'm not even there, and turns away and opens a door where he's got clothes hanging in a closet.

I watch the movement of his muscles. His ass. Those little cut lines that ride his hips. His back as he pushes clothes around on the rack. The hills and valleys of his arms.

"Like what you see?" he asks, still facing away from me.

"I'm not looking at you," I say, reaching for my phone on the bench. "I'm checking voicemail."

"I can see you staring, Tiffy, there's a mirror in here."

Oh.

"It's OK. I like your body too. So next time you get naked in front of me, I'll stare all I want and we'll be even."

“There won’t be a next time.”

“Right.” He starts pulling on a pair of tan trousers, neatly creased down the middle of his legs. He doesn’t button them, but instead turns back towards me and shrugs on a crisp, white, button-down shirt that he also leaves hanging open.

He’s got no boxer briefs on this time.

“Going commando?”

“I forgot them. But if you want to go up to my room with me, I’ll be happy to put some on.”

His room is a definite no. I need to stay the hell out of there. He’s just too hot to ignore. And if he makes another play for me, I’m not sure how strong I can be.

You want Cole, I remind myself. *You’re doing this for Cole.*

Right. I realize that. But Cole does not look like a Greek god just came to life before my eyes. And Fletcher Novak does.

He messes with the collar of his shirt, shrugging his arms around, trying to arrange the fabric over his muscles, and then he starts buttoning it from the bottom up. I stop focusing on his fingers and look up into his eyes. He’s smiling at me. “What?”

“Nothing,” he says, shaking his head a little. He stops buttoning and reaches for a necklace hanging on a hook inside the closet. Dog tags, I realize, as he slips the beaded chain over his neck and tucks it inside his shirt.

“Were you in the military?”

“What?” His smile drops, and then he looks down his shirt to the tags. “Oh. No. These aren’t mine. My gramps was a patriot. Left me one of his tags in the will.”

“Oh.” I’m not sure what to say to that. No mention of gramps in the Wikipedia entry at all.

"You look nice," Fletcher says, slipping his sunglasses on his head and then rolling up his long white shirtsleeves. "I like the other outfit better, but no one cares what I like, so let's go."

We make our way back upstairs to the lobby and then Fletcher guides me out to the valet area with a hand on my upper arm. I feel a little like a prisoner, but his hand is warm and it's touching my bare skin, so I don't really mind it.

We stop alongside a large black limo and Fletcher waits for the driver to open the door before motioning me in. "Wow," I say. "Mr. Moneybags. You always take a limo to the golf course?"

He raises his sunglasses and smiles. "It's your car, Tiffy. I just told them it was for you."

"Oh." I giggle. "Well, you definitely get points for resourcefulness. So tell me, what exactly am I supposed to do at this bar?"

"Just initiate conversation. Play along, some small talk. And then use your tricks to make him see you as sexy."

"You said you'd give me a new one." I can't wait to hear this.

"OK," Fletcher says, turning his body towards me and leaning in a little. He smells like soap, but it's manly soap. I inhale him in and then stare at his lips as he talks, getting a little lost in how lush they are. I picture him licking me on the roof. The feeling of his hair as it dragged along my inner thighs. The way his eyes looked when he glanced up between my legs.

"Got it?" Fletcher asks.

"What?"

"It's easy, right? So now you have that to try too."

Holy shit. I just missed the whole tip. I look out the window as we roll along the mountain road towards the golf course and wonder what it might've been. Well, if it's anything like lick your lips, I think I can improvise.

"So when's the next time Cole will be in town?"

"Oh. I don't know. They need him in San Fran right now. So he might not come back."

"Then I guess we'll have to go to him, then."

"Why?" I turn to look at him again and try not to notice the way his tongue presses against the back of his front teeth when he's being playful.

Why is he being playful right now?

"You have to practice. If you really want him, that is."

"I do. And that's what we're doing here today, right? Practice. And anyway, I don't want you grading my performance with Cole. It's weird."

"You're gonna have to sign a waiver for that, you know."

"What?" I just blink at him.

"Satisfaction guaranteed was the promise, Tiffy. How can I guarantee you satisfaction if I'm not there to see how you perform?"

Did he just say perform?

"So when we get back to the hotel I'll have you signing that if you don't want to have a date with Cole under my eye."

"God, this is so weird. How the hell did I let you talk me into this?"

"Oh, good, we're here. OK, Tiff, just go in there, kid, and do your thing. You look around the bar, choose one guy sitting alone, and go right up and talk to him. Got it?"

"Wait, where are you gonna be?" Suddenly the thought of him watching me isn't so bad. It's better than walking into a strange place by myself with the intent of hitting on a stranger.

"I'm right behind you, princess. But we don't want to appear to walk in together."

"Right." I take a deep breath. "Are you sure I need this? I mean—"

"Tiffy, you want Cole, right?"

"Right," I say. It comes out a little weak.

"OK, so just hit it out of the park, babe. Little bit of lips, little bit of tongue, and then finish it up with the toe-leg combo."

Toe-leg what? Holy fuck. I really did miss something when I was daydreaming in the car.

"Got it?" Fletcher is leaning into me, holding onto my biceps, like he's some coach asking me to go win one for the team.

"OK, got it." I just need to get out of this car before I realize everything I've done since I met Fletcher Novak is completely nuts.

The driver opens my door and I slip out into the bright summer sunshine. I shield my eyes and Fletcher calls out, "Over to the left, Tiffy. Go get him!"

I look around nervously to see if anyone is watching, and yeah. Like forty-seven bazillion people are in this parking lot looking at me right now. I cup a hand over my eyes to hide my face, and power-walk my way over to what looks like a clubhouse.

I slip through the door and thank God for the darkness inside. This is my kind of place. Lodge-y, and dark, and cool.

"Bar?" I ask a waiter at a podium.

"Just off to your left, madam."

"Thank you," I call out cheerfully, heading in that direction. I walk down a bustling hallway filled with happy people who like to hit little balls in the summer heat, and then enter the large open bar and restaurant.

"Do you have a reservation, ma'am?" the next waiter asks me.

"For the bar?"

"Oh, no. The bar is always open. Seat yourself." He smiles and takes his attention to the couple behind me.

OK, Tiffy, I say, looking at the packed room. *The sooner you do this, the sooner you can leave.* I scan the room, looking for a lonely man who is not fifty, stuffing his face with crab, or gay—thank you, Claudio, for my exceptional gaydar. It's saved me more than once.

But there is only one guy who qualifies. And he's sitting at a table, not the bar. I walk slowly past all the filled barstools and find an empty one as close to hot target's table as I can get.

And this *is* sorta hot. I mean, hey, if you have to practice flirting with someone, it might as well be him.

"Excuse me," the man next to me says.

I turn in my seat and give him a look. He's not bad either. Tall, fit, early thirties. He looks like a lawyer or something. "Yes?" I answer.

"I heard there was a clothing-optional beach here in Tahoe. Do you know where it is?"

Oh, boy. This guy is a loser. Who says that to a girl? "You can try the internet." I smile sweetly. "Excuse me, I found my friend."

His mouth opens to say something back, but I turn away, tossing my hair in the process, and walk over to my target.

That guy was OK, but this one. Holy fuck. He's like Fletcher. A lot like Fletcher. A little older, maybe early thirties. He has well-defined muscles, his hair is a little unruly and he has those bright blue eyes. He's got a little more scruff on his chin than Fletch, but wow. They are very similar. Similar enough to make me want him more than I should.

"Excuse me," I say, stopping in front of his table. "I heard there's a clothing-optional beach around here. Do you know where I can find it?"

He looks up from the newspaper he's reading with a scowl. "Really?" But then he stops when he sees me, tilts his head, and laughs. "Huh, I was gonna lay into you for such a lame pickup line, but OK. I can take a minute to chat you up about a nude beach if you want." He winks at me.

I let out a long breath. "Can I sit?"

"Sure. What's your name, darling?"

God, he sorta sounds like Fletcher too. "Tiffany," I say, taking a seat across from him. "But my friends call me Tiffy."

"Yeah?" he says, putting a hand up to stop a waiter. "A drink for the lady? What will it be?"

"Um, how about a Scotch on the rocks?"

"Scotch it is," he says. "Top shelf." And then he winks at me. "I'm Walker, Tiffy. Nice to meet you."

I fidget in my chair. "Nice to meet you as well." Shit, now what? That was so much easier than I expected.

"What do you do? Here with your husband for a long weekend?"

"Oh, no." I laugh. "Not married. Not yet anyway. I'm here… well, I work at the Landslide Hotel and Casino and I'm just here to relax today."

"Got a tee time? Maybe I'll join you?"

"Oh, no. All done with that. Just need a drink now. What do

you do?"

"You played alone?" he asks, ignoring my question.

"No, um, I was on a date, but it didn't go well. So I left him on the course and came in here to wind down before I have to ride back to the hotel with him."

"My lucky day then." He smiles big and lifts his drink, just as mine is delivered. "Cheers," he says.

I clink his glass and take a long sip of alcohol. Shit, I'm nervous. Now what? The obvious stuff is out of the way. On to the tips, I guess. Tongue, bite lip, play with lip, and something called the toe-leg combo.

"Tiffy?"

"Yes?" I ask, coming back to the present.

"Daydreaming?" He laughs.

"What'd I miss?"

"What do you do at the hotel?"

"Oh, I, ah—" Shit. I can't tell him I'm Tiffy Preston. This is not a great example of making good decisions. "I'm a dancer."

What the fuck? How did that come out of my mouth?

"Dancer," he says, his eyes lighting up. "What kind of dancer?"

"Well, err, you know, like a showgirl."

"Wow," he says, sipping his drink while giving me a coy look. "I'm gonna have to come see you perform."

"You really should. Tomorrow night." I laugh at that, knowing full well Fletcher's show is on tomorrow night.

He lets out a chuckle that sounds a little bit like a growl. "It's a date."

"Shit, I was kidding." I say, laughing.

And then he reaches up and scratches his scruffy chin. My

eyes immediately dart to his fingers, and then his lips. Lips, Tiffy, I tell myself. Do the mouth thing.

I take another sip of my drink, letting the sticky liquid cling to my lips, and then my tongue darts out and sweeps a small drop into my mouth.

His eyes are fixated on me. So I improvise. Because hell, I'm on a roll here. He's right where I want him. "So what are you doing here alone?"

"Stood up," he says.

"What? No way. You? Who would stand you up?"

"You'd be surprised." He grins, taking a sip of his beer. "So I figured I'd wait around and see if my luck changes, and sure enough, here you are."

OK, Tiffy. Concentrate. Toe-leg combo. What the fuck can that mean? Why didn't I listen to Fletch in the car? I run all the possibilities through my head and only come up with one thing. Footsie? Is that still a thing?

I have no idea. But it's as good a move as any. So I slip my shoe off under the table, cross my legs, and start swinging them. I hit his leg after a few tries and look up to see him smiling at me.

"What are you doing?" he asks with an air of amusement.

"Sorry, I didn't mean to bump your leg. So, what do you do?" I ask again.

"I'm… an investor."

"Oh, nice. My father does that too. What do you invest in?"

"The usual. Stock, bonds." He nods in the general direction of the bar. "And now golf courses." He stares at me. Hard. And then I feel something touching my leg. His foot is bare too. And it's rubbing up and down my calf in long, slow caresses. He has a look of amusement on his face and the whole thing makes me draw in some air with surprise. It's almost like he's using Fletcher's moves against me.

"What the fuck are you doing here?"

I stand up at the sound of Fletcher's voice and bump into his back, that's how close he's hovering.

"Fletcher," I whisper. "Keep your voice down. This is my new friend, Walker. Walker, this is—"

"Nice to see you again, brother."

"Brother?" And that's when I see the beaded silver chain around Walker's neck and the other half of what is probably the grandfather's dog tags.

"Fuck you," Fletcher spits out. "We stopped being brothers nine years ago. Come on, Tiffy, we're done here."

"Is this your disappointing date, Tiff?" Walker says, standing up and staring straight at Fletcher. "The one you walked out on?"

"Um, I'm not sure what's happening," I say. But Fletcher has a grip on my hand and he's already pulling me through the bar towards the door. Everyone is looking at us, and the heat of embarrassment creeps up my neck and flushes my face.

I look down at my feet as I'm tugged back out into the parking lot. The limo is gone, I'm sure not expecting us to leave so soon. And the parking lot is packed, so I doubt it found somewhere close by to wait. Fletcher pulls me along the asphalt, not saying a word until we reach the edge of the golf course and he walks me into the woods. We follow a dirt trail until the sound of people and traffic recede, and then he lets go of my hand and grabs his hair with both fists.

"What the fuck were you doing with him?"

"What? You sent me in there to flirt with a guy. How the hell was I supposed to know he was your brother?"

"I sent you in there to flirt with Jim. The guy at the bar. You blew him off and made a beeline for my fucking brother!"

"I didn't know he was your brother! What is your problem? And why did you have someone in there? Did you set me up?"

"Tiffy," he says, taking a firm grip on my upper arms and shaking me a little. "What kind of man do you think I am? I would never send you into a bar to pick up a stranger. Jim is the guy who works with me. He's there to play a role and watch over you. I would never put a girl in danger like that. It's all controlled. It's all set up. It's all—"

"Fake," I seethe. "Everything about you is *fake*, Fletcher. Not one thing is real, is it?" He just stares at me, that tongue of his doing a dance against his top teeth.

"Well?"

He shakes his head at me and pulls out his phone. "Roger, we need to be picked up. South entrance, near the putting green." And then he ends the call and starts walking the way we came in.

"Fletcher?" I call out.

"Follow me, Tiffy. Now."

"No," I shout. "No! I'm not going anywhere with you until you tell me what the hell is going on. Is this matchmaking thing fake too? Do you plant men for these girls to reel in, so you can pull it off? Are their relationships fake? Did you sell each girl to the biggest bidder? What kind of men do they marry? Foreigners looking for a green card? You're some kind of sex slaver! So when will they find that out? After they give them their hearts? After those few get married? Will the guy get pissed off one night and tell her their whole life is fake?"

Fletcher turns back to me slowly, his face nothing but anger. "Don't pretend like you know me. And don't," he seethes, "accuse me of fraud."

"Then why was that guy there to meet me?"

"I told you," he says in a lowered voice. "To keep you safe."

"So I was supposed to flirt with him. And then what, Fletcher? Was I supposed to win or lose that game?"

He just stares me down.

"Lose, I take it. So you could be the good guy and come to my rescue. Make me feel better about my failure? God, you're sick."

"You don't even want that guy. So what do you care? If it was Cole, it would be real."

"How do you know? You're just a conman, Fletcher. You trick people. You lie and you cheat. I'm done with this, OK? I'm going back to San Francisco the first flight I can get. And just fuck you, OK? I'll send someone to replace me and they can decide what happens."

I start walking back the way we came, and he reaches out for my arm as I pass him.

"Don't," I say, yanking my arm away. "Don't even touch me. You're everything I thought you were that first night at the show. Everything and more. You're the most pathetic mess of a man I've ever met, Fletcher. You're nothing but a pretty face with a dark soul."

15

"Come in," I call to the knock at my locker room door in the gym.

"Helloooo?" Tiffy's BFF, Claudio, calls as he peeks his head inside.

"I'm packing, asshole. I'll be out of here when I'm done. So tell Miss Preston to calm the fuck down and—"

"Whoa," Claudio says, putting both hands in the air. "Hold the phone, cowboy. Unpack your bags, take a deep breath, and put on your I'm-not-an-asshole hat because I told Tiffy you had one."

"What?" I squint as he enters and closes the door behind him. "I got a pink slip in the email this morning. So I'm just gonna do everyone a favor and be on my way."

"Plans have changed, Fletcher. Randall Preston is coming here tonight to see the show."

"What?"

"And Tiffy asked me to come down here and ask you to stay for tonight. She says she will make sure you get a bonus if you stay."

"Tiffy sent you?"

"Mm-hmm," Claudio says, his lips pressed together tightly in a hard smile.

"She wants her old man to do the honors, or what? She wants to humiliate me in front of him to make herself look better? No fucking thanks."

"It's just one show, Fletcher. And he's not coming to fire you. He's coming because TravelXpress is going to be here to rate the hotel for a deal they are running next month online."

I just stare at him.

"Have you heard of TravelXpress?" He looks stressed.

"Sure, it's like a booking website. They charge a fee though, so I don't use them."

"They charge a fee, Fletcher, because they are the biggest online booking agent in the world. And they visit and review every hotel, every flight, every car rental company they put up for special promotions. Cole has managed to get the Landslide up for a review, and they are coming tonight. A five-star rating from TravelXpress would be a very big deal."

"So now Tiffy needs me." Bitch.

"They're here to see the show too. It's the headline act, so if they rate you five stars, it could be a boon to your… career."

I laugh at his hesitation to call what I do a career. "Can you be any more condescending?"

Claudio stares at me for a minute and then lets out a deep

sigh and turns away. "There's more, Fletcher. And I shouldn't tell you this, but you need to understand. Mr. Preston is leaving Tiffy this hotel. It's all she's going to get in the will."

"Will?"

"He's dying, Fletch. He's got an inoperable brain tumor and was given six months to live. And that was five months ago. He's deteriorating fast and he's made some… unusual decisions about his money in the past six months. For one, Tiffy will get this hotel and nothing else. Not even her trust fund. She will be prohibited from selling the hotel for ten years. If she can make it work, she gets the trust fund once it matures. If she sells it, or it goes bankrupt, she loses everything."

"What kind of asshole does that to his kid? Jesus Christ."

"I know what you're thinking," Claudio says, shaking his head. "But you're wrong. I've known Mr. Preston most of my life. And I know why he's doing this. He talked it over with me before that brain tumor was ever diagnosed. So it's not some whim from an eccentric dying man. It's got solid logic behind it."

"So Tiffy wants me to save her hotel so she can cash in on the trust fund money ten years from now? Fuck that."

"Tiffy doesn't know, Fletcher. She has no idea he's made these changes to the will. He sent her here to take things over and learn the ropes before he dies."

"You just said she sent you down here to beg me to stay."

"She did, but only so when her father gets here, he won't be disappointed in her. She wants the hotel to get a good rating, but not for the reason you think."

"Ah, I see. She wants some bonus money, I get it."

Claudio grunts. "Wow. You really are an asshole."

“I just call it like I see it.”

“She doesn’t know he’s dying, Fletcher. She doesn’t know the will has been changed. She doesn’t know anything. All she knows is that the hotel will be rated this weekend and she wants to make him happy. She knows he’s sick, he had a small stroke and a heart attack last year and some other minor things. But he’s been lying to her. He says it’s stress. That his heart is weakening. Things like that. They worry people, but they don’t make them break down and be sad. And when she finds out he could die any moment, she will break down. Tiffy is not Mr. Preston’s biological daughter. Her mother, Tessa, met him at one of the Preston Resorts in New York City where she was a waitress. Tiffy was four and they were living in a hotel fifty blocks away, so her mother would bring her to work and hide her with the maids. The hotel manager found out when Tiffy took some toys from a room while she was waiting for her mother to finish work. Tessa was about to be fired when Mr. Preston stepped in and saved her job. They became friends. He adored Tiffy. Treated her like a daughter. When they married three years later Mr. Preston decided to adopt her. He’s been a good father, Fletcher. Her mother died a while back, and Randall never wavered in his love and support of Tiffy.”

“Then why cut her out of the will, Claudio? It’s fucked up.”

“It can’t be helped. Mr. Preston was a lot older than Tessa when they married. In fact, he’d been married three times before. He’d resigned himself to the fact that he’d have no children, he’d never remarry, and he pledged his entire estate to a multitude of charity funds. They’re counting on him to deliver. And he’d never go back on a pledge.”

“So Tiffy is left with nothing.”

"Nothing but this hotel. And she doesn't know it yet, but she's worked for him since junior high school and he's been investing her paychecks this whole time. It was enough to purchase the Landslide a few months ago. He's trying his best to set her up for success."

I rub a hand down my face as I take all this in. "And now he's dying?"

Claudio nods. His face is very sad.

"And Tiffy doesn't know?"

"No. Nothing. Not even that she owns this hotel. Not the part about losing her inheritance. None of it."

God. Life is fucked up.

"And I know you two are in some kind of argument, but Fletcher, she needs this to go well. Not for the hotel, don't think that's why I'm here begging. She needs to please her father. All she wants in this world is to make him proud. And if you leave, the show will fail, the hotel will get a subpar rating, and she will feel like she's failed him. She's a sweet girl, Fletch. You have to see that."

"She is," I agree. "I think she's genuine. And nice. But she doesn't believe in me, Claudio. She thinks I'm scum. So why should I care if she gets her wish? Why the hell does her happy ending have to depend on me when all she sees when she looks at me is a conman?"

"I understand," Claudio says. "I do. But… just give it some thought. Just take a few hours to think things over. Don't pack yet. Please."

I look at him and see a true friend. Tiffy is lucky to have him on her side. He loves her. He just wants to protect her from the reality that will come crashing down soon enough. He wants to give her one more win before that happens. "I'll think about it."

"Thank you," he says, backing up towards the door. "Thank you." And then he turns and leaves.

I sit down on the cold wooden bench alongside my locker and put my head in my hands.

Nothing is ever what it seems.

Katie, the girl I put under contract. She's perfect on the outside, but so damaged on the inside, she paid me money to fix her.

Tiffy, rich beyond belief. Well-educated and polite. A daddy's girl from top to bottom. And her heart is about to be broken in teeny-tiny pieces. I can see that coming. I can tell she loves her father from the few times she's mentioned him in conversation. She does care what he thinks. His opinion of her is the one thing that defines her. Just like the opinion of that asshole who hurt Katie is the one thing that defines her.

I can see why Tiffy wants Cole. And not because he's rich and would take care of her. Especially if she has no idea her inheritance was never hers. I think she likes Cole because he's dependable. A mountain that stands tall and strong in a valley filled with storms. She needs to feel safe. And even though Randall Preston has provided her with that since she was a small child, there is still that feeling deep down inside her that knows.

It can all be taken away in an instant.

I slam my locker closed and walk out. I walk past all the rich assholes who feel the need to be perfect so strongly that they work out while on vacation, and then make my way up the stairs to the lobby.

I spy Tiffy talking to the people at the front desk. She's dressed much like she was yesterday. Cream slacks instead of tan. The shoes are high and fancy, but they are a light peach color, like her flowing blouse.

Everything about her screams perfect.

But she doesn't feel perfect. Even I see that.

She's afraid. And she's right to be afraid.

She spots me looking at her and opens her mouth, like she might call out for me. Ask me to help her with this show tonight. Ask me to stay by her side.

But then she presses her lips together, straightens her posture, and turns back to the front desk people.

I turn away too and walk towards the casino. You can get to the beach from the basement, or take the front stairs from the lobby. But I don't want to walk past Tiffy, so I weave my way through the slot machines and tables until I get to the shops and take the back entrance.

I need to get the fuck out of here.

16

Lake Tahoe is one of the most beautiful beaches in the world. It's been developed, sure. But it's been protected too. There's a lot of private land surrounding the crystal-clear water. And the Landslide has quite a bit—relatively speaking for such high-value real estate—on either side.

I kick off my shoes and walk diagonally across the sand. It's packed with people. Families with kids. Newlyweds. Gamblers asleep under the alpine sun. I weave my way through them and head for the rocks on the west side of the hotel where I go to think things through when the doubts creep in.

And they always creep in, right? No matter who you are—no matter how successful your career, or your love life, or your family—those doubts are always there.

I climb over the slate-colored boulders until I find the spot. It's just a little bit hidden from the hustle and bustle of the hotel beach, but it's usually enough distance to get some peace.

The water here is so clear. When you think of a lake, you think of a mud-covered bottom. Reeds and silt muddying the water. But Tahoe is the closest thing you can get to clear blue water and not be in the tropics. The sand is white down below, as I gaze down from the rock, and a crawdad goes bustling by on the bottom.

When I was a kid it used to freak me out to know those things were down there with my feet, ready to pinch me. But I never got pinched. My childhood was good. My family was good. Almost everything was good up until I was eighteen. Then life reared its ugly head and taught me that there is no such thing as fair. My dad died that year. And the shit just kept coming. It never stopped. And my brother?

Seeing him yesterday was a shock. It's been… I count the years on my fingers. Nine of them all told. Nine long years since life fucked me over again.

"Fletcher?"

Fuck. Tiffy must've followed me. A few seconds later she stumbles over and falls in the water, her arms flailing and her face shocked from the cold. It's a mountain lake, after all.

She sputters out some water as she surfaces. "Oh, my God!"

"Hold on," I say, scrambling over the boulder and then reaching down for her. She grabs my hand and I lift her up out of the water and let her scramble the rest of the way up the side of the rock. "What the fuck is on your feet?"

"Huh?" she says, her teeth chattering. "Shoes."

"Four-inch heels, Tiffy? Really?"

"It's what I had on. Jesus. I didn't know there was a dress

requirement. I called your name and you ignored me. And I really need to talk to you."

"I didn't hear you." I picture her trying to walk across the sand in those things. I have to turn my head away to laugh. And I'm not ready to talk to her yet. Not after all those things Claudio told me.

"I j-just," she stutters through her chattering teeth, "needed to ask you a…" Her eyes lower a little along with her mouth. Her frown is one of worry, not sadness. But if she only knew how much she had to be sad about. "A favor."

Here it comes. "What favor?"

"Will-llllll you… will you do one more show with the Mountain Men? I know you quit, and you're not obligated to give notice or anything. But I'd really appreciate it if you'd take my request into consideration."

"I thought I was a fraud. A cheat. A liar."

She scrunches up her face. Probably because she really thinks those things and can't admit it right now. She needs me. "I don't know. OK? I don't know what you're doing with those contracts. Or your many, many one-night stands. Or me, for that matter. You're confusing, and calculating, and hiding something."

"Hiding what?" I snap. I'm so sick of this shit. "You don't even know me, Tiffy. I'm just some dumb stripper to you. I'm a conman, remember?"

She opens her mouth to protest, but I put up my hand and say, "Save it, all right? I'll do the show. So you can stumble back to the hotel and get changed."

She takes a deep breath and lets it out. Her arms are hugging her body, and her clothes are sticking to her skin. And then she reaches down and unbuckles her shoes and throws them in the water, one at a time.

What the fuck is this?

She slips her shirt over her head and then stands up on the rock and wiggles out of her pants. She lays them both out on the large boulder very carefully, and then sits and props her hands behind her, tipping her face up to the sun.

"What are you doing?"

"Drying off," she says. "I'm not walking back there soaking wet. And this rock feels good. It's hot and I'm cold. The sun is making me tired, and it feels good on my skin. I haven't had a day at the beach in… hell, years."

I wait for her to say more, but she's silent. And then she lies all the way back, sighs deep, and closes her eyes.

I take off my shirt and do the same. The sun beats down on my stomach and it's good. "I haven't either, really."

"Why not?" she asks in a sleepy voice. "You live here. I'd take advantage of it, if I lived here. It's small, and peaceful. Not like San Francisco. All city blocks and bustling people on their way somewhere."

"Busy, that's all."

"Well, I guess you have time now."

I open my eyes and stare at her. She's not pasty, but she's not tan like me. Mine's from an airbrush though, not the outdoors. I can't even remember the last day I had off. "Not really. I have another job. Two actually."

She open her eyes and meets my gaze. "What kind of jobs?"

"Just some side things."

"Matchmaking?"

"I guess that makes three."

"Why do you need so many jobs?"

"Money. I've got bills, just like everyone else."

"You make pretty good money at the hotel. Five hundred dollars a show plus tips. What's that bring in? Three or four hundred? So that's not a bad living. Plus you get a free suite at the Landslide." She props herself up on her elbow and stares at me. "Why do you need so much money?"

"Why do you need to know?" I say, picking a loose rock from the side of the cliff and skipping it across the surface of the lake.

"Because you don't add up."

"Neither do you," I say, skipping another one.

"I'm really not complicated."

"Your life sure is."

"What?"

"Nothing." She has no clue. None at all. "So your dad's coming and you want the show to be perfect because the travel people are gonna rate the hotel."

"How'd you know that?"

"Claudio told me this morning. He said you were worried about disappointing your dad. So I guess that's why you're here. For him."

She sits up all the way now. "What's that mean? You're so damn confusing, Fletcher. You want to have sex with me, you want to fix me up with Cole, and you want to keep your job. But nothing about that makes sense."

"It's not really complicated, Tiffy. And anyone who wasn't raised as a billionaire's daughter would understand it. I need money. I have bills. I'm trying my best to make shit work out, so

I do what I have to do. People like you just want to stick me in a box. Put a label on me. Make me into something I'm not. But the truth is, I'm not what you think." I look up at her. "You have no idea who I am."

"You're right, I don't. Because everything you've told me is a lie."

"I never lied to you. And you know what? Just go back to the fucking hotel and tell Chandler I'll be there. OK?" I get up and start climbing past her, but she grabs my arm as I try to pass over her body.

"Wait."

"Why?" I growl. "So I can sit here and listen to you judge me? I'm not a fraud. I'm not a conman, for fuck's sake. That brother of mine you were flirting with yesterday, he's the conman. I'm just a guy doing the best he can. So you can stop now. Just stop acting like you care about any of this bullshit, and just go back to your perfect life."

I regret those words as soon as they leave my mouth because I know her life is not what it seems either. I'm just saying these things to hurt her now. So I guess I am an asshole.

"Then tell why you want to fix me up with Cole."

"You asked me to fix you up with Cole, Tiffy."

"Why did you sleep with me?"

"And there it is," I sneer. "You're just like all the others. I promised fun, you agreed, and now you want to attach some secret meaning to it. It was a fuck, Tiffy. I like to fuck, like every other normal man my age. And it was fun. OK? You're a good fuck. And if you were still interested, I'd fuck you again. But you're not. That's all there is to it."

"Would you still do your job if I said you didn't have to quit?"

"I just told you, I'll do the show!"

"Not the show," she says, gripping me tighter. "Your job with me." Her face is serious. Even a little sad.

"Teach you to be sexy?"

She laughs. "I was wondering what word you used for it. Is that what it is to you then? Teaching girls to be sexy like you?"

"Like I always say… Sexy doesn't sell, it's for sale."

She laughs again and it makes me smile. God, what will happen to her when her father dies? I can't imagine. "You don't need me to teach you that, Tiffy. I already told you, you've got sexy in spades."

"Not according to Cole. Because I asked him if he'd like to have dinner tonight, just the two of us, and he said he was too busy. And if you were interested in someone, and they wanted you to eat with them, then you'd say yes, right?" She looks at me, wanting me to say no, but knowing I won't lie to her.

"I'm not sure." Maybe Cole is distracted by her dad's illness and doesn't have time for that kind of stuff right now? Maybe his job is the most important thing in his life? I can relate to that. It's why I don't have girlfriends. But maybe the fact that she won't inherit any money takes her out of the running? And if Cole knows about that then…

It's that last part that gives me pause. If that's the reason I will kick his ass. I don't care how big that motherfucker is. I will kick his ass if he's been using her and her dad all those years for money.

"Look," I say. "I don't think you're serious about Cole, Tiffy. I think you want a boyfriend and he's just as good as the next. I think you want to replace whatever is missing in your life with him. And I don't think you trust me one bit. So just say it."

"Say what?" she asks, equally annoyed.

"Just admit you can't walk away from my sexy."

She laughs and hides her face.

I like her laugh. She doesn't do it enough. I bet she's been on this road to respect since she was adopted by the old man. A little girl is suddenly thrust into a world of the rich and powerful. Parties, private schools, and all that other shit that comes with it. Pony lessons, ballet, tutors, and most of all… expectations.

"Say it," I repeat. "Tell me I'm sexy and you need me. And then I'll help you. Just let all that other stuff go. If you want the fantasy, then let me be your fantasy."

She rolls her eyes and presses her lips together.

"I know you think it, Tiffy. Everyone thinks it. You can deny all you want. But I'm hot."

She snorts. "It's not hot to *know* you're hot."

"Sure it is." I stare at her green eyes as they sparkle with the reflection of the water. "Sure it is, Tiffy. In fact, when I look twice at a girl, it's not their body I'm looking at. Lots of people have nice bodies. Lots of girls have pretty faces. When I take a second look, it's because she has confidence."

"Then why did you look at me?" She's serious now. She holds her hand up and shields her eyes from the sun and I can see them peering out at me from the shadow she creates. "Because everything about me says second best."

"Wow. Who did that number on you? Normally I'd accuse your father, but I don't think it was him. So who called you second best, Tiffy? It wasn't Claudio. It sure the fuck wasn't me. Was it

Cole? Did you turn his disinterest into self-loathing? Because I'm gonna be honest here. From my perspective, everything about you says winner. Everything points to strength, independence, and intelligence."

She drops her hand from her eyes and bows her head. "Thank you."

And that's a good answer. She can accept a compliment, at least. I have known lots of girls who couldn't even do that. But Tiffy's reply comes off as well-bred manners instead of confidence. It's something she's been taught to do. Be polite.

"I'll do the show and keep our deal about Cole."

She looks up, but the smile is gone.

"I'll do it. But I want something from you in return."

"I'll make sure you have a job—"

"No," I cut her off. "I'm scrappy, Tiffy. That's not what I want. I can find my own way in this world. I don't need your handouts. Fuck the job. I've already written it off and have three ideas for replacing the money."

She squints at me, suspicious. "Then what do you want?"

She has every right to be suspicious. Because I'm smiling a devious I-am-sexy-fucking-Fletcher-Novak smile. "A lap dance, Tiffy. I want a lap dance. Right here. Right now."

17

"You're kidding."

"I'm not." And he isn't. I can tell. Because he stands up and walks across the large flat boulder to another one that is the perfect height to sit on. "Come on, show me your stuff. Show me how sexy you are. And if you do that, I'll give you everything you want."

"Fletcher, I'm not a stripper."

"Neither was I nine months ago. My first lap dance was hilarious. Chandler laughed his ass off. I had to do him, by the way. So at least you've got me to entice. Just imagine trying to be sexy with a dude like him."

I laugh as I picture him. "But you're different. You're good at this stuff. Girls look at you and imagine ripping your clothes off. Guys look at me and imagine the granny pants I have on under my suit."

"No," he says with a laugh. "I'm pretty sure the thought going through my head that night I saw you at the show was, *She looks fuckable*."

"It was not. I was a prissy bitch to you that night."

"You were a sex kitten, Tiffy. Even your name is sexy. You opened that door and the look on your face said insatiable sexual appetite."

"Fuck you," I chuckle, trying to hide my blush. "It did not. I was thinking about how to fire you that night."

"Lap dance. Come on. Get up and do it."

"I don't even know what a lap dance is. I've only ever seen one at your show."

He eyes me suspiciously, considering if I'm lying or not. And then he stands up, takes my hand, whirls me around and pushes down on my shoulders. "OK, I'll go first then. But you're not getting out of it."

I take a deep breath as I look up into his blue eyes. My heart starts to beat a little faster as I imagine what it would be like to watch him try to seduce me with a dance. I blush. Fiercely.

He shoots me one of those grins that light up his face. "Ready?"

I nod.

"Pay close attention, Tiffy." He says this as his hips begin to move back and forth. I'm already mesmerized. But when he places his hands on my shoulders and straddles my legs, I have to gulp down air. "You have to make contact, Tiff. It's the most important thing. I touch you here," he says, his voice lowering as he rubs my shoulders, "and if you're into me, a chill should run through your body."

It does. It so does.

His hips are right in front of my face now, and I can't help but stare at his torso. My eyes slip down to his belt. And then his hands are there, playing with the waistband of his jeans. "And then you direct my eyes down to your hips. Just like that."

I glance up at him to see if he's laughing, but he's got a serious look on his face. And if I didn't know better—if I didn't know that this was the infamous Fletcher Novak, the guy who fucks anyone he wants, whenever he wants, and doesn't have a flavor of the week, but a flavor of the day—then I might think he's into me.

"When my eyes are on your hips, you tease me with them. Be my fantasy, Tiffy. Make me imagine what you'd look like with no clothes."

Jesus. I can imagine. I saw him that first night. I saw him naked the next day. I sucked his dick looking up at him like this. It's very easy to imagine him naked. He certainly qualifies as my fantasy.

He begins to play with my hair, taking the long dark strands into his fingers, caressing it in a long dragging motion until I feel a feather-light touch on the top of my breast. I look up at him again.

"Touch my chest first. Soft strokes that make me feel like this is all real."

It's not real, Tiffy. I say it to remind myself. It's not real. This is a job to him.

His fingers slide between my bra strap and my skin, sweeping up until they're on top of my shoulders. "It's a tease, though. That's the most important thing to remember. It's just a tease. You want me to look at you with lust. You want me to look at you with desire. You want me to think I have a chance."

You have no chance, Tiffy. Oh my God. Why am I even thinking these things?

"You want me to imagine taking off your bra." His hand slips down my back as he pushes his whole body even further into my lap. And then it's on the clasp of my bra.

I swallow hard.

"You want me to"—he unsnaps my bra like a pro, and it comes loose, billowing out in front of me with the soft current of the wind—"think about making a move."

He's making a move all right.

"And then, just to keep the fantasy going"—he slides the bra down my arms until it's in my lap. My nipples perk up from the light spray of the lake waves as they push against the rocks—"you take something off."

"Fletcher—"

But I stop. Because his hands are behind my neck, pulling my face into his weaving hips. He threads his fingers through my hair and up my scalp. That chill up my spine turns into a full-blown tremble.

"You want me to think you'll kiss me, Tiffy." He releases my hair and then his palms are alongside my cheeks, cupping me with force. Not hard, but not soft either. Like he's preparing me for what's to come.

What's coming?

He bows down, his forehead pressing against mine, but he is still too far away. "You want to make me want you. More than anything else, you want me to want you, right now, in this moment."

I want him. Holy fuck, I want him. *Let me be your fantasy, Fletcher.*

His knees rest on either side of my thighs, and then I feel his ass moving across the top of them. Back and forth. Slowly and then even more slowly. He gyrates against me, the heat of his sex appeal crashing against me like the waves against the rocks.

"You want to make me touch you, Tiffy." I know he's still in teacher mode, but I don't care. I reach for him. My fingers find his belt loops and hook around them. I tug him just a little bit closer as I stare into his eyes.

"Then I'll say, *Kiss me, Tiffy.*" And his head dips down further, his lips so close to mine, the kiss is all but inevitable.

But he pauses. I can feel his breath on my lips. I can smell his scent in my nose. He smells like a man. And sweat. And sand. And water. And wind.

"But remember," he says, tipping my chin up a little so our lips bump ever so slightly against one another, "you have to make me beg for it. I have to beg for it or you don't give it up. Because the lap dance, Tiffy, is a test. It's your chance," he whispers over the music of the lake, "to be sexy. To be desired. To be in control. You're all mine. But it's a fantasy, and I have to beg for it."

And then I can't stand it anymore. I move that fraction of an inch and taste him.

He grips my head, pushing his mouth against mine. His tongue doesn't dance like last time, it's hard and pushing. Seeking more from me.

I give him more. I unhook my fingers from his belt loops and slide my hands down his thighs. His legs are well-muscled and his jeans are hot from the sun.

He moans into my mouth, reaches for my hand, and places it over his hard cock.

God. I have never wanted a man to fuck me so much.

I pull back for a minute and we both catch our breath. The next few moments float in my head. "How would you beg for it, Fletch?" I ask him. "How would you make me want you back?"

He kisses me one more time and then moves backwards.

Holy fuck. He's gonna leave me like this.

"You don't have to worry about that, princess. No man in his right mind wouldn't want you right now. And I'm no different."

We stare at each other for a few seconds. And then he picks up my bra and places it in my hands. "But we better get back. I think your clothes are dry and I've gotta get ready for the show."

He gets up off my lap and goes hunting for his shirt. I watch him as he pulls it over his head. taking note of the defined muscles in his abs. He doesn't look at me once he's dressed again, just gathers up my drying clothes off the rock and turns back to hand them over.

"I hope you plan on getting dressed. Because if you try to walk home naked, I'll be kicking a lot of ass on the way."

I shake myself out of his trance and slide my bra up my arms. But before I can reach around to hook it, he's there, his fingers light as they brush against my back and do it for me.

He takes my hand once my bra is on and pulls me to my feet. And I stand there as he dresses me. The shirt is mostly dry, and it flutters over my head and settles on my hips. He opens up my pants and holds them open for me. "Step in, Tiffy. We gotta go."

I place my hand on his shoulder and feel a chill run through him.

He looks up at me and we've traded places from a few minutes ago. I lift a leg and step in, and then do it again. He stands, tugging my pants up with him.

He leans in and whispers, "I can't wait for my turn."

18

I think about her the whole walk back. She wanted me. I can feel it. She wanted me to take her right there. She'd have let me fuck her, just like she did the other night on the roof.

But is it the fantasy she wants? Fletcher the stripper? Fletcher the teacher? Or something else?

It's impossible to tell, and that's the problem with the job I do. You can't ever tell if people like you for *who* you are or *what* you are. I know what I look like. I've never had a problem getting girls. I lost my virginity when other guys were still trying to make it to first base. Hell, I even had a few moms making eyes at me back in high school.

But they always wanted something out of it. The teenagers wanted to go to dances with the quarterback. The college girls wanted to get fucked by the lacrosse star. The patrons at the show want to say they fucked one of the Mountain Men. And not just any Mountain Man, the lead.

It's tainted me, so what? I get to have an opinion about the hand I was dealt, just like everyone else. And I'm not saying I'd want to be anyone but me, because I don't.

I just want girls to look at me with something more than the size of my cock on their minds.

"Hey," Chandler says as I pass through the backstage door. "I was beginning to wonder if you'd show up."

"I'm here, aren't I?" And for the first time, I wish I wasn't. Tiffy's father is gonna be here. She wants me to… what? What kind of first impression is that? *Hey, Dad, this guy wants to date me. Don't you love that he takes his clothes off at our hotel every Wednesday and Saturday?*

Yeah, that's gonna go over well.

Wait, what? Since when do I care what kind of impression I make on a girl's parents? Like I ever had a chance with Tiffy. She's smart, rich, beautiful. And she wants Cole. She hired me to get Cole. And yeah, I can tempt her all I want with lap dances. But the fact is, I'm not the guy who gets a girl like her. She's a one-night stand if ever there was one. And our one night was up a few days ago.

So fuck it. I might as well do my job and do it well.

I go into my dressing room and push the costumes around. Saturdays are a little more wild than Wednesdays. For one, we sell more tickets. We take out some tables and put in cheap seats. There will be a few hundred more people in there tonight. So we do it right. And the new routine we came up with is the first act.

I'm not gonna waste any more time thinking about Tiffy. I'm

just gonna go out there first thing and find me a girl to erase this shitty life I've set up for myself. Erase all the shit that's piling up. Forget that my job is hanging by a thread. Forget that people are depending on me. Forget my fucking brother came back to town on the one day I wish he'd just drop dead.

Forget all that shit.

I go back out into the common room where all the guys hang out and do my thing. "What's Sexy Man have to say this week?"

Mitch throws the weekly tabloid at me and hits me in the chest. "We laughed about it yesterday, asshole. You've just been too caught up in the boss' daughter to even remember we exist."

"Yeah, well. She's been trying to fire me all week. What was I supposed to do? Let her get rid of me?"

"You should read it," Steve says, pointing to the magazine. "It's got you written all over that shit. We laughed so hard last night in the bar."

I grin and open the trashy paper to the weekly columns and start reading.

Dear Sexy Man,

I got a problem. A girl showed up who's way above my league and I fucked her blind in my office. The problem is, she's my boss. And now she wants more and I just don't know how to tell her to get lost without losing my job. Help!

Signed,
Cock on the Clock

I let out a laugh. God, this shit is priceless.

Dear Cock on the Clock,

Never, ever, fuck the boss, son. You have two choices. Marry the bitch or quit your job and move on. Boss bitches never get over it. So declare your independence and fly free, young man. Learn your lesson well. It's a memory for the books, that's for sure. There's nothing better than getting off with a woman who's forbidden. But the cock gods demand to be paid. So next time you're tempted to fuck where you work, ask yourself, 'Is this the girl I want to marry?' And if not, then tuck that cock back in your pants and move on.

Love ya,
Sexy Man

"Classic shit," Bill says, grabbing it out of my hand. "You know, Sexy Man was getting lame there for a while. Talking all serious. I was beginning to think he was gonna pussy out and say he's in love, that's how boring it got."

"He's still funny," I say. "He's just been doing this for a while, that's all. You run out of things to say."

"He gets letters, dumbass," Sean says. "All he's gotta do is pick the funny shit. Hell, I've sent in a few and he never picks my stuff. And it's good, man."

"Like hell. You're as dumb as a hammer," Mitch says. "You couldn't write something funny if your life was on the line.

Fletcher, now he's funny. You ever send a letter into Sexy Man, Fletch?"

"Never," I say. "The last thing I want is to spend my free time thinking about that stupid column."

"I still think it's funny," Steve says, pulling on his cowboy boots. "Where's your costume, Fletch?" he asks, eyeing my regular boots.

"I've got five minutes, Steve. What's the rush?"

"Get a move on, Fletcher," Chandler says, slamming the door behind him. "If you're back, then be back. Not that you've even been here the last few days. You missed three practices this week."

"Corporate, man. Blame them for that shit."

"They wouldn't even be here if you weren't fucking off."

"Well, I have a feeling my days are numbered. Mr. Preston is gonna be here tonight and I'm pretty sure this is not his idea of a good marketing plan. I've also heard that there's some big shots in the online booking world coming to rate the place. I can only imagine the look on Preston's face when he realized his only shot at this opportunity hinges on six guys taking off their clothes."

"I think he knows we're his money-makers, Fletch," Chandlers says. "I've talked to him about it. He just said keep it clean."

"Keep what clean?" Mitch asks. He sounds as annoyed as I feel.

"Yeah," Steve says. "We don't do clean. Those women don't want clean. They want dirty as fuck. I'm not giving up a whole night's worth of tips to keep that asshole happy. Especially if he's just looking for a reason to shut this show down."

"Calm down," Chandler says. "It's one night."

"One night is nothing to you, I guess," Sean says. "I've got bills to pay. And I count on tips to make that happen. It's not like we're raking in the cash with this gig. It's Tahoe, for fuck's sake. Not Vegas."

"Listen," Chandler says, clearly getting pissed off. "If you want to keep this job, then do what I say. Preston wants a clean show. It's his fucking hotel."

"It's not his hotel, actually."

"What?"

They all turn to look at me and I'm sorry I mentioned it. But once you say it, you gotta explain. These guys won't let me off that easy.

"It's Tiffy Preston's hotel. Her old man doesn't own it. She does. And I'm pretty sure she wants to get a good rating. And the way we do that is to do the best show ever. That's not pulling punches. That's making those women scream our names, cover their mouths from embarrassment, and tell all their friends this was worth every penny. With any luck, the reviewer will be a woman."

"Don't even, Novak." He walks over to me and stares me in the eyes. "I'm telling you all right now, we're gonna clean it up and do as we're told."

I stare back at him, my fists clenching right along with my jaw.

"You got it?"

"I got it," I snarl. "You have another job waiting, so you could give a fuck if we fail."

He pushes me hard in the chest and I have to take a few steps back. "Fuck you, Fletcher. You're the problem here, not me. You're the one they want to get rid of, not me."

"I quit yesterday, asshole. And I'm the one who's still here. So I'm obviously not that expendable."

"Wait," Sean says. "What does he mean you've got another job?"

"His pussy-whipped ass took a job in Reno because his girlfriend was bitching and moaning about the show. Didn't he tell you?"

I know he didn't. It was between us. But I know my time here is just about over. So fuck it. Chandler isn't gonna pull rank and act like he cares what happens to this show. Not after all that's happened this week.

"Is that true?" Mitch asks. "You're bailing and you want us to basically throw the fight so you can… what? Get a severance bonus if the hotel gets a good ranking?"

Chandler stares at me with squinted eyes. I crossed a line with him. It was a secret. And he's got plenty of secrets of mine too, so I should've been respectful of his. But the last man standing doesn't get there by being a pussy. "Tell them, Chandler."

"I'll tell them a lot more than that, Novak."

I throw out my arms. "Go ahead. It's my last night, anyway."

"OK," Steve says, pushing himself between us, one hand on each of our chests. "Let's just relax and get through the show. Then we can all have a day to cool off, and discuss it on Monday." He looks at me. "And Fletcher, for fuck's sake, you're not getting fired. I heard Claudio talking you up on the phone earlier today to Preston. I think her father is a good guy."

"So I've heard," I say. But that asshole is gonna leave Tiffy alone in this world, struggling and afraid, just to make her prove herself. I can see a guy doing that to his sons. But girls need protection. They need safety nets. And it pisses me off that he's fucking her over like that.

But I don't say any of that. That really is crossing a line. Tiffy doesn't deserve to find out about her dad from my big mouth. I'm not sure where I stand with her from one minute to the next, but I do know I don't want to hurt her.

Chandler stares me down for a few more seconds and I wait to see if he'll spill any of my secrets. But it's one thing to tell the guys he's leaving. We've been expecting it for a couple months. It's something else to tell them what I'm up to.

So he takes a deep breath and turns away. "Fifteen minutes until show time. Keep it clean. That's an order." And then he walks out of the dressing room and slams the door behind him.

19

The atmosphere for the show is different today than it was on Wednesday. People are louder, more animated. Drunk. Lots of bachelorettes in this crowd, and I bet each one wants a piece of these men tonight.

I crinkle my nose at that thought, just as Claudio comes up and taps me on the shoulder. "Tiff," he says in that voice I dread. It's his concerned voice. One that immediately tells me that something is wrong.

"What?" I can't hold back the trepidation that spreads throughout my body like a wave. "What's happened?"

"Your dad isn't feeling well. He said he's going back to San Francisco tonight."

My dad has been sick for months. He had a slight stroke last year and some heart problems the year before. And even though he recovered, he's been having dizzy spells. And he doesn't like to talk about it with me, so I'm always the last to know. "Maybe I should go with him? I'll go pack my stuff."

"No," Claudio says, grabbing my arm. "He's already gone, Tiff. And he said he needs you here to take care of the hotel. He said he'll call you tomorrow."

"He always says that, Claudio. If you know what's going on, then tell me! It's driving me—" I stop and watch Cole walk into the theater with a woman on his arm. "Who the hell is that?"

Claudio opens his mouth to answer, looking a little too relieved about the distraction. "Wait," I say. "Tell me about my dad first. Is he sick?"

"Tiffy," he says, sighing. "I don't know. I think you need to talk to him about it. And he said he was going to call you tomorrow. So ask him then. And as for that tramp"—he motions his head towards the table we're going to share with Cole and now this girl—"she's new at the office."

"Since when?"

"The day we got here."

"Bullshit. Cole never hires people without telling me."

"Well, he did this one. Made her his executive assistant."

"Well, I guess that really is his decision. But…" My words trail off as he pulls the chair out and she takes a seat, smiling up at him like… "Do you think they're dating?"

"Not yet. So if you want him, you better make a move soon, girlfriend. Because he's about to make his and it won't be you on his arm tonight."

Holy shit. "I'll be right back."

I don't even wait for Claudio to answer before I'm making a mad dash towards backstage. The security guy waves me through and I enter the dimly lit hallway and pass the dressing rooms as I make my way towards the back.

When I get to Fletcher's door, I knock. "Fletch?" I call. "You in there?"

I hear a faint, "Come in," and so I twist the handle and peek my head in.

"You busy?" I ask. He's standing in front of the mirror buckling a holster onto his hip. He's got a cowboy hat on, faded jeans, and cowboy boots.

He looks fucking hot.

As usual.

"Not any busier than normal five minutes before the show opens." He yells over Chandler's booming voice from the stage. "What's up?"

"Cole is up! He's got a girl out there. He brought a date! He's here with a girl from the office!"

"Calm down, princess." He gives me a little rumbling chuckle and then that grin I've grown to love. "How do you know it's a date? Maybe it's just business?"

"What kind of girl goes to see a stripper with her boss?"

"I don't know," he says, leaning his perfect ass against the dressing table and crossing his arms over his chest. "What kind of boss invites her employee up to her room?"

"I was going to fire you. And it's not the same. You don't really work for me. This girl is his"—I make air quotes—"executive assistant. How's that for bullshit?"

Fletcher grabs my hand and pulls me towards him. All kinds of nerve endings start firing in my body from his touch. "Are you jealous?" he asks, putting his hands on my hips once I'm within a few inches of his chest.

I'm about to scream, *Hell, yes!* when I stop. "I don't know if I'm jealous, exactly. But I'm pissed. This was supposed to be my big night. I had this all planned. We," I stress, "had this all planned."

His hands slide up my body until his fingertips are pressing on the back of my ribs and his thumbs are right underneath my breasts. I have to take a deep breath. "What are you doing, Fletcher?"

"Making you crazy."

"Stop and help me get rid of this girl!"

He stands up straight and leans into my neck. "How should I do that?"

Fuck. Why is Fletcher so hot?

"Should I pick her out of the crowd? Make her feel special? Take her to my room?"

Sometimes I wish he'd take me to his room. I got a taste of his magic that first night and holy fuck, if Cole and Claudio weren't there and we'd had time alone, I might've fucked him that night.

Focus, Tiffy.

"Um, yeah?"

"That sounds like a question. Do you want me to take this girl home tonight, Tiffy? Ruin her chances with Cole?"

"Sorta. I just want my chance, ya know? I just want my one opportunity to make him see me as a possibility. And this was gonna be it. I was going to use all those tricks and get him to notice."

A knock at the door interrupts us. "One minute, Fletcher," some stage guy says.

Fletcher looks down at me with a small smile. Not the grin he had on a few seconds ago. “I’ll take care of it, Tiffy. OK? And then you can have another date with him tomorrow and that one will go perfect.”

I nod, unable to take my eyes off his face. That smile isn’t happy, it’s… sad. Something is wrong. And I’m just about to open my mouth to ask why he’s sad when I hear Chandler announcing the guys on stage.

“Just go sit down and be patient. When the girl is gone, make a date for dinner with Cole. I’ll take care of her.”

And then he walks out the door to do his thing.

20

Tiffy is right. That asshole brought a girl with him. And she might be his assistant, but she's a whole lot more than that.

I walk out on stage with the rest of the guys dressed up in our cowboy gear and I automatically do the line dance we've been working on the past few weeks. But my eyes never leave that girl. Not once. I don't care if I'm on the other side of the stage, doing the stripper version of the cupid shuffle, I'm looking at her. It takes her a few minutes to catch on, but by the time we hop down on the floor to flirt, she's not looking at anyone but me.

Cole frowns as I walk up to the table and take her by the hand. On Saturdays we choose three girls. One in the beginning, one during our solos, and one at the end. She's gonna be my pick all night long.

Her hand is sweating as I lead her up on stage with the rest of the first picks and motion for her to take a seat on one of the chairs lined up. She nervously sits in the middle chair with two girls on either side of her.

Chandler squints his eyes at me once he realizes who's in my hot seat, but we're on stage, so what is he gonna do about it now?

I chuckle a little as the rest of us guys line up behind the ladies and start the next dance. This one invokes a trick that each of us do using the chair and the girl as props.

Steve is up first, and his trick is that little chair-rung jumping I used on Tiffy last Wednesday. His girl squeals and covers her mouth, and I spy Tiffy chatting with Cole while I wait my turn.

Steve straddles his girl, grinds her face into his dick for a ten count—that makes me laugh—and then jumps off the top rung and lands a perfect backflip off the stage.

They go wild for Steve. He's like some former gymnast or something and does all that fancy flipping shit. That gets the tips going like crazy.

Bill is already on top of things, though. And he sits down on his girl's lap and does his own version of the dance I did for Tiffy this afternoon. I look over at her again, and she's paying attention now. Her eyes dart to mine and I wink at her. She takes a deep breath and that makes me grin like a kid.

But then my eyes dart to Cole as he leans in and whispers something to Tiffy.

She shakes her head, but doesn't look at me again.

Hmmm. Asshole.

Bill finishes up with the girl on her knees in front of him as he does the wobble in her face.

I look at Chandler, who is fuming now, since that was not

part of Bill's script, but fuck it. He did his job and his girl is happy.

I start my dance behind the secretary, moving my hips for the crowd, not her. And then I start peeling my shirt up, just a little peek here and a little peek there. The ladies scream for more and the secretary gets antsy, twisting her body to try to see me. I reach down, grab her under her thighs, and swing her legs over my shoulders so she's upside down and her face is smashed into my abs. "Lift my shirt up, darlin'. Let's give them all a peek before you take it off."

"Oh my God," is all I hear from her. But her little fingertips reach under my shirt and begin to lift. The crowd goes wild again, and that's when I smack her ass, flip her back down, place both hands on the back of her chair, and jump over her head.

More cheering. But I'm not finished yet.

I pull her up out of the chair and yell, "What should she do?"

"Take it off!"

I laugh. Fucking horny bitches. So I turn to the assistant and say, "You heard them. Proceed!"

I wiggle around a little as she lifts my shirt up and since she's short, I make a game of not letting her get it over my head. The crowd laughs as I tease her. *She* laughs as I tease her. And then, when she's finally got it over, and she's real close up next to me, I whisper, "I want to fuck you tonight."

But before she can answer I push her back down into her chair, swing it around so she's facing the curtain, and then—so the whole place can see it—put her hand down my pants and make her squeeze.

I look at Tiffy and she's beaming. I'm pretty sure if Cole wasn't sitting next to her looking like he was gonna kick my ass, she'd be thumbing me up.

But Cole is mad as hell. And I watch him while Mitch and Sean do their opening acts.

Usually, once we're done with this part, we walk the girls down the stairs so they don't faint or pull some other girly bullshit, but I walk Ms. Executive Assistant all the way back to her table and kiss her hand before I leave.

I go back to my dressing room feeling more satisfied than I have all day.

Pounding on the door a few minutes later forces me to tuck that shit away.

"Hey, asshole," Chandler says, barging in without waiting for an invitation. "What the fuck did I tell you?"

"That was a clean act. One dick grab is all it was. I didn't even pretend to eat her pussy."

"It's the general manager's fucking girlfriend!"

"Girlfriend? I heard that was his secretary or some shit. Figured she wanted to experience the show like a VIP. Oh, by the way, where were the VIP's?"

"Newsflash, dickhead. She's sitting at a table with him, then she's his. Off-limits."

"You gonna tell me Tiffy's off-limits too?"

"She is, Fletcher. And you will not choose her tonight. I do not need another lecture from Cole like last time."

"What lecture?" This is news to me.

"He was all over my ass after he heard. He said to keep you away, and I plan on it, brother. You're not gonna fuck up my job—"

"You're quitting your job, Chandler. Everyone knows this."

He just stares at me.

"You're quitting, aren't you?"

"Cole offered me a position in Vegas. And I'm gonna take it."

"What position?"

"Dude, you know I'm only doing this show because it's all that was available. Well, they've got a hotel show in Vegas that needs a producer. And Cole offered it to me."

"In exchange for what?"

"Just..." He stops to let out a long sigh. "Just to get rid of you, asshole. And you're ready to move on, anyway. So I said yes."

"Thanks a lot, you dick."

"You're done here, Fletcher. You and I both know it. So don't hate me because I have solid plans."

I point to the door. "Get the fuck out of here. And fuck you and your plans."

"You gotta grow up sometime, Fletch. You had a good run, but it's over."

I kick the trashcan and it goes flying. And then I hear Chandler introducing Steve and start putting on my next costume. I fucking hate that Cole guy. I don't know what it is, but he's a douche. I'm going to ruin his night by making his girl compare him to me. And I'm going to do it right in front of his face.

XOXOXOXOX

By the time I'm back on stage doing my Navy officer act, Cole and the secretary aren't even sitting next to each other at that table, and Tiffy's smile is so bright she lights up the room.

God, she's pretty. That whole conversation this afternoon where she called herself second best was shocking.

I start my act, barely paying attention. This one is not new. I've been doing it since the first show I was ever in. I salute, click my heels, and then start stripping by peeling the white gloves off my hands one finger at a time.

The crowd is wild tonight. I've got three bridesmaids flashing their tits before I even get rid of one glove. And by the time the shirt is coming off, I've got two girls fighting to stuff dollars in my pants in the front row.

But Tiffy, man. Her self-image earlier surprised me. This is what I mean, though. Take Katie, for instance. She's a successful… whatever you call her position at that law office. It's not romantic and thrilling like they make it look in the movies. It's corporate shit. She sits in an office all day, has a few meetings, goes home to a nice apartment. She's got all that career shit figured out. But she's unsatisfied. And she can't find a guy who interests her and vice versa, so she blames herself.

But it's not her. It's assholes like me who make her feel like it's her. Assholes who never call back. Assholes who take her out and expect more than they should. Assholes who can't commit.

I grab the sides of my pants at the thighs and rip. The snaps all give way, and then I throw them behind me. Bitches will steal your clothes if you're not careful.

I take my attention back to the secretary and point at her. She smiles wide and her face goes red. She gives Cole a half-glance, but then raises her shoulder closest to him.

The brushoff.

She heard my offer and she's all in.

I glance at Cole and almost bust out laughing. Jesus, he does not have a poker face. He's bright red too, but with fuming anger.

I don't know if Tiffy's like Katie. I don't know Katie all that well. But so far this week when I've called Katie, she's been receptive, realistic, and ready to do anything I've asked.

Sometimes that involves lowering expectations. But in Katie's case, it's more about retargeting the right kind of guy. She wants a bad boy who wants to settle down.

I chuckle at that. Don't they all.

The secretary gets up on her feet as I jump off the stage and make my way to her. I let the girls push those dollars down my briefs and make sure they don't get too excited.

They all do. Want that bad boy who wants to change and be a dad and a husband, that is.

But those guys don't exist. And most women need to hear that for a few weeks. They need to fail at this shit so bad that they get it.

I do, of course, set up the bad guys they meet. I've only been in this stripping business nine months, but I have connections from previous jobs.

Katie saw through my first asshole immediately. Oh, Axe was hot, and he was bad. Reformed prisoner. But Katie has good instincts, and never called him back on Friday when he tried for date two.

Then there was Brian Friday night. If Axe was the president of Bad Boy Inc., then Brian was middle management. Katie agreed to see him again on Saturday for a day date, but I got a message last night that she was not interested.

Which means she likes the idea of a bad boy. Not the bad

boy himself. She wants a guy who works out, wears hot ripped jeans and white t-shirts on the weekends, but has a brain and a legitimate job Monday through Friday.

Like me. If you can call what I do a legitimate job.

Except this secretary bitch right here… all these bitches in here… all they see is Axe. They have no idea who I am. They have no idea what I do. And they have no interest in finding out.

And that's OK with me.

I take the secretary's hand and whirl her to the beat of the thumping music. And then I pull her close in one quick move, crashing her against my rock-hard chest. She's a little stunned from the quick change and even more so when I hold her tight. We do a little slow dance. I watch those faces all around me for the look.

That look that says, *Awwww. I want to take him home. He's bad, but good at the same time. He makes her fist his junk on stage and then slow-dances to the beat of lust in a room full of heat.*

Fletcher Novak is a keeper, they sigh.

But Fletcher Novak is taken. They just have no idea because no one looks hard enough. All they see is this guy here, because that's all they want to see.

Stripper.

Player.

Liar.

Asshole.

And they love it. So fuck this girl in my arms with her head resting on my chest like we are high-school lovers shuffling around on prom night. I don't give one shit about her. She's a job, just like all the rest of them here in this room.

She's just another job to me.

21

Elizabeth was her name. But she's gone now. Fletcher marked her as his the first act and that was that. He never took his eyes off her. And by the time the last act came along, he never let her go either. She disappeared backstage with him and never looked back.

"She's the new employee?" I ask Cole, both of us looking at the curtain with disbelief. "Your assistant?"

Cole grunts and then reluctantly turns back to me. "I'm sorry your dad cancelled. I know how much you wanted to see him."

"Yeah," I say, a little sad about the fact my father didn't show. It's like he's lost all interest in me lately. "I am." But I'm not here to talk about my dad. I'm here to get a date with Cole tomorrow night. "I miss him. It's been months since he's had time for me."

"Well, being a billionaire hotel mogul keeps him busy, right?" Cole's eyes dart to the curtain when a stage hand appears to start cleaning up the equipment. And the other guys are all lined up for their lap dances. That will go on for a while.

"Where do you think she went?" I ask, just to see if he's jealous of Fletcher.

"He's probably fucking her backstage."

"What? Do you think?" I fake it. Sorta.

"Why?" Cole snaps. "You like that asshole too? You think he's sexy? He's hot? He's worth the hassle he comes with? Why didn't you fire him?"

"I didn't have to. He quit. I asked him to come back and do this show for my dad tonight. And the reviewers." I look around for their table and two of the women are already in line for a lap dance. "I guess they want the full experience."

"Yeah, well, if he wanted to impress them, why didn't he stick around for the lap dance?"

"Are you"—please, God. No. He can't really like that girl. She was just… there. Right?—"dating Elizabeth?"

"Dating? God, no. But she's on company time, Tiffy. What kind of employee goes off to fuck the star stripper?"

Hmmmm. I have nothing for that one. I did it myself. In fact, I bet Fletcher took her up on the roof. I bet he's getting that blanket out of the trunk right now. Telling her he's never fucked anyone on it because he makes them stand.

Asshole.

"He's bad news. You fire him tonight. Your father's not coming out here. I know that for sure."

I scrunch my eyebrows together. "I'm supposed to be here for another few weeks to get things in order. He doesn't even want to visit me?"

Cole reaches across the table, his interest in the backstage curtain on pause, and takes my hands in his, giving them a little squeeze. "It's not about you, Tiffy. It's just business."

I force a weak smile. "I know." And then I get an idea. "You want to go grab some dinner tonight? I haven't eaten yet."

He gives the backstage one more glance. "Nah, I've got work to do. Let's go say hello to the reviewers and let them know to contact us if they need anything."

And before I can even register that he shot me down again, he's dropped my hands and walked off towards the two in line.

Hmmm. He's way too preoccupied with his missing assistant.

I spend the next thirty minutes pretending that I'm not noticing how Cole is wasting time to see if Elizabeth will reappear looking well-fucked. But that's what he's doing all right. His conversation is directed to the reviewers but his attention is only on the backstage curtain. Like she'll come out from there.

This is not turning out how I imagined it. "Hey, Cole," I say, inching my body towards his until our arms are touching. "Wanna have dinner with me tomorrow since you're busy tonight?"

The reviewers are preoccupied with their turn in line for lap dances, so they aren't listening. But Cole shoots me a dirty look and shushes me into silence.

God, I'm losing bad right now. I need Fletcher's help. He'd know exactly what to do. But he's on the roof with that tramp.

It pisses me off almost as much as it does Cole. I need him and he's busy fucking someone else.

Asshole.

"OK, well, I'm tired. So I'm turning in for the night. See you tomorrow?"

"Sure, Tiffy. Goodnight." Cole walks off towards the backstage curtain.

I turn on my heel and walk off as well. I spy Claudio in line to get a lap dance with Steve. And I should put a stop to that, but I need to find Fletcher. This is not working. He promised me it would work.

I head straight up to my floor on the penthouse and turn right towards the door to the roof. There is no stone in there to prop it open, but my keycard opens all the doors, and I don't see why this one would be any different. It opens. So I creep up the stairs and prop my head against the door as I crack it just an inch.

Silence. Just some residual party noise from the pool down below.

I slip through the door and tiptoe to the garden shed.

And stop dead.

What if I see him?

I bite my lip and a sick feeling takes over my stomach as I realize I don't want to see him. He was fucking me in there a few days ago. Who knows how many other girls he's had up here since then, but I never knew about them. This would be catching him in the act. And today, out on the rocks, I almost got the feeling he liked me. Maybe not desired me. Not the way he did the other night when I was his conquest. But still. I have this idea that we're friends. That maybe he's doing this because he really does think I'm pretty and I deserve a good guy.

I let out a long breath. Jesus Christ. I'm fantasizing about him. Just like all those other girls do. And he made it perfectly clear it was a one-night-only thing.

Tiffy, my inner voice says in that calm way I've trained it to do, *better to know for sure that he's a lying, cheating player than let this dream of capturing his heart go on any longer.*

So I start walking again, this time not taking care to be quiet. Maybe he will hear me and stop whatever it is he's doing?

When I reach the door I pull it open with force, slamming it against the side of the building.

But it's empty.

Hmmm.

Where else might he have taken her? Out to those rocks? God, he could take her anywhere. He probably took her off the hotel grounds. So I go back the way I came and pull out my cell phone, tabbing my contact at the front desk.

"Landslide Hotel and Cas—"

"It's Miss Preston. Does Fletcher Novak have an assigned parking space?"

"Yes ma'am. Next to the valet, spot…" Her keyboard clicks as she looks it up. "Spot 55E."

"Thank you," I say, and end the call. I'll check there next. If he's gone, then there's no point in looking anywhere else for him, right?

But when I get to the garage and ask the valet guys where the space is, they point to a classic red Camaro with a white racing stripe down the center of the hood. A very Fletcher Novak kind of car.

He didn't leave.

I check the pool next. But even though there are probably a hundred people out there at the weekly Saturday night adult swim, Fletcher is not.

I walk out towards the beach, which has far fewer people on

it, and scan that too. I might be missing him, since it's dark. But I don't see any couples alone on the beach.

But I do see Elizabeth. I don't know how I know it's her, since I only just met her. But I do. And when another familiar shape walks across the sand and stops alongside her, my heart almost stops because it's Cole.

I can't hear the argument, but I know what those gestures mean. I've known Cole for years. I know what he looks like when he's annoyed.

So he does like her. He went looking for her and now that he's found her, he wants answers.

But if she's here alone, then where is Fletcher?

I leave the beach and walk towards the parking lot, looking at them as I make my way to a tree.

I'll just wait this out and see if Fletcher comes back. He's probably gone to get her a drink.

A few minutes pass, and then Cole reaches down to Elizabeth and pulls her to her feet. His quick embrace tells me more than I wanted to know.

He might *really* like her.

They leave together and disappear into the crowd near the pool. At least he didn't take her up to his room. I still have a chance.

Fletcher has to be around somewhere. So I head towards the front desk and wait until the girl at the counter is finished with a few guests, chewing my lip the entire time as I try to figure out what's happening to my plan.

"Can I help—Oh, Miss Preston. Did you find Fletch's car?"

Fletch. She must be on good terms with him. I'm sure they've fucked on the roof too. "Yes, but I'm looking for him. Have you seen him around?"

"Oh, yeah, he's in his room. He called down for room service like an hour ago."

"An hour ago?"

She gives me a flustered look and starts to answer, but I don't wait. I just turn on my heel and go back to the elevator. An hour ago? That means he wasn't with Elizabeth for very long. So what's he been doing?

I walk quickly to the North Tower elevators, pressing the button repeatedly until it opens and a bunch of people spill out dressed up for a night of fun. I smile politely and get in after they leave, and press the button for his floor.

The doors close and I slump back against the mirrored wall, trying to figure this all out. What is he up to?

When I get to fifteen I exit the elevator and head straight to his suite at the end of the hall. I press my ear again the door and listen. There's some music, but it's not loud. Does he have another girl in there? How many can he have in one night?

I knock hard and wait. I don't hear anything, but the door locks disengage and he pulls the door open. "'Bout time, ass—Tiffy? What are you doing here?"

I'm speechless. He's got no shirt on, so my eyes sorta get stuck on the topography of his abs. There's a light dusting of blond happy trail that leads me to the fact that he's only wearing a pair of cut-off sweat shorts that end just below his knees, and before I can stop myself, I'm staring right at the bump of his package under those shorts. "Ummm." What am I doing here? "Cole… he found Elizabeth on the beach and…" I look up and meet Fletcher's gaze. He's squinting at me, confused. Shit. I've been stalking him all night and if I tell him that he's gonna think I'm crazy. "I need more tips, Fletcher. I think he really likes her." Fletcher shoots me a dubious look. And that's when I notice how different he looks. "You wear glasses?"

He smiles, like he was just caught doing something bad, and pulls them off his face. "Just when I'm working."

"You're working? But it's Saturday night."' I lean over to look past him. His dining table is littered with papers and an open laptop. He really is working.

"You wanna come in?" he asks. "Or are you just here checking up on me?"

I blush. Because that's exactly what I'm doing.

"If you want Cole, you have to make him jealous, Tiffy. I pegged him for a guy who wants what he can't have the very first time I met him. So come in," Fletcher says, opening the door wide. "I've got a plan."

22

Tiffy Preston is a tease. And she doesn't have to bite her lip or bare her leg or any of that other bullshit for me to know this. She looks at me like she's hungry. She did it last week when I took her up on the roof and she's doing it right now because her eyes are tracing all up and down my body in a way that makes it necessary to adjust myself under my shorts.

"What plan?" she asks, barely able to drag her stare back up to my face.

I wave her into my room, acutely aware of the stacks of papers on my table, the open laptop on my table, the TV blaring this week's predictions from repeats of the Friday stock reports, and my lack of clothing. Not that she hasn't seen everything. But I'm pushing my own self-control here.

There's another knock at the door and I breathe out a sigh of relief as I go answer it.

"Hey, Fletch," John the waiter says. "Sorry it took so long. We're swamped down—" He stops when he sees Tiffy. "Oh, um, hi, Miss Preston."

"Tiffy and I have business," I say, motioning to my out-of-control paperwork. "So we're eating in tonight."

"Oh, sure," John says, pushing the cart into the room. He starts setting up the food and then notices he only brought one plate and serving set.

I stop him before he opens his mouth. "I'm not hungry, John. So Miss Preston will be the only one dining."

"OK," John says with a smile.

A minute later he's walking back to the door and I slip him a twenty. "Do not say she was here. You got it?"

"I got it, dude," he says with a fake salute. "Later."

I close the door and turn back to Tiffy. She's leaning over the room service cart, inhaling the aroma. "Hungry?"

"Sorry." She laughs. "I never got dinner." She gives herself a little mental shake to get back on point. "I asked him out, Fletch, and he said no. So I asked about tomorrow, and all he was interested in was that trampy assistant. I'm not a good player. There is no way he's interested in me."

I'm not listening to any of that. Maybe two words get through my brain. Because her hair is all crazy disheveled, like she's been in bed. Or out by the beach. I inhale as her lips move and I think I smell the lake on her. That sweet scent I grew up with. It reminds me of home. And that thought derails everything.

Fucking home.

"You listening to me?"

"Yeah." She's got another summer dress on. It's yellow and

stands out against her perfect skin. Her eyes dart up and down my body as she talks and when she notices me noticing that, she closes her eyes and blushes a bright pink.

I think I get hard from that.

"Fletcher!"

"What?"

"You're not listening."

"You think he's not interested. But he is." How the fuck could he not be? Something is off. "I mean, you're friends. And he's nice to you. So that's a tell that he's interested. He's just not motivated to make a move right now. The signals are getting all crossed and shit. So all we gotta do is line those signals up so they connect."

"How? I asked him to dinner—"

"Fuck dinner. Well, not literally." I take the silver lid off the platter and stuff some fries in my mouth. "I'm starving. Wanna share my hamburger?"

She lets out a long sigh, but it comes with a smile. So she's starting to relax. "OK."

"Come on, sit down and we'll eat." I grab all my papers off the table and stack them up.

"What's all that?"

"Taxes. Fucking taxes. They're the bane of my whole existence."

"It's August. Why are you worrying about taxes now?"

"Uh..." Shit. "Quarterlies are due next month." *Good recovery, Fletcher.* "I like to keep on top of it. Gotta report those tips, right?"

"You report tips?"

"It's the law, babe."

"Pffft. OK." She grabs a French fry and stuffs it into her mouth and continues to talk. I cannot even stop watching her lips. And her tongue. Holy fuck. I'm horny. I'm goddamned horny for Tiffy Preston. I've been in denial all week, but when a guy thinks chewing is sexy, he's got a problem.

"Right?" she asks.

"Right," I reply.

"You did not even hear what I said."

She's right. I didn't. "You just need more moves, Tiffy."

"Exactly! That's what I just said."

"But I'm starving. So let's eat first." I grab a knife and slice the burger down the middle, then take one half and give her the plate. I stuff most of that thing in my mouth with one bite.

She picks hers up and starts to nibble on it. Two minutes later I'm finished and I'm eyeing her and her burger like I'm about to eat them both.

"What?" she asks, looking at me with her mouth open, mid-chew.

"What?"

"Did you just say you want to eat me and the burger both?"

I laugh. "I sorta do." I realize that's a bad move if I want to keep this job going a little longer. "I'm starving."

Tiffy raises an eyebrow at me.

"And I was thinking about that girl tonight. She showed me her tits as soon as we got backstage and I put her off."

"Hmmmm. Why'd you do that? I thought you had a new girl for every show?"

"She's a skank." *And you've ruined me,* I don't add. I get one little taste of a lady and I'm ruined. "Those women at those shows are just not my type this week." I sigh and go for the truth, just to see if she believes me. "Not for many weeks, if I'm honest."

Tiffy pauses, rolling that admission around in her head. But what she thinks about it, I have no clue. Because she changes the subject. "So how should we make Cole jealous?"

I should take the hint. Getting more involved with her than I already am is a monumentally bad move. But I realize I don't care. So I smile that smile she seems to like, and play a card in a game I decide I'd really like to win. "Let's practice that lap dance, Tiffy."

"What?" she gasps. "No, Fletcher. Cole isn't—"

"Cole is," I stress. "Every guy is, Tiffy. Maybe Cole doesn't do strippers, but even guys who like the nice girl want the stripper in the bedroom. So I think you should go out there tomorrow, drop some very subtle hints, and then when you get him somewhere private, you pull out the bad girl you're keeping in your pocket."

She's shaking her head the whole time I'm talking and I almost laugh, it's so cute. "There's no way I can seduce him like that. I mean, I can do some lip-licking and some leg-swinging, but—" She looks down at her body. "I'm not that girl. I'm not. I have sex in the dark, Fletcher. I like candles and under the covers."

"I almost fucked you against a wall on the roof, Tiffy."

She draws in a long breath and closes her eyes. My dick swells again. So much that I walk up next to the room service cart to hide it. When she opens her eyes again she finds my face. "That was not me. I don't do that stuff. It's just, you were a little overpowering in your… sex appeal, I guess. I don't know why I went up there with you. But I do know I can't do that with Cole."

I think about this for a minute. Considering what she's saying. Wondering if she's right or not. And decide she isn't.

"You went up there with me, Tiff, because you got caught up in my spell. That's it. That's all. So you just need to get Cole caught up in your spell."

"I'm not a sex witch, Fletch."

I move away from the cart and walk up next to her. God, she smells good. I take her hand. That move makes her swallow and I can tell she's nervous. But when I place her hand over my hard-on she sucks down air like she might stop breathing.

"You make me hard, Tiffy Preston. And all you did was walk into this room. So I'm pretty fucking sure you can do the same for Cole."

"Fletcher," she whispers as I place my hand on her hip and draw her closer.

"Just relax," I say in a low voice. "I'm not gonna make a move. I'm just saying you're sexy as fuck, Tiffy. All you need to do is capture his attention and let his desire take over."

"And how the hell do I get him up to a room to do a lap dance?"

"Fuck the room. We've got a dance floor downstairs."

"Oh my—"

"You dance with the guy, Tiff. And do a little imaginary striptease. Like this." I grab both her hips and pull her close to me, my body moving to the music in the background. My fingertips flare over her ass cheeks, rubbing the muscles beneath her thin dress. My dick is fully erect under my shorts now, so I start pressing against her to stimulate myself. "Relax," I whisper into her neck. And then I grab her hands and lift her arms up above her head. "Keep them up here and move your body like this."

I grind against her as I look her in the eyes. I'm feeling heavy with lust for this girl. She bites her lip and it's not a fucking move. It's real. I almost lose it. I want to bend her over my bed and fuck her so bad.

"Like this?" she asks sweetly. She's moving a little. Trying to do as I ask.

Calm the fuck down, Fletcher. She's here to learn how to seduce Cole. But holy shit, I want her. "You gotta try harder than that if you want the guy, Tiffy."

She takes a deep breath and bends her knees, swaying her body as she dips down. "I can dance, you know. I'm not a complete social moron."

A smile creeps up my face as she does her little wiggle move. Her mouth is so close to my dick, I might explode. "It's not bad," I say playfully. "But you need to practice."

"Hmmm," she says, standing back up. Her hands are in her hair now, and she rips out the little ponytail holder, letting her long brown locks spill over her shoulders. "See," she says with a smile that reaches all the way up to her eyes. "I can seduce you."

"You sure the fuck can," I mumble.

"But you're horny and shit, Fletcher. You live for sex. Cole is..."

"Boring? Blind? Gay? Maybe he's more interested in Claudio?"

"Oh, God." Tiffy bursts out laughing. "Claudio wouldn't sleep with Cole if he was the last man on earth. He thinks Cole's pudgy. Besides, he's sort of in lust with Steve."

"My Steve?" I laugh. My cock starts to calm down with the fun conversation. "They'd make a good couple, actually. Maybe I should set the two of them up instead. Keep you for myself?"

She laughs a little more, but her arms are still swaying above her head and she does another little dip before standing back up and turning her back to me. She peeks over her shoulder like a flirting professional, batting her eyelashes, a move that never works on anyone—except me, right here, right now—and says, "I'm not your type, Fletcher. I'm serious and conservative. And you're not."

She turns her head, and I have to look in the hotel window to see the reflection of her face. Her eyes are closed now. "But maybe you're right. Maybe I should let you teach me how to seduce him with a lap dance."

And then she stops and walks over to the dining table and pulls out a chair, facing it towards me. "Here. Sit. Let me at least try."

I'm suddenly without words. But my feet know when to accept an invitation that my brain has a hard time coming to terms with. So two seconds later I'm walking to that chair. "Your move, Miss Preston."

23

Fletcher is easy. He's always looking for a fuck. Cole is not. Fletcher is a professional seducer. Cole is a professional… well, professional.

So maybe Fletch is right? I need to make Cole want me. I need to make him desire me. I need to seduce him. And I think I can do the dancing. I'm not inept at that. I've been clubbing with Claudio enough to have those moves down.

I'm not a one-night stand kind of girl. But I had that with Fletcher. I was witness to one of the best flirts in the business as he tried to seduce me. So all I really have to do is be the Tiffy Preston version of Fletcher Novak, right?

But if I think about who I'm practicing on too hard, then I'll lose my nerve. So when Fletch gets to the chair, I push him into a sitting position.

"What?" Fletcher laughs.

"Shhh," I say, laying a single fingertip across his lips. "Don't talk or you'll scare me off."

His mouth drops open but he stays silent.

I think back to the rock earlier today. How he was moving his body in front of my face. Demanding my attention. I take a step forward and straddle his legs. The sensitive skin on the inside of my thighs brushes up against his soft sweat shorts, and a shiver runs up my legs—straight through my core.

Just the thought of my panties rubbing against his hard cock is enough to start the throbbing. So I bend my knees a little and lower myself down. Just enough to brush my pussy over the open air between his legs.

I reach for his hair and when I brush the tips of my fingers against his scalp, he lets out a small, "Fuck."

"Like this, Fletch?"

He nods. His eyes are trained on mine. I have his complete attention. "Yeah," he whispers, and swallows hard. "That's pretty good, Tiffy."

I ease forward, my hips swaying back and forth just above his zipper, my legs pressing hard against his. And then I ease down into his lap.

I like this, I realize. I like him. It's dangerous, I know that. But I can't stop now. Not even if I wanted to, and I don't.

The moment my clit feels his cock, I let out a breath of desire. Will he fuck me again if I go too far? Or will he stop himself and obey his own rules? Should I try for it? Should I try to make Fletcher Novak want me?

But his hands on my ass again blow away my thoughts. He's playing along. He rubs the muscles under my dress, and then a moment later they're underneath. Caressing that tender spot between my upper thighs.

I want him to take it further. I want him to want me. But I don't know what to do next. So I hear myself ask, "Now what?"

"Now," he growls, "you close the deal."

"How?" I whisper, leaning into his neck like he did earlier.

He grabs the hem of my dress and lifts it up, exposing my thighs and rubbing them all at the same time. "Take this off."

Jesus. If I do that I have a feeling we might not stop. I know he's a one-night guy and we had that already. But what if I succeed at this seduction thing?

"Do it, Tiffy. Stand up and take the fucking dress off. You make him crazy, just like I make those girls crazy on stage."

A striptease, I realize. He wants me to do a striptease. "I don't know—"

But he stands up and pushes me back. "Take the dress off." He sits back down on the chair and leans back, spreading his legs slightly and getting comfortable. Like he's ready to enjoy a show he typically gives instead of gets.

I'm suddenly flushed with embarrassment. I just know my face is turning red. But I want to do this. I want to learn how to make a man crazy with lust. I want to make Fletcher feel that insane, overpowering want he made me feel last week on the roof. The kind of want that drives men mad. The kind of lust that makes a man throw away all caution, and inhibitions, and rational thought. The kind of desire that has him screaming in his head, *Fuck the consequences*. I want him to crave me so bad, he can't say no. I want that power, and I want it bad. "Where do I start?"

"Tease me," Fletcher says. "With your dress. Lift it up, give me a peek, and then drop it again."

I blink a few times. But the power is within my reach. I can feel it. I might not be a sex witch, but Fletcher Novak is about to be under my spell. So I grab the thin fabric and start rubbing it up and down my thighs. He lets out a breath, watching my fingertips as they do a dance with the dress.

He scoots forward in his chair and wraps the warm palms of his hands behind my knees.

I am immediately wet. I can feel it pooling in my lacy underwear.

He rubs small circles against the sensitive skin on the back of my legs and it feels so good, I lift the dress up and show him my panties.

"Fuck," he mutters again.

I let the dress fall, and then lift it again. My body starts moving now, the way he does when he's performing. I close my eyes and enjoy the beat of the music in the background.

"Take it off, Tiffy. And make it sexy."

"How?" I say, opening my eyes so I can stare at the desire in his face.

"Slow," he says, gripping me harder and pulling me towards him.

I bite my lip and think about all the ways I can make this more seductive. I turn, making his hands drag across my thighs until my back is to him. He starts rubbing my upper thighs, inching higher and higher as I continue to sway.

I reach behind me and grab the zipper of my dress and drag it down a few inches. "Pull it down for me, Fletcher."

His hands take advantage of every opportunity on their way up my back. He caresses my hips, presses the pads of his thumbs into the muscles on each side of my spine, and then reaches around as they travel upward, brushing against my nipples, turning them into tiny peaks.

I moan when he withdraws them, grabbing the back of my dress and the zipper with each hand. I lift up my hair with both hands to give him access and find myself throbbing with anticipation.

The zipper lowers with a small ripping sound, and then his hot mouth is on the bare skin in the middle of my back. One hand finds its way under my dress again, and he presses his fingers against my clit.

"You're wet," he says.

"I can't help it," I whisper.

"Don't try."

I slip one strap of my dress over my shoulder and look back at him. His hands are eager now, one tugging my panties aside and his fingers finding their way into my wet folds.

"Watch me," I say, looking down at him. "I want you to watch me."

"Fuck."

I take that as a good sign, and slip the other strap down my shoulder. He gives the dress a little tug, and it falls away from my breasts, landing at my hips.

I turn back around to get a better look at his face. His eyes immediately find my cream-colored lace bra. He cups both breasts in his hands, squeezing hard.

I moan from that. God, I want him. I probably want him

more than he wants me right now. I want all that hard stuff he did up on the roof.

Patience, that little voice in my head says. *Give him a show. This is all about anticipation.* So my fingertips find the bunched-up fabric stuck on the curve of my hips, and I shimmy a little. Until it works its way over the hourglass shape and then falls to the floor with a soft whoosh.

I swallow then. Hard. I'm not naked yet. But I am standing here in his room, exposed and vulnerable. His gaze takes me in. Every inch of me. And then his hands are exploring. He cups my breasts again, and that hard squeeze comes with it. He pulls one bra cup down and exposes my nipple so he can take it in his mouth.

He sucks and bites. Not softly, but not enough to make it too painful to endure. Just enough. Just. Enough. To make me crave his cock inside me.

I reach behind my back and unclasp my bra and let it hang there, the way he did this afternoon on the rock.

Bu this time he waits for me to take it off. His hands slide down and rest on my hips, caressing the bones that protrude slightly underneath my panties.

"Don't stop now," he growls.

I have no intention of stopping. But I can't say that out loud. So I lean forward enough to allow gravity to let the bra slip down my arms and fall to the floor.

He stares at me.

I shift my feet in my heels, making them click on the tile floor, and let him look.

His mouth presses into my belly, his hands pressing into my

thighs, and then he is kissing me in a tender way that takes me by surprise. Almost everything about Fletcher is hard. His muscles. His cock. His attitude. His gaze.

But his mouth is soft in all the ways I've ever dreamed of.

"Should I..." I swallow. "Should I take my panties off?"

He looks up at me, still kissing my stomach, still rubbing his hands up and down my legs. "Only if you want me to fuck you."

I stand there silently for a moment. We watch each other. I'm filling up with questions, but the only things I see in him are answers.

Fletcher Novak is my answer to every mystery there is.

So I thread my fingertips under the slim elastic lace and work the panties down the curve of my body the same way I did the dress. He watches my face as I do this. And my heart skips a beat.

Never have I felt so naked.

But then he moves his gaze down to the action and leans back once more. So he can take in the view. So he doesn't miss the show. So he can enjoy himself.

My final piece of clothing falls to the floor and once again I step away from them. And in the process, I move closer to him.

I'm begging inside. Begging.

"Fuck me," I say. "I want you to fuck me right now like I've never wanted anything else in my life."

24

There is always a moment when you realize things have changed. You see a girl from across the room and something grabs you. Her legs, maybe. Or her hair. Or the look in her eyes. You can't explain it, that feeling is just there. You watch her walk, you listen to her talk, and it's never enough. You just want to stare at her. Take her all in. Memorize her. It doesn't make sense, but that feeling is there.

I get this feeling now. Tiffy standing here in front of me. Naked. Exposed. Wanting me.

And I have two choices. Yes or no.

It feels like everything hinges on this moment. Like life will flip upside down either way.

Say no and it will hurt her. I know that. If I tell her no, she's never coming back. She's never going to make this offer again. She's never going to let down her guard for another man, period.

Whatever little piece inside her that's damaged can be cured with one nod of my head. But shake it the other way and that damaged piece grows a scar. A scar that might never go away.

And maybe I'm full of myself. Maybe I'm delusional to think that I have this kind of power. But I saw the look on those girls' faces the other day when they came to confront me for the scars I gave them.

I can't do that to Tiffy. I can't. I know it's wrong. She wants someone who can take care of her and I'm not capable of doing that. So if I was an honest guy I'd give her that scar and hope for the best. Because saying yes to this tonight means I will just crush her later. When she finds out who I am, what I'm doing, and how many lies I've told. All for money.

If I was a good guy, this wouldn't even be an issue. I'd put her clothes back on and tell her we can meet up tomorrow to get the guy she really wants. Cole. Cole, the man who can provide for her. Cole, the man she's been fantasizing about for years.

But he's not what she thinks he is either.

So even though I'm breaking all my rules, even though I'm going against all my instincts, and even though I'm gonna regret this in the morning, I say…

"Sit on my lap."

She spreads her legs to straddle mine and eases herself down onto my legs. I can feel the heat of her desire through my shorts and when I look down at her pussy, her lips are spread open, just slightly, giving me a peek at her clit.

I look up at her face. Her long brown hair is draped down her shoulders, the tips reaching for her perky nipples.

I reach behind her, cup her ass, and hike her closer to me so that her opening is pressing against the hard bulge in my pants.

"Touch me," I whisper.

"Where?" she asks back in a scared, quiet voice.

"Anywhere you want."

She reaches for my face and strokes her fingertip up and down my cheek. It's tender and sweet. And it takes me back for a second. I expected her to touch the hard muscles of my chest. Or the hills and valleys of my abs. Or grab hold of my shoulders like she never wants to let go.

Not the face.

"You're beautiful," she says, letting the word out with a long, slow breath of air. I laugh, but the pad of her thumb touches my lips to make it stop. "No, really. People look at you, Fletcher, and they ask themselves, 'Why don't I look like that?'"

"No one wants to be me, Tiffy. I promise you."

"You're wrong," she says. "Everyone wants to be you. You have everything at your fingertips. You're smart, and gorgeous, and happy, and outgoing, and confident, and sexy."

I feel even worse for taking advantage of her right now. Because I'm so far from all those things, she has no idea. "Sexy is on the inside, Tiffy. The inside is the only thing that matters."

"You can say that because you're one of them. One of those beautiful people who don't realize how lucky they are."

I huff out some air. "I could say the same thing about you, ya know. You're all those words you just used to describe me. Only you're the real deal."

Her lips tugs down to make a frown and she shakes her head. "Fuck me. I just want to feel you against me tonight. And I promise, I won't overreact tomorrow when everything goes back to the way it's supposed to be."

The way it's supposed to be. I have a million questions about that statement. But I want her too. I want her mouth on my mouth. I want her legs wrapped around me and her heart beating against mine as I enter her.

So instead of talking, I give her what she's asking for. I cup her ass and stand up, walking us over to the bed, then bend down and lay her on the rumpled covers, spreading her legs as I ease in between them.

"It's your turn now. To watch."

I step back and reach for the waistband of my shorts. Her eyes are fixed on my actions. And when I tug a little, exposing the light trail of blond hair that hides under the fabric, my thick, hard cock is growing as I release the waistband and let the shorts drop to my ankles and kick them aside. I step forward, grab her hair with both hands, and press her face up to me.

Her breath is hot, and then her tongue is pressing against my shaft. She opens her mouth and begins to kiss the fabric of my boxer briefs. Softly.

Everything Tiffy does, she does softly. She is gentle and sweet. And this just makes me want to love her. Not fuck her, like she's asking. But love her. Even if it's just for one night.

So I fist her hair and push her back again, until she's lying all the way back on the bed, and my hands go to my boxer briefs. She swallows down something. Maybe fear. Maybe regret. Maybe something else.

But she's waiting for more, so that's what I give her.

I yank my briefs down and step out, kicking them across the smooth wooden floor where the shorts are in a pile. At the same time, I lean down and kiss her stomach. Small, light, fluttering kisses that aren't part of my normal repertoire. I swirl my tongue around her little belly button. There's no piercing. No tattoos on this girl. No rebellious pink hair or edge to her voice or mannerisms that scream, *I'm a rebel.*

Because she's not a rebel. She's a nice, sweet girl.

So I'm gonna fuck her the way she deserves.

Her fingertips thread through my hair, urging me lower. But I go up instead of down. I fist both of her firm breasts as my mouth finds her nipples. She moans, and spreads her legs wider underneath me.

We are naked. Skin against skin. Not like the last time when it was hard and fast and we were partially clothed.

I take my kisses up to her neck and she shivers from my soft touch. I kiss her diamond earring and then breathe softly into her ear. "Fuck," I say.

"Please," she begs me back.

I scoot up a little more, kneeling on the soft mattress with my knees pressed against her ribs. My fully erect cock is reaching for her. The tip bumps up against her lips and she opens her mouth to let her tongue dart out. She swipes it over my head and then she reaches for my shaft as she opens wider and urges me forward.

I lean down, my hands flat on the bed on either side of her face, and angle my hips until my cock begins to disappear inside her mouth.

She sucks, and oh my God, she feels good. I pump a few times, making her grip tighten around my shaft. She shakes her head a little to let me know I've gone too deep, so I ease back just enough to let her take control for a second.

But the pause only lasts a second. Because her tongue is doing a little swirling dance now, and I can't stop what I want. I want to bury my cock down her throat. I know she's not capable of this, so I force myself to take it slow.

She responds by trying harder to take me in. She opens her mouth wider and then presses her lips down. The pressure is enough to make my head fall backwards from the pleasure.

And then her face moves forward, taking a little bit more.

Be patient, Fletcher, I warn myself. *Be patient.* She's willing to try, so I let her take me any way she wants.

She sucks me like that for a few seconds, and then she reaches down to play with my balls. "Tiffy," I say. "Fuck."

Just as the word comes out of my mouth, she opens and thrusts forward one more time. Not swallowing me, but doing her best. And it's enough. Fuck, yeah, it's enough.

I pull out and lean down to kiss her mouth. "You make me feel so good," I whisper into her mouth. "Scoot up a little."

She braces herself on the bed and does as I ask, finding her way to the middle of my bed. Her legs are still open and the look on her face is one of hunger.

I've seen lust before. But I see more than that in Tiffy. I see what I want to see, because I see love.

I let out a long breath, knowing it's a lie as soon as the thought completes in my mind. She's confused. I did that to her. But I don't care. Because I want her. Not just for a night. I want more.

So I grab a condom from my nightstand and tug it on. And then I ease on top of her, my legs alongside hers, my elbow resting on the bed now, so I can use my fingers to play with her hair as I kiss her mouth.

She kisses me back and I take some pleasure in the softness of her response. She's not looking for the wall sex on the roof. She's happy with what I'm giving her.

So I leave her mouth and kiss my way down her body and give her what she wanted a few minutes ago. When I get to her stomach, I hike her legs up, pressing on the back of her thighs so her knees are up to her chin.

And then I lick her pussy. She's neatly trimmed. Perfectly trimmed. My tongue sweeps up and down, flicking against her clit when I get to the top, and then reaching for her little bud of an asshole on the downswing.

And with each lap around her pussy, she writhes. She reaches for my hair and grips it tight, and her little squeaks become more intense. Her hips begin to jerk from side to side, and I know it's too much. But I'm not stopping. Not until she comes in my mouth. So I clamp down on her forearms and pin them to the bed. I take her clit between my lips and suck. Gently at first, to get her to calm down. And as soon as she does, I flick it wildly. Back and forth.

"Fletcher," she moans. "Oh, shit, Fletcher!"

I'm too busy to answer because I know she's close. But I let go of one arm so I can reach down between her legs and insert two fingers inside her. I pump a few times and she lets out a little scream.

"Oh, shit," she says again. "Oh my God." When I look up at her face to gauge how much more she can take, she's biting her lip so hard, it draws blood.

She's so close.

So I withdraw my fingers and strum her clit, just as my tongue thrusts up inside her pussy and she clamps my head between her legs with a long moan. Her whole body twists and I can taste her come in my mouth. It flows down to the rhythm of her orgasm and all the tension is released in that moment.

When I look up again, her eyes are closed and her head is to the side. She's panting hard, taking long draws of breath as she basks in the afterglow of her pleasure.

I kiss my way back up her stomach, angling my body and my legs so my tip is poised just outside her entrance. And then I ease into her slick pussy.

This time I moan. She's so fucking wet. And so fucking tight.

I push harder, making her arch her back. But her eyes are still closed when I check her face to see if I should stop.

I don't stop. I press down on her breasts with my chest and take her mouth with mine. "Taste it, Tiffy." She kisses me back without hesitation. Her nails dig into my back, clawing their way up as I pump inside her. Hard. And then harder. "I did that to you," I say. "I made you taste like that."

"Mmmm," she moans, meeting my thrusts with her own. "More," she mumbles. "I want to feel that again."

I reach underneath her and roll us over, my cock never leaving her pussy. She's too tired and too satiated to sit up and ride me, but that's not what I want, anyway. I want her close. So I wrap my arms around her waist and upper back and hold her down on top of my chest. She hikes her legs up, so she's practically on her knees, and lets me pound her from below. I grab her hair and pull her head back, not able to stop myself from getting a little rough with her. But she responds like we've been doing this for years. Like we are two parts of a whole. Like we're a matching set.

She knows just what to do.

She looks me in the eyes, arches her back, and then we come together. I slide against the walls of her pussy. She's gushing now, that's how wet she is from coming twice. My contractions go on and on, semen spilling into the condom as wave after wave of pleasure fills me up and washes over me. I press my head into her breasts and bite one, just as the feeling begins to subside.

I ease out, rip the condom off and throw it into the trashcan on the side of the bed.

"Come here," I growl, turning her body so her ass angles into my cock. I wrap my arms around her waist and hold her close as I kiss her cheek. "Fuck, Tiffy. That was amazing."

"Mmmm," she mumbles, snuggling into my chest. "The best sex I've ever had."

I fall asleep with her words echoing in my mind.

Me too, is all I keep thinking. No other sex even comes close. I can't even call this sex. And even though I know I should not be getting attached to this unattainable girl, I get attached. I hold her close. Her breathing deepens and she drifts off to sleep.

It takes me a lot longer to give in to the call. Because I lie there for a long time thinking about how all I want is to keep her for myself.

But I do drift off. Eventually that hope makes it into my dreams.

That's all it is though.

Because when I wake up to the bright sunshine coming through the hotel windows, she's gone.

So I do the only thing I can think to do to make it right. I pick up the phone and call a girl.

25

My only saving grace is the fact that Claudio is out screwing around with Steve. Because if he was home, he'd know immediately. And he'd know it was Fletcher. Then he'd whoop and holler and do that stupid little I-told-you-so dance until he convinced me that Cole is a jerk and Fletcher the stripper is the man of my dreams.

But let's be real. Fletcher is an asshole. No, not last night. But pretty much every other night. He's an asshole. He uses girls for sex and… whatever. I don't know his problems. Everyone has them, and I'm sure he's no different. But he's got a free room in a luxury resort, a job that maybe requires him to work thirty hours a week, and a paycheck that is far higher than a guy whose main claim to fame is making women scream his name deserves.

Not to mention his side business. If you can call that a business.

I let the water from the rain shower pound down on my shoulders and spit some out.

But fuck if he isn't hot.

And experienced. *Very* experienced.

God, just thinking about his tongue on my pussy and the way he fucked me afterward. Holy Jesus. I could get used to that. And the way he was last night has me reconsidering things.

Tiffy.

I know. I cannot fall for a stripper. I still remember my mom struggling when I was little. I've seen pictures of my real father. He was an attractive man. Too attractive. Like Fletcher. These guys are never satisfied. They're always looking for something better. Better girl, better job, better house, better car. All that bullshit.

My mom didn't have it easy before she married into the Preston family. And neither did I. It sucked to have no father when I was little. It sucked to have to have that empty pit in my stomach every time I thought about the man who didn't want me.

And even though my new dad was the prince in my mom's Cinderella story, she told me over and over as I was growing up that princes don't normally save the day. I should not count on being saved. She pounded it into my head that all choices have consequences. Both the good and the bad.

If you find a good guy—one who provides, one who cares for his family and is faithful, one who works hard and still knows how to relax at the end of the day—well, you don't let him go. No matter what.

And I can still hear my question after she told me that the first time. It was a couple years after she first started seeing Randall Preston, but she was still working the night shift.

What if I don't love that guy?

Love is an illusion, she said back. *Love is what you make it.* She smoothed down my hair and smiled a strained smile, her lips painted a bright red for her job, her hair piled on top of her head in a dramatic updo. *Don't make the same mistakes I did, Tiffany Marie.* When she used my real name I knew I had better listen up. And I did. That conversation has stayed with me all these years. *Find a good man. A solid man with a good job and a soft heart. A man who won't hit you, or yell, or walk out on you and your children. And you never let him go.*

I thought her long silky dress was something out of a fairy tale back then.

It took years to realize my mother was a hooker and Randall was her client. When Fletcher said Cole might be using one, I feigned ignorance. No one knows what my mom used to do. Not even Claudio.

Everyone has a secret they're desperate to keep hidden.

Yes, my mother had the Cinderella story. But she never loved Randall. And he never loved her that way either. I have felt, from the first day we moved into his huge mansion in Monterey, that I was the glue that held them together. He never had kids and I was his one chance. He was the perfect father. A fairytale father.

But he cried at her funeral. I took his hand that day. I was only fifteen when she killed herself, but I knew that Randall felt responsible. They didn't fight. Ever. Not in my presence, anyway. It could've happened in private, but I don't think so. My mother was the perfect wife on the outside. She never raised her voice.

She never complained. She was simply grateful and satisfied.

Maybe that's not how you take life by the horns and make the most of it, but it worked for her. And it gave me opportunities that I would never have had.

Randall loved her in a way a man loves a woman he wants to save. And even if she didn't love him back, she respected him and he treated her well. Gave her everything she ever wanted.

Then why did she kill herself?

I have asked myself that question since the moment I learned it happened. She was supposed to be at the Four Seasons for a spa day, but they called and said she never showed up. We didn't start to worry until she didn't show up for dinner at home. She was always home for dinner. It was a constant thing in my life once Randall took us in. We were a family, he said. And families eat dinner together.

The police found her car off the side of a cliff.

And there was a note. All it said was, *I can't go on.*

Why? How could her life be that bad? My therapists said she was depressed and didn't seek help, so it overpowered her.

But I don't know about that. I've never been convinced. Something was missing from her life and I always felt that even though Randall was perfect, she was infatuated with my real father.

Maybe infatuated isn't the right word. In fact, maybe it wasn't love she felt for him at all. Maybe it was the idea that she wasn't good enough to keep him around.

Fletcher reminds me a lot of that man, the sperm donor who walked out. And Cole reminds me a lot of Randall, the prince who saved us. Maybe it's unfair, but what reason, beyond great sex, has Fletcher given me to think otherwise?

I turn the shower off and wrap myself in a towel. My body aches from the sex. I can still feel Fletcher's touch from last night. I can still feel his breath on my neck as he held me close as we slept.

But what does any of it mean? And why would I throw away a good possibility with a man like Cole for those brief moments with Fletcher?

But God, it felt good. And not just the sex. Why can't the hot guy be the prince? Just once?

Maybe Fletcher is a prince?

It's a novel idea for me, since I've only seen him as a player with all the right moves to win the game.

But then I swipe my hand across the mirror so I can look myself in the face. Tiffy Preston might be rich, and educated, and cultured—but she is still the girl who was left behind. Just like her mother.

It would be a monumental waste of time to explore the idea that Fletcher Novak might be a real possibility. I know nothing about him beyond what I've seen here at the hotel. And I have to admit, reluctantly, that none of that looks good for a future with him.

He's an expert in one-night stands, seduction, and helping girls manipulate their future husbands into loving them.

I reach for my phone and text Cole. I'll give him one more chance.

Want to meet for dinner?

No answer.

Maybe all men are assholes? Maybe I should just give up

on them altogether and just concentrate on my career? Maybe I should hang out with the gays and just have fun? Maybe I should—

Are you working today? he texts back.

No, I'm taking the day off.

Good, he replies a few seconds later. *Your father thinks you're working too hard, so I told him I'd arrange a spa day for you. They're expecting you at ten this morning, so don't be late. And dinner will be fun. What time?*

I laugh as I start texting. Yes! He's thinking of me. *How about six o'clock?*

Sounds good, Tiffy. I've got meetings all day, so I'll just pick you up in your room.

OK, bye!

I lie back on the bed and smile with relief. He's not avoiding me after all. He's just busy. And arranging a spa day for me is sweet. I really needed this ego boost.

My phone rings and jolts me out of my little daydream world. I look at the screen and moan. Fletcher. He's gonna want to know why I left without saying goodbye.

"Hello?" I say into the speaker.

"Hey," he says, a little hesitation in his voice. "You left me cold this morning."

"Oh, Cole planned a spa day for me, so I needed to get back to my room and clean up." Clean up? Jesus. What a way to bring up the fact that we fucked like teenagers last night.

No. Not exactly teenagers. It was pretty amazing. But that's what the bad boys do, right? They hook you with great sex and then leave you. So why not leave him first?

"Oh." He pauses, thinking probably.

"I got a date with Cole tonight though. So we're still on for Operation Jealousy? Or is this a good sign and I should stop with the games?"

"Date, huh?" He sounds unsure. But that's typical, right? He probably wants another one-night stand with me. And honestly, I should not have had sex with him again. One night is OK, I guess. It's a fling. But we've been taking this too far. "I think you're probably on your way to bagging your man. So you don't need me anymore."

Hmmm. His usually friendly demeanor is gone. In fact, if I didn't know better I'd think he was jealous.

"So he's the guy for you, huh?"

"Yeah, right? That was the whole point of all these things we've been doing the past week."

"And you love him, right?"

"Well, I'm not sure about love, Fletcher. Do you love every girl you bang?"

He huffs some air into the phone.

"Don't get weird on me, OK? You're the one who wanted a one-nighter."

"You were the one who wanted last night, if my memory serves."

"Yeah, well, I was feeling dejected."

"And I was just there?"

"What the hell, Fletcher? You're not interested in me. You're interested in a job, remember? You wanted us to use each other. And we did. And now you're trying to pretend you actually like me? You want me to feel guilty for going for the guy who was the goal the whole time? Wow."

"I never said I was pretending to like you, Tiffy. I picked you out of a crowd for a reason."

"Yeah, to fuck me for one night and then throw me away like trash. Just like you always do."

"So you're gonna get the jump on that, then? And throw me away before I have a chance?"

"So you admit it!"

"I'm not admitting shit, other than I had a nice time last night and I'd like to do it again."

"Oh, so we're just gonna keep this going? An endless string of casual sex with no commitments? I don't think so. I'm not that kind of girl, for one thing. And I'm not interested in casual."

"How do you even know I was thinking casual, anyway? Did you ever ask?"

"You have it written all over you, Fletcher. Your sign says *Don't get attached, because I sure won't.* And so I took your warning to heart and now you're mad at me? How is that fair?"

"I'll ask you again. You're just gonna throw this away and not even give it a chance?"

"Give what a chance? I'm having a hard time understanding you, Fletcher. Do you even know what you want? Do you even know *who* you want? Why me?"

"Huh," he says, laughing out the word. "Classic self-loathing, Tiffy. You don't think you're good enough. You're so sure I could never like you for real, you decide to fuck it all up and ditch me first before you can get hurt."

"What are you talking about? We fucked last night, nothing more."

"Really? That's all it was? You didn't feel any connection with me at all?" He pauses again, but I get the feeling he's got more to say and I can't help but be intrigued. So I stay silent. "Because I did. It was fun, Tiff. But it was more than fun. It was nice. And I was seriously hoping you had real feelings for me. Because I'd like to get to know you better."

I don't know what to say to that. A childish insult just seems wrong. What if he is sincere? Would I want him?

He's definitely hot. So yeah, I guess there's that. But his personality, God, what do I do with that? He's a callous player. He thinks love is a game. He's out for himself. And he's a stripper, for Pete's sake. How will a man like him care for me? He's a I'm-gonna-walk-out-on-you kind of guy if ever there was one. I just know it. The minute I depend on him, those true colors will come through and he'll leave me. Just like my real father did to my mother. Cole is the stable choice. Just like Randall was the stable choice for my mom. "It's not about me being good enough for *you*, Fletcher. It's whether you're good enough for *me*."

Silence.

And then hang-up beeps.

I just stare at the phone. What the fuck was that? Since when does he have feelings? Like any feelings? He's Mr I Have No Feelings! And we have one night of great sex and I'm supposed to believe he's changed? How the fuck does that make sense?

Just put him out of your mind, Tiffy. He's no one. He's using you. He's the worst kind of player. Because maybe he does have an inkling of emotion in him beyond lust, but I just know he's a flight risk. I can see it now. I tell him what he wants to hear, we have a few great weeks of hot sex, and then he's on to the next project. That's all girls are to him. Projects.

"Fuck that. I'm not a project."

But I am. Because I made a deal with him to get Cole.

No. It's not the same, Tiffy. Nothing he did helped me. Cole wasn't interested in me when I was flirting. He was the opposite of interested. He only became interested when I was real. When I put myself out there without any help from Fletcher and made my move. I'm the one who got him excited about having dinner with me today. I'm the one who took a chance. And Fletcher had nothing to do with that. Cole likes me when I'm me. Fletcher just likes me when I'm naked.

I take a deep breath and pull on some shorts and a tank top. I'm going to the spa. I'm gonna relax for the whole day, and then get prettied up and meet Cole for dinner. I'm not gonna waste my chance with the possibility of a maybe from Fletcher Novak. No way.

26

My spa time is anything but relaxing. My conversation with Fletcher dominates my thoughts. Why now? Why, when life seems to be going just the way I planned, does he have to try to convince me he's changed his stripes?

I don't understand. I'm not equipped to understand, if I'm being honest. I'm not a player. I should never have gotten mixed up with Fletcher. He's way out of my league.

And that thought stops me again. Do I really think that? Is he right? Do I think he's too good for me and all that shit I spewed at him this morning was just a way to cover up the fact that I feel unworthy of a looker like Fletcher?

"Owww," I whine at the masseuse.

"You need to relax, Miss Preston. Your neck is bunched up tight as a fist. Let go and let me help you."

I let out a long sigh and try to relax my shoulders. God, even the staff thinks I'm uptight. "You know what? I'm just not into it today. I've had enough." I sit up, clutching the towel to my chest. Marie, the masseuse, looks hurt. Like she did something wrong. "It's not you, Marie. I just have too much on my mind. I can't relax right now. How about I come back later this week and we try this spa day again?"

"OK, Miss Preston," she says, gathering up her oils. "You just give us a call when you're ready and I will clear my schedule for you." She squeezes my shoulder. "But don't let it go too long. Stress isn't good for you."

I smile, get up off the table, and let her walk me to the door. "Thanks. I'll try."

I leave the massage room and go back to the lockers to take a hot shower and wash off the oil. The water feels good, but it's not enough to calm me down. My heart has been beating fast since I hung up with Fletcher this morning. I just can't get his words out of my mind. What are the chances that he's genuinely interested in me?

But then I hear my dad's voice in my head again. *You will never know if people like you for your money or just for who you are.*

He's right. Fletcher seems to be preoccupied with money. So much so that he took me on like a charity case to keep his job. There is a very real possibility that the only reason he's interested is because of who I'm related to.

But I don't know. That little speech he gave me out on the rocks seems to contradict all those assumptions. He's scrappy, he said. He can take care of himself. He doesn't need my job offer and he's got other jobs already lined up.

So how do I fit these pieces together?

I don't know.

I just get out of the shower and tug a new pair of shorts and a tank top back on. I grab my purse and slip my feet into my flipflops and head to the stairs that will take me back to the main lobby.

As soon as I get there, I smell food from the bar and realize I haven't eaten all day. Maybe that will ease my nerves? Some good old comfort food from the bar. I ease my way past the bustling waitresses and the customers and make my way to an empty booth in back. A waitress I haven't seen before nods to me and holds up a finger, telling me she will be over in a minute.

I settle back in the booth and let out a sigh and then gasp.

"What the—?"

Cole is across the restaurant, sitting at a table with a beautiful blonde girl.

"I thought he said he had meetings?" I whisper to myself.

"Oh, he's got meetings all right," the waitress says. "Maybe this one will stick."

"What?" I look up at her dumbly. "What do you mean?"

"He's got a new meeting," she says as she does a little upper body shake and stresses the word, "every afternoon."

"You mean, with vendors?" I try, hopefully.

The waitress snorts. "No-ho-ho," she says through a laugh. "At least I've never seen him kiss the vendors."

"He's been gone half the week—"

"Oh, he's here all the time, Miss Preston." She squints at me. "You didn't know?"

I get that sinking feeling in my stomach. That one that comes when the doubts creep in. "Know what?" I ask, feeling the truth before the words ever come out of her mouth.

"He's been coming here for almost three months. Except…" She pauses, like the thought just occurred to her that she should shut up.

"Except what?" I prod, looking back over at Cole and his blonde bimbo.

"Well…" She looks over at her shoulder at him as well. "We never knew who he was until you came together. Usually he's just here for fun."

"With that woman?" My heart is cracking.

"Oh, lots of them, I guess. At least a dozen meetings since I first started noticing him. And when he showed up with you I figured he was spying on us. He is, isn't he? We were all told when the merger went through that the Landslide was on a short list for liquidation."

Since when? I want to scream. My father gave me control over the Landslide as soon as the deal went through. But I hold my cool so she doesn't realize how my tension is ramping up and my heart is beating even faster than it already was. "Hmmm. I'm not sure. Maybe my father sent him."

"I bet that's it." She smiles at me. "At any rate, I hope he's found what he's looking for in this one. He's met with her three times already last week. And each time they get a little more cozy. I guess Fletcher really does know what he's doing."

"What?"

She cocks her head at me with a quizzical look. "I thought you were working with him?"

I stare dumbly at her again.

"A matchmaking deal. Sorry." She laughs. "I'm nosy. And Fletcher is so interesting the way he works. I can't help but take notice every time he meets a girl for lunch. That girl there with Mr. Cole is Fletcher's last week's client. Fletcher works fast, right? Did he find someone for you yet? If he does, you can bet he'll be a keeper. My girlfriend swears by his pick for her. She's already engaged."

I want to throw up. But I take a deep breath and say, "Can you get some water with lemon?" instead.

"Sure, Miss Preston. Be right back."

She gets distracted with other tables, and I take that opportunity to slip out of the restaurant and make a dash for the elevators. When I get to my room, I hope and pray that Claudio isn't there. He's been gone a lot with that stripper, Steve, and my luck holds. Still out from last night, probably.

I lock myself in the bathroom and turn on the shower, just in case he comes home. I am in full-on hiding right now. I need to come to terms with what I just saw and heard.

Cole has been coming here for months.

Rumors of a selloff.

Either he was sent by my father to spy on the operations, which is highly unlikely, or he's been using the Landslide as his personal fuck palace.

Jesus Christ.

And Fletcher. He said he was helping me get Cole's attention, but the whole time he was setting up his other client with Cole?

I feel sick. So sick, I lift the lid of the toilet and dry-heave into the porcelain bowl for several minutes. I wait out the revulsion, the cramps in my stomach and the hurt in my heart. I wait until the knotted-up tension in my neck becomes a full-fledged ache in my head.

Fletcher set me up. He used me. He played me. Like a fucking chess piece.

And not only that… he *humiliated* me. How many other people here know about our deal? How many other people here know about Cole and his women?

I sit back on my butt and wipe the sweat off my forehead.

How stupid do I feel right now?

I have no words to describe it, but crushed comes to mind. Broken, maybe. Mortified. Embarrassed of my naivety, ashamed of my trust in men.

And not just these two men. All men. My mother was right to marry my father and forget about the worthless piece of shit who couldn't get out of the picture fast enough.

She was right. Love is a dream some people were never meant to have.

I don't cry, and that surprises me. Instead, I get up off the floor, take a deep breath, and go looking for Fletcher Novak.

27

I head to the elevator and take it down to fifteen. The walk down the hallway to his suite—his free suite that my hotel provides for him—feels longer than it should considering it's only thirty feet. But by the time I pound on the door, my heart is racing, my armpits are sweaty, and my mouth is dry.

No answer. I press my ear against the door, almost afraid I'll hear the moans of women in the throes of passion. But there's nothing but silence from the other side.

He's not here.

Well, he's here, I bet. Somewhere in this hotel. And I'm gonna find him.

I go back downstairs and peek into the restaurant, but Cole and that blonde woman are gone. *Thank you, God, for small favors.* I cannot see him yet. It's not his fault he was a pawn in

Fletcher's game. I mean, we weren't a couple, right? Cole was just doing what men do. Trying to get as much as he can from as many women as possible.

I can almost forgive him for that. It's in their nature, after all.

But Fletcher is something altogether different. Fletcher is a conniving liar, a conman, and a grade-A scumbag for what he did.

And he needs to pay.

I dial his number, but it goes to voicemail. Does he know I'm on to him? That waitress had to know she said too much. So if Fletcher came by, she might've pulled him aside and given him a heads-up.

I try the front desk. There's a young girl free at one of the computers and she greets me by name with a smile. "Good morning, Miss Preston. Are you having a nice day off?"

Her smile seems genuine, but I'm clearly not well-versed in the appearance of good intentions. I give her the benefit of the doubt anyway, and force a smile. "Have you seen Fletcher Novak? I have to talk to him about his schedule." The one he will no longer have after I get done today.

"Oh," the girl says, pointing at the door. "I think he just called the valet for his car. Try outside."

Valet. It pisses me off to no end that Fletcher Novak thinks he can come into my hotel and—*Later, Tiffy. Focus.* "Thank you," I say with my sweetest fake smile.

Then I power-walk over to the front doors of the lobby, searching the valet line for his blond hair and tall build.

I spot him getting into that classic red Camaro near the front of the line, and before I can even shout his name, he revs the engine and pulls out towards the street.

I whistle at a taxi that is just pulling away after dropping off guests, and he slams on his brakes as I run towards him and hop in the back seat. "Follow that red car, please." I try to sound calm and not like some dame in a noir movie from the nineteen forties, but I'm not sure I succeed, because the driver shoots me a look over his shoulder. "I'm serious, don't lose him!"

"Sure thing, lady."

I sit back and try to keep the car in my vision. He gets ahead of us a few times as he turns corners, but we find him again on US-50 going north up the shore of the lake. The driver keeps glancing back at me, but each time, I just say, "Keep going."

"What if he's on his way to—"

"I don't care where he's going, we're following him, understand? I've got a credit card, so you don't need to worry about it. Just keep going."

He shoots me the bitch look after that masterpiece of high-class manners. But I don't care. We keep driving. We wind past the curve of Zephyr Cove, past Lake Tahoe State Park, and almost an hour later make our way into Incline Village at the northern tip of the lake.

He's from here, I remember from our conversations. Hmmm.

I know very little about Fletcher Novak other than the few conversations we've had and the Wikipedia entry that may or may not be true. But I'm about to find out more.

We take a left onto Country Club Drive and then a right on Lakeshore Boulevard. The cabbie pulls over on a side street and we watch Fletcher's car enter a gated community called Windshore Estates.

"Unless you got a house here, lady, this is the end of the line. That's Billionaire's Row, and it's got security. What do you want me to do? Because I'm not going to jail for trying to get in."

I take a deep breath and make a decision. "Wait here," I say. "And leave the meter running. I'll be back in a little bit."

I don't give him a chance to argue, simply slip out of the back seat and slam the door behind me. I'm looking both ways for traffic as I cross the road and then I walk up to the gate. I have an in, I realize. My father's old friend lives in Incline Village, I know him well. My father even mentioned him a few times after the merger. Told me to look him up while I was up here. I just hadn't gotten around to it. The guard is out of the gatehouse before I even get within ten feet.

"Can I help you, ma'am?" he asks, his hand on his belted radio.

"Hi, I'm Tiffy Preston and I was down the street at a friend's house when I remembered that Montey Silverman lives in this community. My father is an old friend of his and asked me to look him up, so I decided to take a walk and—" I giggle and put a hand over my heart. "Oh, he's probably not home, but can you call him up and tell him I'm here and see if he'd like a visit?"

The guard eyes me. I'm sure walk-ups to this private neighborhood are pretty rare. But if what I say is true, then he'll be in a lot more trouble for refusing my request than he would if he discovers I'm an interloper.

"Wait right here," he says, going back into the guardhouse, leaving the door open so I can catch the conversation. "Yes, this is the guardhouse. I've got a guest here for Mr. Silverman. Says her name is—" He looks at me for help.

"Tiffy," I say. "Tiffy Preston." I smile as he repeats my name and then begins to nod at whatever the person on the other end of the line is telling him. A few seconds later he looks at me. "They'd like to know if you need a ride up to the house? You can walk it, if you're after the exercise, but they'll send a golf cart."

"I'd rather walk."

He relays that back and then hangs up. "Just head left—" He begins to give me directions.

"I remember where it is," I say quickly. "I've been here before when I was younger."

"OK, Miss Preston. Come through the gate." He motions to a walkway a few feet to the left of the guardhouse, and when I reach it, a buzzer sounds, letting me in.

I smile over my shoulder and set off at a brisk walk that turns into a run as soon as the pine trees block the guard's view. God only knows where Fletcher is in this neighborhood. All I have to go on is his red car, and I'll never find him if he's got it in a garage.

I peek down all the driveways as I run. These lots are not too big. The lakefront real estate is premium. But I don't see his car anywhere. There is a long hedge, easily six feet tall in height, that runs the length of several average-sized lots, and I peek down that driveway in the name of being thorough, not expecting to find what I'm looking for.

But my breath catches in my chest when the red paint flashes through a gap in the trees lining the driveway.

There is a gate at this house, but it's open. Like a car just drove through. I slip past the invitation and creep up the pavement, looking over my shoulder.

What the fuck is going on? Who lives here that Fletcher

knows?

I stop in my tracks when I hear the squeal of a little girl. Fletcher's gruff voice echoes back, also laughing. I duck behind a tree when they come into sight.

"Hey, baby," Fletcher says. He's talking to a little girl, about eight years old, clinging to him like she never wants to let go. And then… and then…

And then he leans into a tall, pretty woman who looks so much like the child, there is no mistaking who she is. And he kisses her on the cheek as he pulls her into a hug.

I turn away.

Holy fuck.

Of all the things I expected to see here, a woman with a child was never even in the running.

I look back and he's got the little girl in his arms, twirling her around as her blonde hair fans out from the spin. She laughs and giggles, and I see that smile. That same smile that I've seen on Fletcher the few times he's flashed it in front of me.

There is no mistake who these two people are to him. It's written all over their happy smiles.

Fletcher Novak has a family.

I run back to the guardhouse, burst through the gate, and then yell at the guard, "Can you tell Mr. Silverman I had an emergency and had to leave?"

I don't wait for an answer. I just run all the way back to the cab, get in, slam the door, and say, "Take me back to the hotel."

28

"Hey, Sea Shells, when we going to the Seychelles?"

Shelly laughs that little eight-year-old laugh that picks me up and makes my day every time. She's in love with the tongue-twisters. I have to shake off a mental image of me holding a shotgun at the door when her first boyfriend comes knocking—trying to twist his way into her life like the words that are twisting out of her mouth.

"I can't say it!" She giggles, still trying as she hugs my waist.

I pat Shelly's head and then look up to Samantha. "How'd your week go?"

Her smile is fake. I've known her since she was fourteen, so I can tell. She swallows hard. "Walker called a little while ago."

Fucking hell. With all the shit going on, I'd forgotten about my piece-of-shit older brother. "What'd he want?" I growl. But I know what he wants.

Sam shrugs. "Just to talk, I guess."

I squint my eyes at her. "You talked to him?"

"I hung up on him. I can't do it again, Fletch. I've been over and over it in my mind and we didn't do anything wrong. Walker and I broke up." She looks up at me, pleading. "You and I didn't do anything wrong. Right?"

I pull her in close for a hug. "Of course not. Forget about him."

"He says he's coming over. Says he's got things to say. Things he's been wanting to say for a long time now. But I told him you weren't coming home today." She looks up with watery eyes. "He didn't believe me."

"Did you tell him about—" But I don't have time to finish, because I can hear the rumble of the car he's been driving since he got his license. A twin of my own nineteen-sixty-nine Camaro, but in blue, and received one year earlier. Our grandfather was a collector and we each got our pick the day we turned sixteen.

If he took the blue, then I'd take the red. It's always been like that with Walker and me. One-upmanship. Jealousy. And rage. We were competitive to the end. But the end came sooner rather than later. And I stayed when he left. I got Sam and then, later, Shell. And he got… well, I have no idea what he got. I hadn't seen him in almost a decade before last week. But whatever it was, he came out on the wrong end of that deal.

"Where are the Seychelles, anyway?" Shelly asks, tugging on my shirt sleeve. "And when can we go there?"

"Indian Ocean, Shells. Go inside with your mom. I'll be just a second."

Samantha nods and takes Shelly's hand. "Come on, baby.

Let's get lunch ready."

"I'm starving," Shelly says, as they walk up the front steps of the eight-thousand-square-foot beachfront mansion. It's the biggest house on this end of Lakeshore. Been in the family for three generations. And it's mine now. Everything in there is mine now.

Walker slides his sunglasses up his forehead and opens the car door.

"Don't come any further, asshole."

The pause is short-lived, and a second later he steps out anyway. I knew he would, but I figure he deserves a warning. And that one sentence was all he's getting.

He's wearing clothing that gives him the appearance of acceptable. White dress shirt, sleeves casually rolled up his forearms. Tight black slacks tailored for his athletic form. And fancy leather shoes that could probably put Shells through a year of community college. He looks well-bred and rich. And I guess he is. I guess we both are. But some of us just know how to wear that good breeding better than others.

My fists are clenching before he takes his first step on the stone-paved driveway and my feet are in motion before he takes the next one. "I'm warning you, Walker."

He holds his hands up, palms out, to calm me or piss me off, I'm not quite sure. "I'm not here to start trouble, Fletch."

"The fuck you're not. Why come here then? You need money? I don't have any left over for you. You need somewhere to stay and you figure this place is your home? You're wrong, brother. I bought you out and I will kick you out. I don't care if you're sleeping in your car at the state park tonight. You're not walking into my house."

He lets off a fake sigh. I've known him a lot longer than Sam, so I peg that fake shit right out of the gate. "I just want to talk to her, man. That's it."

"If she wanted to talk to you, she'd be outside right now."

"I heard you, Fletcher. Ordering her around like some kind of boss. Still insisting on calling the shots, eh? Some things never change."

"Some people either," I spit back.

"Those who live in glass houses, Fletcher. Does she know what you do for a living?"

"Why would I lie about that?" She does know. She doesn't like it, but she knows. And Walker can see the truth in what I said. He's not gonna win her sympathy with that he's-a-no-good-stripper bullshit.

"Because you lie about everything else." He shoots me a smile that says he's got something on me. I recognize it from all the fights we had growing up. All the times we tangled over girls, or cars, or hell, the attention of our parents. "I know all about you, *Fletch*. More than you think."

"Good for you," I say, ratcheting down the urge to punch him in the face. "Now get the fuck off my property."

"I traced you all over this country, Fletch. First New York—"

I see red.

"—then LA. You sure get around for a hometown boy. Even found some girls who were more than willing to tell me all about your—"

My fist crashes against his jaw. His lip splits and then I take one in the same place. The blood rushes into my mouth as we start brawling. Samantha is yelling and I catch a glimpse of her running across the well-groomed lawn as Walker and I roll on the ground. I get him in a headlock, ready to choke the life out of him, when he breaks out of my hold with a knee to the stomach. We roll again, and then Sam is grasping at my red-stained shirt.

"Fletcher! Stop!" Sam screams. "Please!"

I push Walker away and we get to our feet, circling each other. He wipes a trickle of blood off his lip, looks at it on his fingers, and laughs. "Yup, some things never change."

I spit out my own blood, and the crimson saliva finds its way to his fancy-ass black dress shoes.

He looks down at that for a moment, like he cannot believe I'd fuck up his two-thousand-dollar shoes, then turns his attention to Sam. The reason he's here. The reason he'd start a fight after all these years. The reason he cannot come one step closer.

I step between them, forcing him to look at me instead.

He speaks directly to Sam at my back. "I'm not here to cause trouble, Sam. I just wanted to make peace with this shit. That's all."

And then he turns away, walks to his car, gets back in, and backs down the driveway, screeching his tires the whole way out.

It's a goddamned miracle he didn't kill someone on the sidewalk with that move.

"Who was that?" Shells asks from the top step of the house porch.

"No one you ever need to worry about, Sea Shells." I spit out some more blood, wipe my mouth with the back of my hand—hoping there's no blood on my lips—and feel relief when Sam smiles and lets out a deep breath. I take her hand and turn her around. “No one important, baby.”

I walk them back inside and clean up in the bathroom as Sam and Shell make us some sandwiches. I wait for the adrenaline to seep out of me like sweat, and then I go upstairs and change my shirt, pulling on yet another plain white t-shirt that came out of the same four-pack as the one I just took off.

Fuck him and his fancy clothes.

At least I earned what I have.

29

I get a text from Katie halfway through lunch and I feel the disappointment in Shelly's face before I even look at her. "You have to go?" she asks from across the table, her mouth still full of the roast beef sandwich.

I force a smile. "Yeah, but I'll be back soon." I get up from the table and squeeze Sam's shoulder as I walk over to Shelly and bend down to let her kiss my cheek.

"You always say that, but you leave for days."

"I gotta work, baby. You know I'd rather be here with you, right?"

She puffs up her lip and pouts. But she nods. She knows the drill.

"I'll call ya later, OK, Sam? If he comes back—"

"I know, Fletch. Don't worry. I called the guardhouse and told them not to let him in again."

I let out a sigh and a little bit of the tension I've been wearing all week slides down my shoulders.

"Thanks for understanding."

She gives me a weak smile and I figure that's all she's got right now, so I take it and make my way to the front of the house.

It's a spectacular house. It's not my accomplishment, so I've never had any reason to be proud of it. But I do love it. And I love that Shelly is growing up here. Just like me and Walker, only without the rivalry.

I don't know why my brother hated me. First child syndrome? Jealousy of the new baby? But it doesn't make much sense. How much jealousy is a one-year-old capable of anyway?

We are sixteen months apart in age. A fact that definitely contributed to the demise of my mother's social life, and then later, her interest in life. She's not even dead, like my dad. Just cut out of the family for lack of ambition after he passed.

I guess I can't blame her. I see first-hand what having one kid does to Sam. Imagining her with two little ones that close in age is enough to make me cringe. It's nothing against Sam at all. It's just a lot of work taking care of one infant, let alone two. I know. I've been there.

So I can cut my mom some slack. My dad was more like Walker than me. Transient would be a good word to describe him. Ask any kid if that's a good quality in a father and even an eight-year-old like Shells will tell you no.

I imagine her thinking that of me as I drive south along the lakeshore. It's late afternoon now. I didn't even get to stay an hour before I got called away. Does Shelly think I'm transient because I stay down in South Tahoe most nights?

I hope not. I do my best.

I lose myself in thought as the miles pass and the minutes tick by. I barely see the beauty of the landscape around me anymore. Tahoe is part of me. I don't leave often. And the fact that Walker knew about my trips to New York and LA has me unsettled.

Does he know who I am?

He might. It's not like I've been super-secretive about any of it. I just figured no one much cared.

But apparently someone does. And it figures it would be Walker. I imagine all the reasons why he came back. Money tops the list. But I don't owe him shit and he's not getting one dime out of me.

Sam is second on the list. And that's the more realistic one, considering that the outfit he was wearing today must've cost him about five grand alone. He's not out of money yet.

I try to imagine a scenario where she'd choose him over me and come up short. Sam would never do that. Never. She's the most loyal person I've ever met.

But… she could. She could still love him.

And if she does, Fletch, then she does. You can't change the way people feel about each other.

And that line of thought brings me back to Tiffy just as I pull onto Lake Parkway and wind my way past the golf course towards the Landslide, their bright copper towers gleaming in the late-afternoon sun. Blinding, almost. The perfect metaphor to describe what goes on inside.

Name your poison—gambling, drugs, stripping, sex—you can get it inside. Those guys at the tables tell themselves it's their lucky day. They snort coke in the bathroom and stuff tips in the bras of the cocktail waitresses. Hell, I tell myself that shit too. It's my lucky day every night I go out on stage and come back with a pile of money.

I pull up to the valet and leave my delusions in the backseat when I get out. *It's a job, Fletcher. Nothing more.*

But Tiffy didn't feel like a job last night. Tiffy felt like a possibility.

Just your delusional mind, trying to justify why you're not a no-good piece of shit.

Whatever.

I stop by the front desk and smile at Kristen. She's not too bright, but she tries hard to please and she always smiles. I like her for those reasons alone. "Hey, Kristen, you got a package for me?"

"Oh, yeah, hey, Fletch. One sec." She finishes typing on her keyboard and then slips behind the partition that separates the front desk from the office. She appears again, barely a minute later, and hands me a thin box with my name on it.

"Thanks, babe. Oh, hey," I say, turning back to her. "Have you seen Tiffy today?"

"Earlier," she says, going back to typing on her keyboard. "Maybe an hour and a half ago?" She looks up and gives me a smile. "Not since then."

I nod. "OK, well, thanks." I head off for the elevators, barely registering her answer of, "No problem," and push the button when I get there, anxious to see what's in the box Katie left.

It can't be good. Well, it can, in a way. But ultimately, everything about this request I had her do for me will turn to shit.

I tap my foot as I wait for the elevator to take me up to fifteen, and then get out and find my keycard in my back pocket as I walk down the hall. When I get to the door, I pass it over the lock and the light flashes green at me.

I push the door open.

Tiffy Preston is sitting on my couch with a stack of papers in her hand.

My mind races as I figure out what might be on those papers. "What the fuck are you doing in my room?"

"Your room?" She laughs. "This is the hotel's room. And I'm the legal representative of the hotel. So this room, Fletcher Novak, belongs to me. You don't even pay for it."

"You better have a damn good explanation for this, Tiffy. I'm not even joking. And those papers in your hands, they had better belong to you, or I'm going to be one pissed-off guy."

"You think you have the right to be pissed off? Ha!" She looks down at the papers in her hand and begins reading. "'Dear Sexy Man'"—she snorts—"'I have a problem with a girl. She's rich and I'm not. She comes from a very prominent family and I work for her father. It's difficult to relate to her, and I'm sure she feels the same way about me. But there is something there that makes me want to try harder. What can I do to close this money gap? Signed, Rich Man, Poor Man.'" She shakes the letter in her hand. "What is this?" Her voice rises a little at the end of that sentence, making me cringe. "Why do you have these letters?" She flips through the pile, dozens of them in her hands. "I've read them all, Fletcher. The one from Self-Loathing in Saratoga where the guy complains about how his girlfriend has such a low opinion of herself, she can't see that he really loves her? What is that?"

I clear my throat, unwilling to say nothing, but not sure how I can soften the blow. In the end, I decide I can't. So I just tell it like it is. "I've been using our conversations to write the letters."

"Obviously," Tiffy snaps. "Are you this… this… Sexy Man? Do you write that column?"

I nod. "I am. I do."

"And you make those letters up?" It's an accusation. One she already knows the answer to, she just wants confirmation.

"Come on, Tiffy. The whole world is scripted. You know this."

"You know what? Yesterday I almost thought that I had misjudged you. That I was pegging you unfairly. That I came here with an expectation that you deserved to be fired. Because you have this smooth voice. And your words are like candy. Soothing and sweet. But you're poison, Fletcher Novak. Nothing but poison."

I give her a sidelong glance. "How would you know?" I growl. "You have no idea who I am."

"I have an idea," she snaps back. "Cole sent me to the spa today to relax. Because he had meetings all day and we weren't going to meet until dinner."

I cringe at the dinner part, just like I did this morning. She's finally wrangled him into a date. Got just what she wanted.

"But I wasn't into it, so I left and went up to the restaurant. And do you know who I saw up there?"

"I can guess," I say evenly, letting out a breath of air.

She stares at me for a moment, looking like she might explode. But then she lifts her chin and steels herself for the next confrontation. "You set up your client with my possibility."

I shake my head no.

"You liar," she seethes. "You liar. I saw you today too."

"Saw me where?"

Tiffy crosses her arms cross her chest. "That mansion you have up in Incline Village? What the hell was that? You're rich? You're married?"

"You had me followed?"

"I followed you myself. I saw you with your… wife, lover, girlfriend… whatever she's called in your sick world. And your daughter. Do they know what you do, Fletcher?"

"She knows," I say, leaving Shelly out of it. "And she knows why."

"So she's OK with you whoring yourself out? Taking home girls, fucking them on the roof, stringing them along so—"

"I never strung you along. You're the one who got up and walked out on me this morning."

"You set Cole up with one of your clients." She snarls the words out. "You wanna tell me why you did that when you knew I wanted him?"

"You can't always get what you want, princess." Her face hardens. "Besides, he's no good for you. I realized he was an asshole the first time I saw him up at this hotel months ago." I wait for the surprise, but it never comes. "So you know he was up here?" I ask.

"I do now. Not that it matters. He and I weren't dating then." Her anger morphs into pain before my eyes. "He and I weren't fucking. You used me. You lied to me." Tears begin to form. "You sold me out, Fletcher. And all I ever did was try to help you keep your job."

I scoff out a laugh. "I told you the other day, you can keep that fucking job. You think this one measly paycheck is enough to pay my bills?"

"What bills? I saw your house today, Fletcher. And I'm not a real-estate expert, but I looked the address up, and comps come in around four million dollars."

"Shit." My laugh is practically a guffaw this time. "If that house was worth four million dollars, my problems would be over. Try thirteen million, Tiffy. Thirteen fucking million dollars. Almost three acres of lakefront property. Two hundred yards of beach. A dock with deep water access so the bigger boats can get in. Eight thousand square feet of living space, home theatre, heated pool in the backyard, and a gym on the lower level that would put this hotel gym to shame."

"Then why do you need money? And is that why you were so interested in me? For my money?"

Jesus Christ. I eye her, considering if I should tell her or not, considering if she deserves the truth. In the end, I let her decide. "Why do you think?" She lets out an exasperated sigh. "I'm serious," I say, before she can protest. "Tell me why you think I need money."

"God only knows. You already admitted to using me for that stupid column of yours. Who knows why you need anything."

"Give it a shot," I growl.

She purses her lips and shrugs. "Drugs. Gambling debt."

"You have a really low opinion of me, don't you, Tiffy?"

"Oh, please!" she chortles. "I have a low opinion of *you*? Try the other way around, Fletcher."

But I'm shaking my head, and then my words come out so low, I'm practically whispering. "I never lied to you. I just don't hand the truth out to just anyone. And I never had a low opinion of you, Tiffy. From the minute I saw you out in the audience, I was hooked. You were beautiful. So fucking beautiful, you caught my eye in a crowd of hundreds. And even though you didn't realize it, I liked you because you were confident. It shone through all the doubts you had. I saw it, even when you didn't. I thought you were sexy. I thought you were funny, and intriguing, and smart. And yeah, the first time we fucked, it was a fuck. But if you think that was fucking last night, then I feel sorry for you. Because you don't seem to be able to recognize love, Tiffy. And that is just sad."

I stare at her as she stands in front of me with her arms crossed, shocked into silence.

"Now, if you don't mind, I'm gonna be busy packing, so get the fuck—"

A knock at my door stops me mid-sentence, and since I could use the distraction, I walk over and open it up.

Claudio is standing on the other side of the door, his face in a long, sad frown. "Is Tiffy with you? She's got her phone turned off and I need to talk to her."

I open the door wide and wave him in.

"Claudio," Tiffy says, rushing forward. "What's wrong? Did something happen?"

Claudio nods, looking at me first, before shifting his gaze to Tiffy. "Your father is in the hospital. They've sent a helicopter to take us to Reno where the jet is waiting."

30

My father died on Tuesday. And the saddest thing about it was that the world went on.

The doctors and nurses in the private hospital suite were too used to death, too wrapped up in the realities of it, and too busy to mark this one particular occasion as special. It wasn't, in fact. Special. And aside from a somber three sentences muttered on the stock report news that night on the cable channels, no one noticed.

I got there in time, at least. I spent nearly forty-eight hours with him before he slipped away. He wasn't coherent though. He hadn't come to the show Saturday night because he'd had another stroke due to the tumor pressing on his brain.

And now that I'm sitting here alone at the cemetery five days later, I feel like shutting down.

At least it's not raining, though. But it might later because

I can see a storm brewing out over the Pacific from where I sit. And it's not quiet. The traffic from the city is all too familiar. It's just an ordinary day marking another ordinary death. I don't mind. I don't care about anything right now.

Claudio and Cole both explained the money situation. I'm not even sure I mind that. It wasn't mine, after all. Why should he let me have it?

No, it's not the money that nags at my calm exterior. It's the fact that being cut out makes me feel like it was all a lie.

Of course, Claudio insists that I shouldn't feel this way. But what does he know about rejection? His parents are still together. They live in the same top-floor condo in Russian Hill as they did when he was five. He's the poster child for unconditional forever love from his parents. He can't possibly understand.

And that's why I'm here alone. I told Claudio I'd talk to him later. I just wanted a few minutes alone with my dad to say goodbye. People who have been loved their whole life like he has can't possibly understand how I feel right now.

I sigh as I wring my gloved hands in my lap. It's warm today, so they're sweating. My whole body is hot and slick under my black lace dress and my matching hat. It feels like punishment for some reason.

It's not the money that bothers me. I'm not sure I remember what it's like to live on a budget, I was so young when Randall appeared. But I'm smart and I can adjust. I can figure it out. So it's not the money. It's the feeling I get about the whole situation. The lies about his illness. The last-minute changes to the will. It's like he left me behind. Like he took it with him, after all. He took everything with him and left me here all alone.

My mind wanders to Fletcher. I think about him constantly. His home up in those mountains. His family. How happy he looked when he was there. A different kind of happy than when I saw him at the hotel. Why does he keep them secret? Why does he cheat? Why does he do anything?

I can't stop thinking about him.

It's like he switched places with Cole, who I have barely thought about at all in the past week. I can't stand to look at Cole, to be honest. Even now, his name starts to make my stomach sick.

A man clears his throat behind me. "Do you need anything, Miss Preston?"

I don't turn. I just shake my head.

"You can stay as long as you want. Do you need a ride home?"

I've been here for more than an hour, just staring at the grave. Contrary to movies, they don't just fill the grave in after people leave. Cemeteries, it seems, run on a schedule just like anyone else. So the shiny black coffin in the hole in front of me only has those few symbolic handfuls of dirt on it. I can hear the machinery off in another part of the cemetery as it works to cover another recently deceased's grave. I might be fucking up their schedule, come to think of it.

But who cares? I guess if there is a moment in life when you can be a little bit selfish about taking up other people's time, it's when you're sitting at a cemetery.

"No, thank you," I finally say. "I have my car."

Everybody disappeared after they found out about the will. It's not official yet, these things take time. But the writing is on the wall. Tiffy Preston was cut out. She owns one struggling luxury hotel in Nevada, and I'm sure they think I'm gonna get nowhere with that, since the whole place is in flux after Fletcher left and Chandler took the job in Vegas that Cole offered him.

Cole. I can't even.

I can't even with that hotel either. I just feel… defeated.

"I'm sorry for your loss."

I turn my head a little at the woman's voice behind me, but not enough to see who it is.

"Thank you," I mutter.

Clothing rustles as she makes her way up to the row of chairs in front of the grave where I sit alone. She takes a seat two chairs down and places a black leather attaché case on the red velvet cushion.

I stare at it, then glance up at her face and frown. It's the woman who was having lunch with Cole last Sunday. "Can I help you with something?"

She smiles. And she's very pretty with her blue eyes and blonde hair, her perfect face with her perfect makeup. No bloodshot eyes for her. No tearstains on her cheeks. Her hair is swept up in a professional do that is sophisticated and sexy at the same time.

"I'm a friend of Fletcher's."

I shake my head and look down. But I say nothing. I just haven't got the energy.

"And he was going to show you this last weekend, but he…" She pauses, maybe trying to find the right words for what happened last weekend. "But he didn't have time."

"I'm not interested." It comes out flat. Devoid of emotion.

"Maybe not." She sighs. "But he thinks you should at least

know." She pats the case and stands. "When you're ready."

I have nothing for that. I don't even have a slight curiosity about what that case might contain. A letter of apology? That makes me snort and the woman halts her retreat mid-stride, to see if I have anything to say.

No, more likely it's more lies.

"He's sorry," she says.

"I bet he is."

She sighs, letting out a long stream of frustration into air that is so damp from humidity, it probably clings to her breath. "He really is sorry."

"For what?" I ask, finally looking up again. "What exactly is he sorry for?"

The woman gives me a little gesture with her hands. Something akin to, *I'm not sure.*

That makes two of us.

"If you have any questions, you can call me." Those are her final words. She turns and walks off.

I stare at the case, then turn around in my seat and watch her retreat. The man in charge here is waiting a little ways off, his hands clasped together behind his back, like he's standing guard.

I look back at the case, pick it up by the handle, and then stand. I peer over into the deep hole that holds the only father I ever knew and feel the sting of sadness as a final tear streaks its way down my cheek. "Goodbye, Dad." My chin trembles. "I just want you to know, I love you. And I don't care about the money. If you feel I don't deserve anything, then there's a reason for that. I'll be OK."

And that's it. That's all there is to say about it. He made his decision and I'm going to live with it.

I walk off, the heels of my shoes sticking into the soil underneath the deep grass with each step. I get my car, place the black case on the passenger seat beside me, and then start it up and drive away.

31

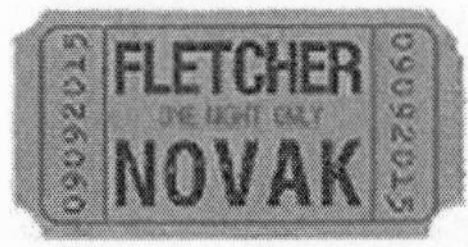

At home, in my Preston Hotels-owned condo in Pacific Heights—how soon will they take this away, I wonder for a brief second—I lie in my bed. The AC is on, and the small one-bedroom condo I've called home for the past two years has allowed me the luxury of hiding under the covers, pretending reality is a dream and the dream is reality.

The phone rings, but I ignore it. It's been ringing all day. There are at least ten messages on there.

The machine picks up and Cole's voice meanders into my bedroom. "Tiffy, we need to talk. I know you're upset about—"

He has no idea what I'm upset about. I barely know what I'm upset about. It's more than the death. It's everything that happened last week end all rolled up into one giant WTF.

"—but I have investors interested in the Landslide. I hadn't had time to talk about the financial situation—"

"No," I say bitterly, "you were too busy using it as your fuck palace to have a frank conversation with me about the hotel."

"—they made a decent offer. So if you need the capital to..." He hesitates here, maybe choosing his words carefully. "... to clear up some financial obligations..."

Wow. That was tactful.

"... I can arrange for the sale. Just let me know."

The message ends. The machine beeps. And then the apartment goes silent with nothing but the sound of the air-conditioning coming out of the vents.

I go back to sleep.

XOXOXOXOX

When I wake the light streaming through the sheer white curtains of my bedroom tells me it's late afternoon. But I don't turn to see the time. The phone is ringing again. I listen to a strange voice claiming she is from the probate lawyers telling me that we have a meeting tomorrow.

I won't be going, so I turn over and fall back asleep.

The next time the phone rings, the sunlight has that new-day brightness to it. This time it's Claudio.

My eyes close and I pine for my mom.

XOXOXOXOX

"Tiffy?"

Claudio has found his way into my apartment. I open my eyes and wait for him to find me.

"Tiffy," he says, walking through my bedroom door. "Oh my God. Jesus Christ, girlfriend. I thought you were dead. Some dramatic suicide—"

"Claudio," I croak out. "Why are you here?"

"I've been trying to call you for two days!" He screams it, jolting me awake. "You fucking bitch!" I look at him and realize he's been crying.

"Claudio," I repeat.

"No," he says, shaking his head in that dramatic way he does. "No, Tiffy. You had me so worried. I came all the way from Nevada. Drove straight through. I asked Cole to come check on you, but he said he'd send someone from his office. And the thought that a stranger would find your body—"

"I'm fine, Claudio."

"It doesn't matter. I thought you..." He sniffs. "I thought you'd..."

"I didn't." The fact that he thinks I'd take the easy way out like my mother stings more than I care to admit. "I just don't feel like talking to anyone."

He comes over to the bed and lies down next to me. He pulls me into a hug that is deep, and sad, and says all the things I needed to hear in one silent gesture. "Please," he says. "Don't do this. Don't give up. We're going to be fine. OK?"

I nod into his embrace. "I know. I do. I just needed... time."

We lie there like that. Me and my best friend. I don't know how long, but it's a considerable amount of time. It slips away from me these days.

"Get up now, OK?" he asks. "I'll make you breakfast and coffee. And we can put things back together."

"I'm not sure I want to put things back together, Claudio. *Cole*."

"Oh, God," he says. "Don't even mention that bastard's name."

"Why?" I turn to him. "What's happened?"

"You mean besides the fact that he's got foreign investors all over the Landslide like he owns it? You need to fire him, Tiffy. Today. He needs to get his nosy ass out of your hotel. He's out there making decisions. He fired all the dancers."

"What?"

"He shut down the show, Tiffy. And the review on that travel site came out today. It was a five-star rating and he's fucked it all up."

"Why would he fire them? They were the only money-makers we had."

"That's the million-dollar question, right? Why would he fire them?" Claudio sucks in a deep breath through his teeth and glares at some image of Cole in his imagination.

But that bit of news gets me moving. Cole fired the dancers? It just doesn't make sense.

I let Claudio make breakfast while I take a shower. I had no idea it had been two days since the funeral. Claudio is right. I need to pull myself together and find a way to get through this. So I pull on a robe, shuffle out to the kitchen and take a seat at my breakfast bar.

"Hungry?" Claudio asks over a griddle filled with pancakes. He flips them and then pours me a cup of coffee, adding in the cream and sugar he knows I love, and then slides it down the counter.

"Starved, actually."

"Yes," he says, pursing his lips and placing a spatula-holding hand on his hip. "Well, forgetting to eat for two days will do that to you."

I sneer back at him, good-naturedly, of course, then I sigh. "It's all so surreal, ya know?"

His sneer becomes a pout, and he walks over and hugs me. "I know, baby. But we'll find a way to survive. We always do."

"We've never really had to, Claudio. Have you ever thought of that?"

"But we're equipped, Tiff." He looks at me seriously. "We are. We're smart, and innovative. I just know it."

I have to laugh at that a little. "We might be. I guess we'll find out."

I get up with my coffee and wander over to the terrace to open the drapes. I spy the black attaché case from the day of the funeral on the coffee table and walk over to it. I pick it up. It's not that heavy.

"What's that?" Claudio asks from the stove.

"I'm not sure. Something from Fletcher. That blonde woman Fletcher set up with Cole—"

"What?" Claudio says. "When did that—"

"It doesn't matter," I interrupt. I can't even go there yet. "She showed up at the funeral and handed me this case. Said Fletcher was sorry and he wanted me to have this."

"Open it up, you crazy bitch." Claudio starts piling food on plates as I turn the case around so the locking mechanism is facing me. I press the tabs and the lock disengages, allowing the top to pop up a little bit.

I lift the lid and peer inside. Claudio comes over with our

food and places it on the table as he takes a seat next to me. "What is all that?"

I stare down at the papers. "Offices of Shalanger, Shalanger, and Shalanger. Fucking lawyers," I say with contempt.

But then I start reading the top letter.

> Dear Miss Preston,
>
> I was hired by Fletcher Rourke to investigate the legality of the last will and testament of your father, Randall Jonathan Preston—

"Fletcher *Rourke*?" Claudio says, looking up at me.

That's just the first of many questions we have as we read the letter together. And when we're done, we sit there and stare at the paper in my hands.

"Cole?" Claudio asks. "Stole your inheritance?"

I'm having a hard time with it myself. He seems to be a no-good slimeball when it comes to women, but manipulating my father into cutting me out of the will with the idea that he will take over the company is a whole other matter.

I put the letter down and take out the corresponding documents, all labeled neatly in lawyer fashion, and start flipping through them.

Some of it is the legal definition of sound mind and body. Some of it is a case study and court ruling precedents. But the part that interests me most is the last piece of paper, signed by my father five days before he died, making Cole Lancaster the executor of his last will and testament.

As such, Cole will be paid two percent of sixteen billion dollars.

Thirty-two million dollars of my father's sixteen-billion-dollar estate will go to Cole while I am left with nothing but a failing hotel.

"That was the day he left me up in Tahoe to go back to San Francisco," I tell Claudio as I massage my temples, trying to stave off a headache.

"That two-timing swine," Claudio says. He looks over at me with wide eyes. "We're not gonna let him get away with this."

"I don't know, Claudio. It says here"—I hold up the legal document explaining what sound mind and body means—"that it's pretty hard to prove someone was unable to make decisions when it comes to a will."

"Your father had a stroke, Tiffy."

"I know that. But he seemed fine to me. So he must've seemed fine to everyone else, too."

"Don't let Cole do this, Tiffy. Please." Claudio takes my hand and squeezes. "Please. I'll help you any way I can, but he does not get thirty-two million dollars by cheating. He just doesn't. He must've known your father was getting sicker. I mean, come on! The man died five days later."

"I realize that," I say. "But that part about me not getting any money was there a long time ago. Look." I point to one of the documents in the case. "There are several copies of the will. God only knows how this woman got these." I pause for a moment as I picture her having lunch with Cole that day I blew up at Fletcher.

"Yeah, but—"

I cut Claudio off and keep going. "And all of them have the same stipulation. His shares in the corporation will be sold and all his money will be given to charity."

"I knew about that," Claudio says somberly. "Cole told me. But that's not the point. Why should *he* get money out of this? And look, Tiffy," Claudio says, taking out another legal document. "The paper trail of former executors. You've been on there since your mother died." Claudio's eyes narrow into slits. "Cole stole that money from you. Your father might've wanted his estate to go to charity, but he never wanted you to be penniless. He never wanted you to struggle."

Tears and sadness overtake me as I look out the window and feel shame. Because I doubted my father's love and I had no right.

No right at all.

32

Katie Shalanger's law office is located in downtown San Francisco on California Street. It's a towering building made of glass with a semi-circle of columns that reach up five stories flanking the entrance. There is a common square in front with gardens and people sitting on the long concrete planters having lunch. More than respectable—it's intimidating. I go inside and security immediately directs me to the reception desk where a pleasant and pretty woman takes my name and checks a list.

"Here you go, Miss Preston," she says, handing me a visitor's badge. "Miss Shalanger is expecting you. Use the pass to access the twenty-fifth floor."

I don't need to have this meeting. And when I called, the receptionist seemed hesitant to give me a face-to-face. I'm not sure if Katie is nervous about how this all went down, or if she thinks I might come to her work and cause a scene.

I get to the elevators and swipe my badge and press the button. The elevator doors close and a second later I'm flying upward. Towards what, I'm not sure. The truth, I hope.

The doors open again and I come out directly into a lobby. Which means they have the whole floor. These Shalangers are nobody you want to mess with if you're on the opposite side of the courtroom from them. Their whole image says they are serious, accomplished, and have considerable assets available for their clients.

"Miss Preston," the woman at the greeting desk says, standing up so I can see her better. "Miss Shalanger will be out in a minute. Can I get you some water?"

"No, thank you," I say, taking a seat in one of the overstuffed leather chairs. I wring my hands for four minutes before a sweet voice says, "Miss Preston?" from the other side of the room.

I stand and walk towards her. Katie Shalanger is tall, blonde, and utterly gorgeous.

And she was a client of Fletcher Novak. He was setting her up with a man.

I don't understand.

I shake her outstretched hand and say, "Thank you so much for agreeing to meet with me."

She gives me a tight smile and then leads the way through the hall and waves me into her office. It's large and clean. Neat and tidy with no messy files like my office in my father's corporate building a few blocks down. Everything here is about appearances.

I take a seat in another overstuffed chair, and Katie takes the one next to me instead of positioning herself in power behind the desk.

"I'd just like to start by saying I'm so sorry for your loss."

I nod, biting back the sadness. "Thank you. And as you can imagine, that's why I'm here. I looked at the files you left me and I understand what they mean, Miss—"

"Call me Katie," she says, take my hand and giving it a squeeze.

"Katie," I say, swallowing. "I understand what you were trying to tell me with those documents. My lawyers have looked them over and, well, they're taking care of things."

"I'm glad… may I call you Tiffy?"

"Sure." I laugh.

"Tiffy, I'm glad. I'm not a probate lawyer. I'm not a lawyer at all, in fact. My father and uncles do that. What I do is investigate for them. And Fletcher is… well, I consider him a very good friend. He went to school with one of my cousins, and she… well…" Katie throws up her hands. "OK, you know he runs a matchmaking business, right?"

"I do," I say.

"So I hired him, and that same night, he hired us. First it was about you and the company. He was just trying to save his job. But then he mentioned that Cole Lancaster looked familiar. So I started digging. Just in case there was something there I needed to know."

"And there was."

"There was. At first it was just about the frequent visits to the hotel. The rooms, the room service billed to the company. Things like that. Things Fletcher could use to prove he did nothing wrong by dating patrons of the show. You see, Cole was"—she does finger quotes—"'dating' plenty of employees himself."

I swallow hard again. "I figured that out too. A bar waitress told me that day my dad died."

"I'm only bringing that up because I need you to understand Fletcher didn't set out to pry into your life. And he doesn't want you to think he did. It started out as a way to fight for his job."

I let out a sigh. "But you found more."

"Your friend Claudio told Fletcher about your father's interest, and he mentioned it to me. Just a little FYI. Sometimes things that don't seem important at the time end up being the crucial details that wins a case."

"And you went on a hunch?" I look down at my feet. "Was Cole that obvious? Was I the only one oblivious to his true nature?"

She laughs. "I doubt that. He had a lot of scams brewing, Miss Preston. And your father's will was just one of them. I think he used your longtime friendship to manipulate you and your father. When you know someone, you have every right to trust them. No one expects betrayal from someone they counted on as a friend."

I feel the tears spring forth, and it pisses me off that I could control them when she mentioned my father, but not this frank admission of what Cole did. "I'm sorry," I say, dabbing my eyes with a tissue I pull from my purse.

"Don't be. It's a sad thing when trust is broken."

"Well, I want to say thank you for all the work you did. My lawyers said we have a solid case. Your research and thoroughness will make sure that Cole Lancaster is not the executor of the will, and that title is given back to me."

She squeezes my hand again. "I'm so glad."

"But that's not the real reason I'm here." I stare at her, willing myself to ask the question. "I want to know if you…" Fuck. "If you know where I can find Fletcher."

She smiles and I already know what she's going to say. "I'm sorry, I don't. I know he left Tahoe. And I have a feeling about where he went. But he is a client of ours as well, so I can't share that with you."

"I understand." I also feel defeated. "But I said some things I'd like to take back, and I was…" My words trail off because her smile is firm. She will not divulge anything about Fletcher to me today. "Well, if you see him or talk to him, can you just let him know I'm sorry for all the things I said?" I shake my head with a sigh. "I don't know who he is, but the person everyone thinks he is, Katie, that's not real, is it?"

She smiles bigger, like I just hit my target. But it comes with a noncommittal shrug. "I'm sure he'll turn up again. One day."

"OK," I say, withdrawing my hand from hers and standing up. "I won't take up any more of your time. But one more thing, Katie. Why did you hire Fletch? I mean, I don't understand why you needed his… services."

She stands with me, and now she's beaming. "Tiffy, surely you've noticed that Fletcher has a remarkable presence. He's charismatic, and fun, and friendly. He knows his way around a woman."

I chortle.

"But not like that. It's not what you think. I can give you this small piece of information, as it's so vague, no one could misconstrue that as breach of privacy. He's not what you think. Nothing about him is what you think. So if you see him again, keep that in mind. And if you don't, don't feel bad about how it ended. He liked you, I know that much. Or he'd never have gotten so personally involved." She laughs. "Especially without a contract."

Jesus. I laugh about that too. "Did he help you, Katie? With whatever it was you were looking for help with?"

Her shrug is as big as the smile she lights the room up with. "He did, Tiffy. He did. I'm a satisfied customer. And no, it wasn't Cole."

I laugh too. "I figured that."

"You're too good for that guy. I'll give you one piece of advice I got from Fletcher the first time we met, before we signed our contract. I think that's fair game. When I first explained my problem to him, he took my hand, leaned down into my ear, and whispered, in the softest voice possible, 'You're way too good for him, Katie. Don't devalue yourself like that. And if you hire me, I'll remind you of this fact for the rest of your life. I'll never let you forget it.'"

I can picture it in my head. So clear. And then the vision morphs into Fletcher and I out on the rocks that day. "Did you believe him?"

She nods slowly. "I still do."

"You didn't feel like you were…" I look down, and then eye her from under the hair that falls in front of my face. "Being used? Like you were being played? That he was just telling you those things because he wanted something?"

"Never." She stares at me for a moment, probably working

out the fact that he told me those things too, only I chose not to believe him. "He's the real deal, Tiffy. I hope you two can work it out some day. I'd really like you to know him the way I do."

We shake hands one more time after she walks me back to the greeting area, and I spend the quick trip downstairs knowing that I will never see Fletcher Novak again.

33

Nine months later.

The bright sunshine of early morning in Tahoe was a sight I missed since I've been gone. June can be hit or miss in the mountains. It can snow one day and be a balmy seventy degrees the next. You just never know.

But this year we lucked out with a mild spring that lingered all the way through the first day of summer. And right now the South Shore is alive, even at nine AM on a Tuesday. I flip up my sunglasses as I walk into the lobby of the Landslide Hotel and look to my right to check the front desk.

None of the people busy with the checkout rush are familiar. But what did I expect? You can't go home again. I scratch the scant stubble on my chin for a moment, considering.

Should I stop and ask about her?

But someone bumps into me, a man with a young family,

his hands filled with a baby and luggage, while his wife is busy herding two small boys under five.

"Sorry," he says, distracted with the baby in his arms as she starts to become upset.

"No problem," I say. Yeah, I think I will skip the front desk and head right down to the training room.

I ease my way through the bustling crowds lingering on the edges of the casino. They're lined up in front of the restaurant that now has a long and colorful neon sign that reads *Breakfast Buffet*.

Looks like she made some changes and the changes were good.

I punch the elevator button with the card Claudio sent me in the mail, and then wait. Patient, but thinking. He asked me to come by, somehow having gotten wind that I was in town on the North Shore finishing up some business.

I didn't ask about Tiffy, but he offered. She doesn't know I'm here. All he wanted was some advice on the all-new and revamped Mountain Man show.

After Cole fired everyone I heard Tiffy shut the show down for good. Maybe with the idea that the hotel needed a new look. Or maybe she was just overwhelmed and didn't care to put it back together. Some magic act came in to replace us, the whole place got a little more family-friendly with the addition of a water park that opened a few weeks ago, and I figured she'd just move on and forget we ever existed. But now the Mountain Men are back.

Claudio found me through Steve. Tiffy tried to call. Many times, in fact. But I never answered that old phone number. Not once. It was a link to a life I was more interested in forgetting than rekindling.

Steve though, he and I remained in touch, though I told him to keep it private. Which he did. Until now.

But it was nice to hear Claudio's voice. And nice to hear the updates on the hotel as well. Maybe being a part of the Mountain Men was never my endgame, but I was invested.

The elevator arrives and opens for me. And as I step in, all the memories of this routine come washing over me. The feeling is as brief as the ride down one floor, though. I get out, flash my badge to an unfamiliar face standing guard in front of the training room, and then pull that door open, allowing the sounds of rehearsal to boom out into the hallway before I can shut the door behind me.

The stage lights and smoke machines are on, and the six guys on stage are in the middle of a routine that looks very much like a dress rehearsal. It's opening night for the new show. They have two stages now, I hear. Claudio filled me in. The family-friendly magician is still here, alternating nights with a comedian and the Landslide's own version of a Shakespeare Festival for those people who prefer air-conditioning to the outdoor amphitheater up on the North Shore.

That might not be her best idea since she took over the hotel. It's hard to compete with a tradition. But she's trying and I'm glad. And hell, what's success anyway without the sting of an occasional failure to spur you forward?

"Fletcher," the familiar voice says from off to my right.

"Claudio." I laugh, surprised at how happy I am to see him again. He's looking very professional and sleek in his expensive designer suit. I extend my hand, but he hesitates.

"Hell, give me a hug, you gorgeous specimen of a man." He pulls me into him and claps me on the back.

I laugh and clap him on the shoulder. "Steve is MC, huh?"

"Snotty bitches are going to be pawing him like an animal once the show opens. I have to guard my heart, Fletch. Keep him on the sidelines as much as possible." Claudio squints his eyes at me and says in a serious voice, "I'm the jealous type, you know."

He makes me chuckle again. "Yeah, I bet you—"

"No!" The voice booms out, and then the music stops. Tiffy Preston walks out on stage. "No, Jerry. Not like that." She strides up to him wearing old jeans and a white tank top that reminds me of a Tiffy version of myself last summer. Her hair is all piled on top of her head in something that says that whole idea of doing it was an afterthought. She bellows, "Music!" It starts thumping again, right where it left off, and Tiffy starts moving to the beat. "Tease them, Jerry. You have to seduce them." She yells it over the noise, the stage lights bouncing off her as she joins the five dancers in the act. "Only show them—"

But I lose track of her words after that. Because she is pulling up her tank top, just a little bit at a time, just like I used to do out there last summer. I get a glimpse of the taut muscles of her stomach as she sways, my eyes glued to her fingertips as she grabs my attention like no woman ever has. Not before she came along and not since.

The hurt pumps through me again. It takes me by surprise, to be honest. I thought I was over it. Thought I had gotten beyond what happened last summer. Thought I had it under control.

Claudio is frowning. "I lied."

"I guess you did."

"She's here. She's been here since she took control last year. Every day, Fletcher. She's been working on this hotel like her life depends on it."

"Then why did you lie and tell me she was out of town?" I'm angry at him, I realize. For tricking me into this. He asked for help, but it's clear now that he and Steve are trying to play matchmaker. And I don't play games anymore.

"I knew you wouldn't come."

I nod, understanding. And it's appropriate, I guess. That I should get played after all the playing I did myself last year. I turn to leave, but Claudio grabs me by the arm.

"Wait," he says. "Just hear me out."

"I can't do it, Claudio. I can't. We're not right for each other and pretending that we are won't change that fact."

"She's changed, Fletcher." He says this as I slip through the rehearsal studio doors and back into the hallway. I walk briskly back towards the elevator and punch the button, ignoring the security guard and the man calling my name behind me.

The doors open and I slip in, but Claudio is right there, out of breath and talking a mile a minute. "It was a misunderstanding, Fletcher. It was—"

I tune him out. Fuck that.

"—and she was manipulated, you know this. She was—"

"She had a very low opinion of me, Claudio. And I'm pretty sure that hasn't changed."

The doors open to the lobby and I walk straight out, Claudio still keeping stride, still making excuses for her.

"Just talk to her, Fletcher. Please. For me."

I stop outside the hotel and wave to the valet to bring my car.

"Why?" I say, whirling back to him. "So she can say she's sorry? It's easy to be sorry when you find out all your preconceived notions are wrong, isn't it? It's easy—"

"She didn't know," he says, almost pleading.

"Isn't that the point, Claudio? Isn't that the fucking point?"

He stops talking as I stare at him, maybe a little defeated or maybe just disappointed in me for my predictable reaction. Then his expression changes to anger. "You weren't fair to her either. So get off your high horse and stop being a prick. Stop being the asshole you want everyone to see you as and be real for a minute."

I look around to find two dozen people staring at us.

But Claudio doesn't care about perceptions right now. He's pissed off. "You only saw what you wanted to see as well. So don't stand there all high and mighty and tell me that you don't owe her an apology. That you don't owe *each other* an apology. Because if you walk out this time, she's moving on. She saw you back there, Fletcher. Her eyes met mine just before you stormed out. So she knows now. She knows you're here. And if you don't man up and get it out in the open, then you burned this bridge."

He plants his hands on his hips and stares me down, daring me to do it.

"I'll be glad if you leave, you know. You hurt her, Fletcher. Bad. She tried to contact you many times and you turned your back. She's my best friend, so I don't take kindly to people who make her sad."

"Please, Claudio. She was—"

"Don't," he says, putting a hand up. "Don't, OK? She did her best with the information she had. You were the one who knew everything. You can't expect people to make the right decisions when they only have half the information. You know that better than anyone."

I growl out my frustration. He's referring to my matchmaking. My fuckup with Cole and Katie. My secrets. All of which are out in the open now, since my name is all over the fall TV schedule.

"And don't pull this bullshit that she only wants you because you're not a stripper anymore, either," Claudio continues. "Because it's not fair. She started that show up again, Fletcher. She did all of it. She held the auditions, she hired the dancers. She found the best choreographer she could and was part of every bit of it. So fuck you and your attitude. She didn't want to be with you because you were a liar, not because you were a stripper."

"Well," I snarl back, "it would've been a lot easier to know that if I was still stripping instead of what I'm doing now, wouldn't it."

"You walked out on her. If you hadn't, she'd have stuck by you. And the only reason you're still pissed off now is because you think she's gonna use you. Well, newsflash, asshole. You used her last year and she looked past it. So just fuck you if you can't extend her the same consideration."

Claudio turns to leave me there, but it's me who catches his arm this time. "Wait."

34

Fletcher Novak.

My eyes meet Claudio's just as Fletcher turns to walk out of the rehearsal room. My breath hitches in my chest and my stomach gets a sinking feeling that I haven't felt in months.

I've done my best to put him behind me. Come to terms with the way I judged him. The way I hurt him. All the many, many mistakes I made with Fletcher Novak over the short time we were… friends.

Because that's what he was to me. In every way. It's just too bad I didn't have the good sense to realize it when I had the chance.

I tuck away the urge to run after him and scream his name. Beg him to forgive me and all my preconceptions about who and what he is. It takes me several seconds. And by the time I look away from the door, the entire troupe has noticed.

Steve shoots me a sympathetic look, then clears his throat and grabs the attention of the dancers so I can recover.

"OK," I say after that moment passes. "Let's do it again, guys. From the top. We've got a show tonight, and we're gonna blow this town away."

They smile and joke, as they take their poisons again. The music restarts and the lights come on, allowing me to make a dignified escape off the stage.

I slump down into the director's chair set up offstage and watch eight months of work finally come together. They are as near perfect as we can get. They are all fit and handsome. All dancers. The music is original, and there is an artistic quality to the show that might set us apart from all the other male revue shows that have cropped up over the past few years.

It's a long shot, I know that. The show Fletcher and Chandler put together before I took over the hotel was fun. It was very good too. And it did get a five-star review, although it was a moot point since Cole shut it down and ruined everything.

But that's OK. It was a long process, regrouping and finding my stride. But I found it. And I'm proud of this show. I'm proud of the men who dance, the stagehands, the lighting guys. We even have a film crew to do promos for us along for the ride tonight.

It's not the same show. It's better. Because it's mine.

Claudio appears again, making his way towards me. He sits down in his chair, next to Steve's empty one, since he is dancing. The three of us are a team now, but even though I talk myself into feeling complete… I'm not.

The hole is still there.

I don't bring up Fletcher, and Claudio is silent as we wait for the rehearsal to be over. Everyone gathers around for a few words of encouragement—the nerves are hard to keep at bay, and it's my job to keep them all focused and positive. Until finally the rehearsal room goes quiet and it's just Claudio and me left.

"He gave me this," Claudio says, holding out a white plastic card. "Said you'd know what to do with it, and I quote, 'if you were interested in talking.'"

I stare at the card and take it from Claudio's outstretched hand. It says Windshore Estates on it, with a beautiful picture of the lake.

"Do you know what to do with it?" Claudio asks. "Because I sure don't."

I nod and turn the card over, studying it. "I think so." I check my watch. It's almost an hour up to the North Shore.

"Go," Claudio says.

"What?" I look up, still thinking of Fletcher. He has been on my mind since the moment I laid eyes on him back at that first show last summer. Even though I knew him such a short time, he dominated my thoughts. The anger when he propositioned me. The rage after he turned my plot to fire him against me. I look back down at my shoes and smile just thinking about it. And then I remember the sex on the roof and feel flushed. I felt betrayed when he set Cole up with Katie, but then cared for when I found out who she was and what Fletcher was doing. Of course, I've found out a lot more about him since that last meeting with Katie.

It wasn't hard. The fake Wikipedia entry is still there. But the name Rourke on those legal papers Katie sent started Claudio and I on a hunt to figure out who Fletcher Novak really is.

Claudio is waiting for me to work all this out and when I look back up one more time, he reaches for my hand and gives me a sad smile. "If you don't try, you'll never know. So just go, Tiffy. It might be your only chance."

I give him a slight nod as I take in a deep breath. "He's not going to care why, Claudio." Claudio starts to protest, but I put a hand up to stop him. "I'm still gonna try," I say. "And OK, he might still hate me afterward, but he might not. So I guess it's better to know one way or the other than let it stay a mystery."

Claudio leans in and hugs me. "Good luck, girlfriend. And don't be late for your show. If he's still a stubborn bastard, just keep your mind on the show. We've got opening night, babe. And those bitches in the new auditorium are going to scream so loud, Fletcher Novak will hear them from the other side of the lake."

I chuckle into his shoulder, trying my best not to cry so he won't complain about tears on his suit. "I promise to remember that."

XOXOXOXOX

The drive up the lake takes almost an hour. This time I know where I'm going and I'm not in a rage trying to follow his red car. So I enjoy it. That's something I've been working on since my father died last summer. *Live in the moment, Tiffy. Don't waste any chances.* Because you only get one life. One trip around the game board. One chance to win.

I pull up to the gatehouse where I lied to the guard all those months ago. It's not the same guy, thank God. Mr. Silverman was very confused by my behavior that day, but he ended up blaming it on my father's sickness and death.

The guard leans down, placing a hand on the top of my car hood, and says, "Good afternoon, ma'am. Can I help you?"

I grab the pass Fletcher gave Claudio to get me past the gate. "Fletcher Rourke invited me to the house and gave me this pass."

The guard's expression changes and a beaming smile comes forth. "Ah, I'm gonna miss him." He backs away a few paces to push the button for the gate. "Go on in, ma'am," he says, waving me through.

I drive slowly down the road running parallel to the lakeshore. Every now and then I get a peek at the brilliant blue water flanked on all sides by the majestic mountains. I see the driveway for Fletch's house. There's a sale sign attached to the gate with an *Open House By Invitation Only* banner running across it. When I pull up, the gate opens automatically and I drive forward until Fletcher's red Camaro comes into view.

I park behind him and get out, dragging my fingertips along the white racing stripe on the hood as I walk up to the front steps. The door is not open, and it has one of those lock boxes on the handle so agents can show the place.

I ring the doorbell several times, but no one comes. I step back from the house and walk back to the driveway, trying to see the backyard. It tilts a little, goes uphill, so I walk a few steps along the stone pavers flanked on either side with brightly colored flower beds, and when I get to the top the view almost takes my breath away.

The thirteen-million-dollar house has an equally impressive backyard. The sand is clean and raked to perfection with the exception of one trail of footsteps and my eyes follow them to the apex of a short dune where I can barely make out a mess of blond hair flowing in the lake breeze peeking out over the top.

I slip my sneakers off and step into the warm sand, my toes digging in deep. It feels wonderful. I have not been on our beach this summer at all. Too busy getting the show in shape. Too busy trying to forget my mistakes last summer. The walk only takes half a minute, and then there I am. Staring down on his sitting frame, his knees tucked up to his chest, his forearms poking out of the rolled-up sleeves of a crisp white dress shirt. Untucked and open in the front so that the slight wind coming off the lake makes it flutter around his body like a sheet in the wind.

"It's a tough sell," he says, his back still to me. "Thirteen million dollars." He turns his head slowly, giving me a sidelong glance over his shoulder. He eyes my tattered jeans first, then his gaze travels up to my white tank top. "Nice outfit."

"I hear it's the uniform."

That gets a half-hearted chuckle out of him as he turns his attention back to the view. But it helps me relax. So I take a few more steps, crest the soft peak of the sand dune, and then slide a little as I descend and take a seat next to him. "Did you sell it?" I ask, my fingertips digging into the sand.

"Got an offer this morning."

"Are you gonna take it?"

A shrug. "I guess."

I nod. "I guess I would too. But it would be sad."

He looks over at me. Another side glance, like he's not interested in meeting my gaze. "She wasn't my wife, you know."

"I know, Fletcher. I know a lot more now than I did back

then. I have investigators too."

He picks up a twig and stabs it into the sand a few times. "She's my brother's ex. And Shelly is my niece."

"You don't have to explain," I say. "I know." He stays silent after that. Just staring out across the sapphire-colored water. I can't see the south shore from here, but it's a long view down the entire length of the lake. Breathtaking. "It must be hard to leave."

"I'm still trying to figure that one out, ya know?" He turns his head again. This time he looks at me straight on. "My granddad was a pretty important golf-course designer back in his day." Fletch takes a deep breath, looks away, like he's wondering if he should talk about it or not, then decides he will, and continues. "He got this land before all the development. Back when it was still valuable, but not outrageously so. It was a partial payment for a course he consulted on. And before he died years ago, back when I was eighteen and Walker was nineteen, he was in a huge fight with my parents. Called them no-good lazy bums." He stops to laugh. It's real and comes with that smile I loved so much last summer.

"But he was right, I think. And that's why he gave Walk and me the house. He wanted it to stay in the family and figured my parents would sell it off the first chance they got." He squints in the sunshine and look over at me again. "They would've too."

I nod. "It's a lot of responsibility, I imagine."

"I did my best, Tiff. I tell myself that, anyway. But I just can't afford it. My granddad left Walk and me about five million each. But after Walker fucked up with Samantha, I bought him out. I spent every last cent getting the title to this place to keep my promise to my granddad and give her a home to live in. A base that Shelly could count on, just like I did when I was a kid."

I want to take his hand as he works through this decision to sell his house and break his promise. But it's not something I can make him feel better about. It's just something he has to come to terms with.

"So it's ironic, ya know?" He looks at me again, the wind tossing his blond hair in a mess of loose curls, his blue eyes shining in a slash of sunshine that cuts across his face. "I'll be so rich if I take this offer, money will lose all meaning. Add in the deal I just made down in LA, and it barely makes sense to me."

I sigh along with his frustration. "That's how it works, right? The rich get richer and they don't even have to try. Money makes money."

"The taxes alone killed me. Every year I scrambled to pay them. Fifty thousand dollars in property taxes. That's not even counting what it costs to maintain this place. The gardeners alone." He shakes his head. "And I tried, OK? I tried to mow that fucking lawn. But it was an all-day job, and half the sod died, and then it just cost me more to hire people to come fix the shit I messed up."

"I can relate. The cost of running that hotel made me throw up when I found out. And then I had to hire someone else to come do it for me, because every time I thought about it, I'd make myself sick. So yeah, I couldn't win. And I can relate."

He stares at me for a moment. "Am I doing the right thing, Tiffy? If I take this offer?"

I look out at the lake now, thinking about how I got here. Not here on the beach, but here, this moment in time. "It's opening night tonight."

"I know," he says with a sigh. "I've been seeing the promos everywhere."

"But it was a long road, and a lot of decisions to get to this night." I smile at him and he smiles back. Not the big one that I love, but I'll take what I can get right now. "My lawyers took all that info you had Katie gather and ran with it. They got the will overturned. Not just the executor thing that Cole tried to slip in, but the whole damn will. It was something of a miracle. The right judge, and all that."

Fletcher raises his eyebrows.

"Yeah, I got all sixteen billion dollars."

"That's a quite a windfall."

"Right?" I ask. "But it wasn't right. Because my dad wanted me to have enough, but not too much. And sixteen billion is way too much. So I did what he asked and I parceled it out the way he intended. I kept the part I got as the executor. And I kept the hotel, obviously, since it was mine anyway. I decided I've been scared of taking chances for far too long. I was going to make a decision and stick with it. See it through to the end. See what I'm made of. And no, running a resort in Lake Tahoe was never how I saw my life when I was younger. I pictured a capable man taking care of me for the rest of my days, to be honest. So I adjusted my dream. Thought about what I wanted. And what I wanted was to be… capable of something. Anything, really. So I'm still here. And I'm staying."

"I get it." Fletcher looks down at the sand and starts running it through his fingers alongside of me. "I was out here last week. Just moping on the beach. And Shelly came out and sat next to me. She put her arm around me and looked up at my face with those wise eight-year-old eyes and said, 'It doesn't matter if you sell it, Uncle Fletch. We can always think about the beach in our heads and it will still be there.'"

"Very wise kid," I say.

"She's amazing. And she was right. So I put the house up for sale the next day, and one week later we had an offer on the table." He stops playing with the sand and stares out across the lake. "I feel so much relief, Tiffy. It scares me. I should feel like a failure. I should feel like I let my granddad down by putting this house up for sale. But I don't. I just feel relief. Like I've finally admitted I was on the wrong path and just accepting that fact is enough to make it right."

"I'm glad." I have so much more to say, but I'm just not sure how to start. So we sit there in silence for a few minutes, listening to the waves and watching jet skis off in the distance.

"I'm going to LA tonight."

My heart wrenches in my chest. But what did I expect?

"How much do you really know about me?" He fills in the silence left hanging.

"Enough to know you weren't who I thought you were."

"Hmmm," he grunts. "I was so pissed about that, you have no idea."

I have nothing to say. So I say nothing.

"You never tried to know me, Tiffy. You never once tried to know me. You didn't make any effort."

"That's not true," I say, feeling a little defensive. "I looked you up on Wikipedia."

It was a joke, but he doesn't laugh. "You saw Fletcher the stripper. Fletcher the player. Fletcher the fuckup."

"To be fair, Fletcher"—my anger gets the best of me—"those were the only parts you showed me."

"Really? You sure about that?"

"You were a man-whore."

"I told you you were special the first night we met."

"That was after you propositioned me at the show."

"You came there to fire me based on rumors."

"Rumors that were partially true! And you outed yourself as the matchmaker, remember? I didn't come up with that idea myself."

He shrugs. "I was trying to help you. And I did help you." He looks over at me, the anger in his heated stare apparent now. "You just never saw it."

"You hurt me too, Fletcher. You set Cole up with Katie and never told me why. You let me find out on my own. You took me to a restaurant to practice—"

"You wanted all that, Tiffy. And I didn't tell you about Cole because I didn't have the evidence until after you broke into my hotel room and went through my private papers."

I don't reply. I'm angry again and I don't want things to end like this.

"I saw you, ya know."

"Saw me where?"

He shakes his head. "Not where, Tiffy. You're so preoccupied with where and when. The only thing that matters is the how and the why."

I sigh. We're going in circles. "You lied to me, Fletcher. And sure, I was no one to you, so I guess you had that right. But you don't get to judge me. Not when our whole relationship was based on the idea that you could change me."

"Is that what you think?" he asks, laughing. "Well, try on this perspective for a minute, Miss Preston. I fell for you the minute I saw you out in the audience. I never wanted to change you, you wanted *me* to change you. I liked the clothes you wore. I liked the sexy you had back then. I liked everything about you, which is why I went out of my way to help you. It was Cole who needed the new and improved version, not me."

I huff out a breath of air though my nose, the anger building inside me. "You don't even know me, Fletcher."

"Ditto, babe," he snarls. "Ditto."

I stand up and wipe the sand off my ass. "Well, I'm glad you're good, Fletcher. And maybe one day we'll be friends again. But I'm not going to sit here and let you tell me who I am. Not when you haven't even asked one goddamned question about me. Not one, Fletcher. You were never interested."

He stands too, grabbing me by the wrist. "So tell me, then. What makes you tick, Tiffy Preston? You figured me out. I had a debt I needed to pay, a family I dropped everything to take care of, a woman and a child who weren't even my responsibility. I left college for them, you know. I put my whole life on hold to take care of my brother's mistake. Scraping by doing this and that. Trying to pay the taxes on this monstrous house and put food on the table. Pay the babysitter while Samantha went to nursing school. And I did my best. Any way I could. I came up with dozens of ideas to get something rolling and that matchmaking business was all I had for years. And I was good at it. I helped those girls, Tiffy, Every single one of them. I changed the way they saw themselves."

"So? What's that got to do with me?" I regret those words and quickly amend them. "Us, I mean. Because even though what you're doing to me right now isn't fair, I'm still here. I'm still trying. But all you seem to want to do is blame me for this fucked-up position you're in. Do you want the money to keep your house, Fletcher? I can give it to you if that's what you need in order to understand I like you."

"Fuck you," he growls. "I was never interested in your money, Tiffy. You're mixing me up with your dream man, Cole."

I look away and shake my head. We are both silent again, perhaps choosing our next words carefully as we try to navigate a minefield of hurt and disappointment.

"Back when I first started the matchmaking thing it was sort of a joke. I had just quit school in my senior year to help Samantha with Shelly after she gave birth. She had some depression and I was a psych major. So I figured if I couldn't finish my degree, I could at least help her out. And it became so clear that Samantha's self-worth was tied up in Walker's opinion of her that I started coaching her on how to feel sexy. Not how to *be* sexy, Tiffy. How to *feel* sexy. There's a very big difference."

I look him in the eye now, seeing a way forward, even if it is by way of a very crooked path.

"And after she started getting better, I began to notice more and more how people perceived me, and how that perception wove its way into my own opinion of myself. Sexy, to ninety-nine percent of the population, is only on the outside. So why not take advantage of that? Why not sell my brand of sexy and buy myself some time?"

"So you became a stripper. Don't you think that's a little self-defeating, Fletcher? On the one hand you're lecturing Samantha and these other girls about valuing themselves for who they are on the inside, but at the same time you're using your looks to make money."

"It was an experiment, that's it."

I can tell he's pissed off about my accusation, but screw it. He brought it all up. "So you wrote a screenplay about what it feels like to be an objectified man taking his clothes off to survive and you sold your story to a network. I'm happy for you, Fletcher. And I think you're going places. Selling this house is probably going to set you on a path to success. And I wish you all the best. But I was raised by a prostitute, Fletcher. So excuse me if I didn't have the highest regard for your path to redemption."

His mouth gapes open for a second.

"Yeah, my mother sold herself to save me. And she got what she thought she wanted too. But she never loved my father. And once I came to terms with that, I started to doubt her love for me as well. It's a shitty thing to be lied to under the pretense that it's for your own good. And you did that to me too. Did you even like me? Or was I just another project? Was I just another girl you needed to fix to make yourself feel important and in control of your own destiny?"

"That's not what it was," he sneers.

"That's because you and I see it from opposite sides, Fletcher. And you're so goddamned sure that you walk on water, you can't even be bothered to wonder if my point of view is even worthy of your consideration."

35

I don't stop her when she walks out.

I don't stop her because everything she just said hits me in the chest like a brick. It stops me dead.

Instead I sit back down and stare out at the water, wondering if Samantha feels the same way about me as Tiffy does. Wondering if, in the process of trying to fix things, all I did was fuck them up more.

I pull out my phone and tab Sam's contact. She picks up on the third ring, kids laughing in the background. "Hey," she says, a little out of breath. "How'd it go?"

Samantha moved out of the mansion last September. She graduated from nursing school and sat me down that night, thanking me for all my help, but anxious to take control of her life and make it on her own. "Got an offer," I say without much enthusiasm.

"Great!" But my silence betrays my thoughts. She knows me too well. "What's wrong?"

"I don't know."

"Fletcher," she says in that stern voice she uses with me often these days. "We've been over this. I don't need that house. And you're selling for all the right reasons. I don't want you to keep it because you think you owe us. Or," she adds quickly, "because you think your granddad would be disappointed. He had no way of knowing how it would all turn out. He doesn't want you to struggle. He wants you to live a good life and put the past to rest. And even with the Hollywood money, it's a big commitment to keep that property."

"I know," I say. But my fight with Tiffy is weighing on my mind right now.

"You don't need to take care of us anymore, Fletch. We're good. And I'm so thankful. But I can't steal your life away just because you feel obligated."

Her words are just another brick hitting my chest. "I'm gonna take the offer," I say.

"Good." She laughs. "Good. I'm so happy for you, Fletcher. Really." There's some squealing of girls in the background and I know she and Shells are at a friend's house for a pool party.

"Well, I'll let you guys get back to the fun." I force the cheerfulness into my voice so she won't ask any more questions. "I just wanted to let you know."

"Congrats, Fletcher. Talk to you soon."

I end the call and lie back on the sand, letting the wind whip around my body. It's hard to let Samantha go. And I bet it was even harder for her to take her life into her own hands and trust that she had what it took to make it on her own. Walker is still hanging around and part of me suspects that Sam wanted some distance from me so she could sort out her feelings for him.

That hurts too, since I was the one who was there for her and Shelly. He walked out, just like his name implies. Too many big dreams to be saddled with a high school girlfriend and a new baby. Walker and I had this competitive gene that hooked us when we were kids and never let go. So I wonder… did I step in for Samantha and Shelly? Or did I just want to prove to my brother that I was a better man than him?

Tiffy's doubts about her mother's love have shattered my preconceived notions about what I have been doing all these years. Will Shelly grow up thinking she was an obligation that needed to be dealt with? Handled like a problem? Will she accuse me of stealing her mother's life? Will she accuse her mother of taking the easy way out? Will she doubt my love for her because I felt the need to provide? Step in and save them under the guise of doing the right thing?

I don't want that.

And it's not gonna happen. But none of these changes were because of me. It was Samantha who took things into her own hands and made the hard choices. It was Samantha who said no to our arrangement and decided there was more to life than… stability.

That word echoes in my mind and more of what makes Tiffy tick starts to make sense.

So I tab another contact and wait for my realtor to pick up. "Take the offer," I say. "And keep me posted."

I listen half-heartedly to his enthusiasm on the other end of the line for a few seconds, and then I end that call too.

I don't go back inside the house. It's just too much right now. They want to buy it furnished, which I can understand. It makes sense if you like the decor. Filling up all that space with new things is an expense that costs both time and money.

But it hurts. I took what I wanted before the first showing. All the things that tugged at my heart. But it still hurts.

So I weigh my next move in my head. Back to LA tonight? Or sort things out with Tiffy?

In the end that decision is made for me. Because when I finally make my way back to the driveway, on the windshield of my car, tucked under the wipers, is a ticket for the opening night of the new Mountain Men show at the Landslide Hotel.

If she's still interested, then so am I.

I'm all in.

36

I stand backstage, peeking out through the curtain, staring at the auditorium doors while everyone else bustles around me getting ready for the show.

"Just go sit at your table," Claudio tells me for the billionth time. "He's coming, I know it."

"What if he doesn't?"

"Tiffy," Claudio says, taking my face in his hands. "The man is in love with you. He hasn't said it yet, but he is. He's coming."

"We had a fight, Claudio. And we didn't part on good terms. And he said he was going back to LA—"

But my words catch because Fletcher Novak walks in.

He's… stunning. Dark jeans that accentuate his legs and taper down just right. A white dress shirt, sleeves rolled up, casually, owning the look like no other man I've ever seen. And his blond hair is combed back, the unruly loose wave of curls trying to break free as they brush against his shoulders when he turns his head.

Is he searching for me?

I take a deep breath.

"Go. Sit with him."

"God, I'm so nervous. What if we argue again? It will kill me."

"He's here, Tiffy. Don't let him get away." Claudio kisses me on the lips, and lets go of my face so he can get back to work. "I'll handle everything, girlfriend," he calls over his shoulder. "Go get your sexy on."

I laugh, and then slip back behind the curtain and make my way out to the auditorium through the side door.

The event is sold out. People called the hotel for months complaining after the show was cancelled. It was the only thing they cared about. The magician is good, and it will be nice to have two shows, but I'm banking on the Mountain Men to make this hotel a success.

Fletcher spots me coming just as he finds the front-row center table I reserved. I had no idea he'd be in town, but I have a feeling Claudio had something to do with that. He was the one who insisted I keep the reserved VIP table for myself.

"Hey," Fletcher says, reaching for me as I walk up. He takes my hand, pulls me close, and then leans in and kisses me on the cheek. "You look pretty."

I blush. I'm wearing a flirty peach-colored sundress that hits me just above the knee and my favorite new four-inch heels. I dressed for him, so that's a huge relief. "Thank you. I'm sorry—"

"Don't." He places a fingertip over my lips. "You don't need to be sorry for anything."

"I know, but I just need you to know that it wasn't fair for me to throw this show in your face. Not when I'm basically doing the same thing. I was wrong to judge you."

He gives me a crooked smile that reaches all the way up to his eyes. "The apologies are over, and you were right about everything, Tiffy. I'm here because I want you. Not the new you, not the old you. Just you. Any way you want to be, I'm in, princess."

I take a deep breath and look him in the eyes. "I'm in too, Fletch. I have never felt this way about anyone in my life. You are always there. Always on my mind. And even though I know I can do it without any help from anyone now, I don't want to." I swallow hard. "I really don't. I want you there with me. Next to me, every night, for as long as you'll stay."

"I love ya, Tiff," he says, pulling me to his chest and kissing my head. "I love ya. I want to be in your life and I'm not going anywhere unless you kick me out."

I check my watch, and then have an idea. "We have twenty minutes before the show starts. Can I show you something?"

"Show away, princess. I'm your captive audience tonight."

I pull him along by the hand, since he's still holding mine, and go out the door into the lobby. "It's upstairs."

He waggles his eyebrows at me. "Sure it is."

We get into the elevator and I lean back against the mirrored wall, fanning myself with my free hand. "I'm nervous."

He just smiles. We get off on my old penthouse floor and he chuckles as I lead him down the hallway. "I like where this is going." I bite my lip as I look over my shoulder at him. "Hey," he says. "No using my tips and tricks against me tonight."

But then he does that little tongue thing where he touches it to the tip of his front teeth, and I laugh. "I like your tips, so feel free to use them on me all you want."

He shakes his head as he smiles. I walk past my old penthouse door and keep going, straight to the one at the end of the hallway.

"The roof?" he asks, his eyebrows up.

"Just wait, Fletcher." We go through the door and walk up the flight of stairs that leads outside.

I stop and look at him for a second, my hand on the knob, ready to show him what I've done. Somehow the fight is over. It's like we needed to say all that stuff back on the beach in order to move forward and now that it's out in the open, everything feels… right.

I open the door and step aside, letting him get a good look at what's beyond.

"Holy shit, princess. You turned my rooftop into the royal gardens."

"Do you like it?" I ask, looking at my recently completed project with his eyes for a moment. The raised beds are filled with flowers and shrubs. The ground has been paved with stones, and little bits of grass and moss peek through the edges, like it's been growing this way for a hundred years. White lights are strung around the perimeter, and the glow is just enough to give it a special ambiance that mixes with the fading sunset.

"I love it," he says, taking it in as his gaze wanders from garden bed to garden bed.

"I just had the trees planted last week. In fact, I just moved up here from my old room a few days ago. And look what I did to the garden shed, Fletch."

I realize when I say his name that we are true friends now. These last few minutes are new and old in all the right ways. He feels like a part of me. He feels like he's been with me this whole time. He feels… real.

37

The wonder and happiness in her face settles my nerves and calms me down. I have never been so filled with apprehension going to meet a girl as I was tonight. Everything raced through my mind as I pulled up to the valet. All the possibilities left hanging between us. All the ways I could fuck it up. Just how easy it would be to lose this girl and how I'd feel if that happened.

It wasn't going to happen, I decided. I wouldn't let it.

So when she came up to me downstairs and let me take her hand, it felt right. Like every decision that led to this moment was right.

She pulls me along towards what used to be the shed. But now it's bigger. The dingy old cinderblock bricks have been painted white. The windows have shutters and flower boxes spilling over with color.

She opens the door to the new and improved garden shed and steps back to let me walk in first. It's not big. Just a room, really. With a small kitchen where the old potting bench used to be and a king-size bed where I laid her down on the floor and ate her pussy until she came.

I shoot her a sidelong look. "How many men have you fucked in this bed?"

She laughs, getting my joke. "None, you sicko. I make them stand."

I walk forward, hungry for her, and take her face in my hands so I can kiss her on the lips and whisper in her mouth. "You get me?"

"I get you, Fletcher," she whispers back. "I do. Everything about you is sexy. But not the way you think. You're sexy on the inside. Your heart is big, and your brain is smart."

"I'm sorry, Tiffy," I say, pulling back a little. "I was guilty of everything I accused you of."

"We always wanted the same things, Fletcher. We were just trying to get them the wrong way."

It makes sense, I realize. She thought she needed Cole to provide for her because her mother taught her to want that. And I wanted to take care of Sam and Shelly to prove I was a better man than my brother. "It's strange how that happens."

"We're gonna miss the show," Tiffy says, still kissing me.

"This is the show, sexy. The only one that matters." I pull back and start unbuttoning my shirt.

Her eyes are trained on these small movements immediately. Her fingertips flutter down to the hem of her dress and begin to lift it up. She shows me a bit of leg as I continue to ease the buttons of my shirt free. When I get to the last one and shrug it off, she turns around and swipes her long dark hair off the nape of her neck.

I reach for the zipper and slide it down as she peeks at me over her shoulder. "Keep going," I whisper. "Please don't stop now."

Tiffy grins as she looks down at my pants, and then my fingertips are on my belt buckle. It jingles as I free the leather strap, and I unbutton my jeans.

She sucks in a little air through her teeth and turns back to face me, allowing one strap of her pretty dress to fall over her shoulder. She chews on her lip a little and I'm about to lose my mind as her tease overtakes me.

I drag my own zipper down and fist my cock for a moment. Her breasts rise and fall underneath the thin fabric as her breathing hitches. She slips one arm out of her dress, then the other, so that it falls to the curve of her hip. Just the way it did last summer when she was driving me mad with desire.

My dick is already hard. Almost throbbing from the anticipation of seeing her body again.

But she's slow and deliberate as she wiggles just enough to make the dress fall to the floor with a whoosh of air that wafts up, bringing the scent of her desire with it.

I drag my cock from the confines of my boxer briefs just as she lowers herself to the floor on her knees.

"Fuck, Tiffy. I think you've been practicing."

"No need to practice, Fletch." She grabs my hard length and gives me a squeeze. "I learned from the best." And then she wraps her mouth around me and I moan.

Her sucking starts slow, but increases in intensity as my head falls back and I fist her hair, pushing her towards me. Urging her on. Wanting more with each passing second. I pull away to stop myself from coming down her throat in a rush.

"I want more," I whisper. "I want to make this last all fucking night." So I take her hand and guide her up off her knees so I can kiss her mouth. "Finish what you started," I say in a gruff voice.

She places both palms on my chest and pushes me back until I bump into the bed and sit down. She straddles my lap, our eyes locked together. "You want me to tease it out of you?" she laughs.

"More than anything else in this world, Tiffy."

She smiles knowingly. The shy girl from last summer has found her stride. She reaches behind her back and unclasps her bra, letting it fall forward just a little bit, just enough to give me a peek at her full breasts as they drape against her ribs.

I moan again. "Fuck."

She slides the straps down her arms until I have a full view, and lets the bra fall into my lap. I reach for her, cupping her soft breasts, and this time *she* moans. I ease my face down to her nipple and take one in my mouth, sucking on her gently.

Her hands wrap around my head, fisting my hair in encouragement. I reach behind her ass and stand up, taking her with me. And then I toss her playfully down on the bed and watch her tits bounce.

"I really want you," I say.

"Please," she whispers back. "Take me."

I kick off my shoes, drag my pants and boxer briefs down in one swift movement, and then kick them aside as I reach for her panties. She lifts her hips to give me access, and those panties go flying off over my shoulder.

Her legs come up, the shyness plastered across her face once more. And I die for that. Just die. I hike her knees up to her face and press my mouth to her pussy, letting my tongue swirl around her clit until she's wriggling beneath me.

But I'm paying close attention to her. I monitor her moans and squeals. The way her legs clamp against my neck when it gets intense. The way she arches her back when I suck on her clit and stick my fingers inside her.

And just when I know she will explode, I stop.

"No," she moans, so sorrowfully I almost feel guilty.

"I want to come with you this time, Tiffy." I grab a condom out of my wallet and roll it onto my cock. She watches me, her attention one hundred percent on what's coming next.

Us.

We're coming next.

I ease into her, filling her up, and she clenches against me. Squeezing my shaft with her muscles and letting me know she's so very, very close.

Us.

That's the next chapter in our story.

Us.

I don't fuck her. I love her. I love her hard and soft. Far longer than I should be able to with the heat of our desire and the rising intensity.

I savor every moment until we peak together and let out months of regrets, filling ourselves back up with a lifetime of possibilities.

We miss the show.

But no one cares.

We are right where we are supposed to be.

Epilogue

One Year Later

"*Life is a game and everyone's a player. Whether you believe it or not, the only thing that matters is the score.*"

I'm so excited, I have to take deep breaths as we watch the season one premiere of *Sexy* in the Landslide bar. Everyone is here. Claudio and Steve. Samantha and my piece-of-shit brother, Walker, who I am learning to like again, even if it's just in small in increments. And, of course, the whole staff of the hotel and the cast of our revamped Mountain Men show.

When I finally forced myself to leave Tiffy's new and improved penthouse, I went back to LA to negotiate the terms of the contract. Since the screenplay was based on my experiences as a male stripper here at the hotel, I wanted the show to be true to how I wrote it. So I offered up the Landslide as the location.

It was hardly a negotiation, since the studio thought it was a great idea. And it kept me close to home while we were shooting.

The hotel has been balls to the wall since the opening night of Mountain Men 2. The show was off-the-charts popular, and we have a franchise in the making with a contract being negotiated for Vegas and a traveling show that will start touring in a few months.

Her dad would be proud. She manages the charities she left his billions to in addition to the hotel. And me. She manages me too.

I chuckle and have to hide a smile so she doesn't think I'm up to something when she drags her eyes from the TV and looks over at me. God, that girl. She's everything to me.

We got married on Valentine's Day on the beach just outside. It was my idea. Who knew I was such a romantic? But I'm fooling myself. I've always known it. And I guess that's why I was so pissed off when Walker left Samantha when she got pregnant. Sam hasn't quite forgiven him for that either, but she's trying. He's trying too. And as Tiffy often reminds me, everyone makes mistakes, so I cut him some slack and let him find his way forward with the family he regrets leaving behind.

Tiff and I found out we're expecting our first baby last week. The first of many, I hope. So in a few months life will be… I have to stop and catch my breath, that's how fabulous life will be. I loved every minute when I was helping Samantha bring up Shelly, so I can only imagine that joy will overwhelm me once my own little person comes into this world.

When I made the decision to sell the house it felt like a failure. For about… five hours. Because that's the amount of time that went by until I met Tiffy at the show that night. And that meeting has changed my perspective on everything.

Each of us gets a life and each of us gets to live it the way we want. I wasn't in debt to my granddad's wishes any more than Tiffy was to her mother's. We do our best and no one has a right to ask us for more. And who knows, maybe one day that house will be up for sale again and I'll be in a position to take it back.

But I'm not waiting around for it.

Because I was right. Life *is* a game.

And there are many ways to win it.

End Of Book Shit

Welcome to the End Of Book Shit (we call them the EOBS for short). This is where I get to talk shit and shit. And shit. Sometimes. Not today though. I have no shit taking today. No for serious, I just talk about the book and stuff.

So this book is special to me in two ways.

First the concept. I was at the Cleveland Author Event in April this year (Yay – that singing is one of the best out there!) and a few members of my Street Team were with me and one of them got us all tickets to go see Thunder Down Under (Thanks, Bella!) And that show barely started when my assistant, Jana, and I looked at each other and said, "We need a book!"

It's not the strippers. OK, yeah, it is. But the whole show as just fun. They took grandma up on stage and stuck her hand down their pants, and grandma giggled like she was a teenager. She got her picture taken and had a great time. They had brides-to-be on stage. They had the girls who did just about anything to get a guy's attention practically dancing on tables. I bet there really are girls who go there for a chance to go home with one and I bet there really are guys like Fletcher who look for a new one every time he goes on stage.

But you know, when I'm looking for a story I see past what's on the outside and try to find what's on the inside. And I guess if Fletcher Novak has a motto, that's it. Sexy is on the inside. So I wanted to bring that out in the characters. I really wanted to get the perspective of a pretty boy in a world where pretty boys seem to rule. And I really wanted to present you with the "perfect" heroine like Tiffy. Because that's how we see people. We see the outside. It takes a really long time to get to know someone, and in the world of social media, that's hard to do. We get snippets of this and that but you never really know someone until to take the time to figure them out.

That's all I set out to do in Sexy. Just delve a little deeper into the lives of these two people who appear to have it all on the outside but on the inside, are just like everyone else. Trying to find their way in a game with no rulebook.

I made this a fun book. No killing in this one. No mind-bending twists. Just fun. I don't write a lot of those. The Social Media series was my first attempt at "just fun" and if you've read it, I got it all twisted up pretty fast. So hopefully this was an easy read that made you smile. I had fun writing it and I read it last night after the edits came back and I caught myself laughing a few times. I hope you did too.

The second reason is a little more personal and I'm not going into any details, but Tiffy and Claudio are real. Tiffy is part of my Street Team and she came to see me at the Atlantic City Signing this past June and brought her BFF, Claudio. I have such admiration for her and her spirit. (Tiffy, bitch you got this! And I love ya, chick. I do. I'm getting all sappy just thinking about you right now. And Claudio is perfect. I'm so glad you brought him to meet me. You two made my day, for reals. Made my day.)

And I just loved Claudio's name so much, I needed a character. So I made Tiffy & Claudio BFF's in the book too. (This book is for you and Claudio, Tiffy. I hope you guys laugh a little. And give him a big kiss for me.)

Krazy Katie, another member of my Street Team got a shout out as well. Haha, she is co crazy! But in the sweetest and good-hearted way. Thanks for your help, Katie. You're so damn fun!

And of course, Jana, my assistant, thank you. (All the books are dedicated to her, she insists. ;))

If you enjoyed Sexy please consider leaving me a review on Amazon. I'd really appreciate it. They mean so much to me and my success as an Indie Author depends on word of mouth feedback from readers and fans like you.

So what is next for me…? I'm doing three major projects the rest of this year. First, a Junco spin-off that introduces Gideon's story after all that shit that happened in the final book, Return. There will be a novella in a boxed set called Red Hot Magic, it will be 99 cents for the boxed set, and I will not release the novella outside of that set because it's the first part of a new full-length book (no cliffy in the novella though). The full-length Gideon book will release end of January 2016.

Second, I have a brand new biker romance series and book one will release on December 2, 2015. That one is super secret but look for a cover reveal in October. It's the first standalone (yes, 100% standalone) book in a four book series (all four are standalones) that will complete by summer 2016.

The second is another secret project that I won't even

mention. But it's based off my life. ;) Should be very interesting. That should release in November if things stay on track.

And the third, which I am so excited for, is a book about the entire Rook & Ronin team called Happily Ever After (HEA). It's a FORD BOOK! Yes, you have been asking for more Ford and I am delivering. This is another novella that will release December 21 and will be 99 cents. Just a little gift to the fans for being so supportive. Five will also have a POV in that book (and his full-length grown-up book will release in mid-2016 as well.)

In addition to all that, my NYT Bestseller, 321, is in audiobook production. I scored a deal with an amazing company called Podium Publishing who wanted to produce it and they promised me amazing. I have several audiobooks in production as well, including FORD, the rest of the Junco series, and Social Media series. They should all release around Christmas or shortly thereafter.

If you follow me on my author page on Facebook or my Twitter account, you know I run a lot of contests. I give away a lot of signed books and prize packages. That's how I like to connect with #fans. So if you want to win some cool stuff, keep in touch! I love interacting with fans and answering any questions you have about the characters or the story.

I have a really great Street Team. The best, in fact. They are awesome and we are like a family in there. I'm not taking new members, we are closed. But I do run a fan group on Facebook called Shrike Bikes. They are in there all the time, as am I. So if you'd like to hang out with us, just click the link and ask to join the group. One of us will approve you as soon as we see the request.

If you want to be notified of upcoming books, sign-up forms for advanced release copies (ARC's), special pre-release teasers, or how to order a signed copy of this book, you can sign up for my newsletter here.

Thank you for reading. Thank you for reviewing. And I'll see you in the next book!

Julie

About The Author

JA Huss is the USA Today bestselling author of more than twenty romances. She likes stories about family, loyalty, and extraordinary characters who struggle with basic human emotions while dealing with bigger than life problems. JA loves writing heroes who make you swoon, heroines who makes you jealous, and the perfect Happily Ever After ending.

Printed in Great Britain
by Amazon.co.uk, Ltd.,
Marston Gate.